I0549656

FAIR FOLK
IN
KNOBS END

By Liz Strange

Talar stepped into the room, taking over from Nerys. "Yes, dear. You see we are from what many call the Otherworld. We are *Tylwyth Teg*, the fair folk. What you would know as faeries. Though that's not a very accurate label."

"Talar," Nerys urged.

"You see, Nerys, along with her two sisters, are in hiding here in the human world, while her parents are fighting for control over our land. My husband and I are here to protect her."

The two were watching for Sophie's reaction with the grimmest expressions. Both were taken aback when she burst out laughing. "You're kidding."

"Not at all, dear."

The laughter dried up in her throat. "Why are you telling me this?"

"Because I believe you are meant to help us."

"Help you what?"

Talar came to kneel before Sophie. "Find the Dagger of Everlasting Truth, of course.

This is the only way to end this challenge once and for all."

Copyright © 2013 by Liz Strange
ISBN 978-1-952979-92-7
All rights reserved. No part of this book may be used or reproduced in any manner
whatsoever without written permission except in the case of
brief quotations embodied in criticalarticles and reviews
For information address Crossroad Press at 141 Brayden Dr., Hertford, NC 27944
A Mystique Press Production - Mystique Press is an imprint of Crossroad Press.
www.crossroadpress.com

Crossroad Press Trade Edition

ANNWN, THE DISTANT PAST...

The wind howled and snapped, rattling the thin glass in the windows, and raising the occupants' level of anxiety tenfold. Inside the dome-shaped cottage a young woman moaned; a terrible, haunting sound. She gripped the jumble of sweat-dampened bedclothes beneath her as she writhed in pain.

An older woman hurried back to the bed with a cool cloth to mop up the perspiration dripping down her charge's face. Her gnarled hands maintained a difficult grip on the fabric, but it did not stop her from providing what little comfort was available. It had been a long, hard labour. With practiced hands she felt the woman's belly, determining the baby had moved. The woman kept her gratitude silent, so as not to raise any unnecessary alarm. It would all be over soon.

An hour later the woman was dead. The silver lining to the unfortunate death was that a healthy, beautiful baby girl had been brought into the world. The tiny lungs emitted an impressive cry, pulling both tears and a smile from the one who'd assisted in her safe delivery. It had been her experience that children of mixed *Tylwyth Teg* and human blood never came easily, and often didn't survive.

This one is strong. Another robust cry confirmed her assessment.

The baby was wrapped and placed inside a hand-woven basket, allowing the woman free movement to clean up and place the proper blessing upon the mother. Without it the young woman might not pass over to the otherworld, forced to linger without her corporeal body. Over the corpse she recited the ancient words, making a continuous circular motion with her fingers to sprinkle the remains with *Wermwd lwyd* and *Swyn-ystres*. In the mother's hands the old woman placed a small bouquet of dried *Ddynhaden*, ensuring that not even the foulest of spirits could prevent her cross-over.

The force of the wind picked up, dragging the branches of a nearby tree against the side of the house, a sound that raised the hairs on the back of the old woman's neck. A bright crack of lighting hastened her departure. With a long cloak wrapped about her misshapen form the woman stepped out into the night. The baby stirred in the basket, now draped with a thin piece of hide to protect her from the elements. There was no time to spare, the child needed to be taken to *Eirianwen*.

The woman stumbled along in the dark, the pounding rain making the path slick beneath her feet. The density of the mud resisted the urgency of her movement, pulling at her leather boots. The effort to keep moving had the woman panting.

Magical ability ran strong in her family, intensified with each generation. Her own gifts were foresight and sensitivity to the natural world, both aspects wreaking havoc on her mind in that crucial moment. Her skin crawled with the sensation of being watched, as though the forest itself was tracking her progress, waiting for the opportune moment to overcome her. The amulet banging against her chest would keep her safe to a certain degree, depending on the power of her would-be foe. Many in Annwn felt cross-bred children should be killed at birth, and kept a vigilant watch for the rare instances.

I have to keep the child safe.

The path took a sudden sharp turn. A flash of light tore open the night, an occurrence the woman met with a grin. It was a silly bit of magic, beautiful in its simplicity, yet a clear indication that *Eirianwen* was near. The sign had been predetermined in preparation for the child's arrival many months before. The woman hurried ahead.

A second flash of light appeared, stopping her. Her heart pounded in companionship with her exhilaration. As the light dissipated words escaped her lips, her arms moving in a practiced motion to invoke the power needed to continue on.

"Bendith y Mamau."

Out of the darkness a crude shelter appeared, the magical cloak lifted long enough for her and the baby to pass safely inside. The tingle at her back let her know the façade had fallen back in place, hiding their location from those who would do them harm.

She lowered her head in a sign of respect as *Eirianwen* met her in the middle of the protected space. She appeared to her as beautiful, young maiden, a visage with no hold in reality. The old woman had no guess as to how old the seer really was, she had simply always been known to her, and too many generations before her time. Her origins were murky, the extent of her scope and power murkier still. She knew better than to question such things. *Eirianwen* was the wisest *Gwiddonod* her world had ever known.

"The child lives," *Eirianwen* said.

The old woman nodded. "Yes."

Eirianwen leaned down to examine the child, who had begun to squirm in the basket. Her fingers lightly brushed one plump cheek, and the seer's eyes slipped closed. A surge of power enveloped them, swirling about as a whisper of cool wind and brushing against bare flesh in a crackle of static electricity. She dared not move, holding her breath tight. Silence filled the space, waiting. Less than a minute later *Eirianwen's* eyes opened. Her eyes turned hard. A dark look flashed across her delicate features, as though something in her vision had troubled her.

A kiss pressed to the baby's forehead emitted a burst of light, for a moment hovering as a glowing halo above both their heads. The old woman suspected a binding spell of some kind, but it was a magic far more powerful than anything she could ever produce. She knew it was not her place to comment or question, only to do as instructed.

"She must be kept safe." Standing, *Eirianwen* leveled her gaze on the old woman, looking deep into her eyes. "I will give you the means to travel to the human world. There you must transport the child to the exact place I instruct, where she will be taken in and raised as one of their own. Do you understand what I say?"

The old woman nodded, trying to hide her reticence. It had been many years since she'd travelled to the human world, in truth a voyage she never enjoyed. There were many things that confused and frightened her there. "Why such precautions?"

"The blood of this child will one day save Annwn from the most wretched of fates.
She must live, so that her descendent may someday return."

The words were a dagger through the old woman's heart. Never has she been entrusted with such an important task.

When the proper spell had been invoked, and instructions imparted the old woman left *Eirianwen's* cottage, venturing to one of Annwn's sacred bodies of water. There she would slip through to deliver the most precious of gifts. She prayed the threat to Annwn would never come, yet she remained fully aware the seer's predictions had never been wrong before.

How could a child of human blood save a world where she did not belong?

CHAPTER 1

St. Augustine's Academy for Girls loomed large and foreboding, a sprawling monstrosity of a building, originally built as a psychiatric hospital in the early nineteen twenties. Attempts had been made to soften the structure's appearance with a cheerful school banner and extensive flower gardens, but nothing could completely disguise the boxy institutional design. Sophie stood on the sidewalk, outside of the property's wrought iron gates, waiting. What she was waiting for, she wasn't quite sure.

"You coming in?" The voice startled her.

Sophie turned her attention away from the school, settling on the face of a girl about her age, whose eyes were the most unusual shade of green she'd ever seen. For an instant she felt trapped by the girl's gaze, overcome with a sensation akin to drowning. Then the girl smiled and the moment was broken.

"I'm Nerys. You must be new here." The girl offered her hand.

Sophie looked at her for a few seconds before shaking it. The girl's touch was warm and sent a parade of tingles up her arm. "Yes, I'm Sophie. I moved here over the summer."

"Well c'mon then. Ms. Blackstone will not be happy if you're late on your very first day." Without waiting for a reply the girl started up the wide concrete steps with feline-like grace.

She hurried to catch up. Nerys was already walking through the giant double-doors at the front of the building, the sway of her red-gold hair mesmerizing. Her new friend possessed a unique, ethereal beauty, which distracted her as they made their way to the office where she picked up her timetable and locker number. Individually her features may have been viewed as too sharp, certainly straying from the modern ideal of beauty, yet when assembled together captivated the viewer.

While standing at the desk waiting for the secretary to hand over her paperwork she found herself taking continuous peeks at her new friend, each time surprised and pleased to find her still there. As luck would have it the girls shared a home room, as well as a number of classes. Sophie was silently grateful not to have to make a solo entrance into rooms filled with unfamiliar faces. The thought triggered memories of the years passed at her previous school, and the terrible episode that had necessitated the unwanted move.

Nerys led her to her locker, which was but a few down from her own. They deposited their bags and continued on to their home room. The hallways were clogged with masses of young girls, laughing and chatting as they headed to their own respective destinations. Sophie thought again about her old school, and Jasmine and Caroline, the best friends she'd had to leave behind. So many losses in the past year.

"Here we are," Nerys said, before ducking into an open doorway.

Sophie followed her inside. Nerys took a seat near the back of the room, her smile never wavering. Sophie sat next to her, conscious of maneuvering her lanky frame into the seat attached to her desk. Though Nerys made no attempt to converse with any one close, she dared a look about at the others already seated. Many regarded her with curiosity, and several girls pretended not to have noticed her at all. One girl with a beauty so sharp it could have cut glass stared at her openly, only turning away to whisper something to the girl beside her.

"That's Carleen. She's very popular. It's always best not to get on her bad side," Nerys informed her.

Sophie didn't want to be on anyone's bad side. The previous year had been the worst of her life. It had been difficult to move away from where she had grown up, and to adjust herself to living with her grandmother. She'd spent the better part of the summer on her own, as her father had already gone on to his new location, far across the world where the army had needed his expertise. Her grandmother Elinor, though into her sixties, still worked as a receptionist at a local doctor's office. Of course she'd been available in the evenings and on the weekends, but there was only so much a sixteen-year-old girl and her grandmother could do together. For the most part she'd read, taken long bike rides, and slept.

A man strode into the room, bringing the conversation to a standstill. He was short and thin, with a neatly trimmed moustache. Sophie didn't think his posture could be any straighter if he'd had a steel bar fused to his spine.

He went to the board and wrote *Mr. Sampson* in large block letters. Then he retrieved a list from his bag and began to call names for attendance. Before saying Sophie's name he'd hesitated. His cool grey eyes met hers as she'd answered. A sudden chill gripped her, as quickly fleeting as it had been intense.

Papers were passed about, while Mr. Sampson gave instructions about the timelines to return completed forms. He kept looking to Sophie as he spoke, causing her to slouch in her chair to avoid his scrutiny. If she could have slipped any lower she would have, but at almost six feet tall it was hard to be unobtrusive. At last the bell rang and they were dismissed.

Nerys steered her out of the crowd with quick determination, as though reading Sophie's mind. She'd hoped to evade a confrontation with the man, he'd made her feel...strange. Something about the girl's presence at her side dissipated the sensation, bringing instead warmth and calmness. Quite simply, her position at Sophie's side erased the discomfort Mr. Sampson's presence had invoked. It was an odd reaction considering she'd known the girl less than an hour.

They continued on to English class, then math, before being released for the lunch hour. She found herself grateful to have Nerys as her guide. The school was enormous and confusing, the layout conducive to losing one's way. Yet it was more than having the girl help her find her way, for whatever reason an undeniable connection existed between the two. There were no awkward silences in their conversation, and despite the substantial difference in their height they had easily fallen into a walking rhythm, their movements mirroring one another. Sophie had been dreading coming to a new school, a worry that had kept her up most of the night before. Nerys had erased all of that within seconds of their meeting. Sophie felt quite certain that she wouldn't have had the same reaction to anyone else, as she found it difficult in new situations. Her mother had liked to say that things happen for a reason. Maybe she was right.

They took their lunches to the back courtyard where tables and benches had been set up in scattered groupings. Students had gathered into small cliques, like any high school, divided by age, status and friendships. A few girls smiled or said hello to Nerys, but for the most part she seemed to glide through those around her without garnering much attention.

They settled on the grass, under the welcome shade of an enormous elm. The day was bright and warm, hanging onto the summer humidity with all its might. Sophie felt the back of her white blouse sticking to her skin. For a few minutes they ate in silence, watching the milling crowd.

"So what brings you to Knob's End anyway?" Nerys asked.

"I came to live with my grandmother. My dad's in the military and he has an assignment overseas."

"What about your mom?"

Sophie paused, and put down the apple she'd been munching. "She died last year.
She had cancer."

"Oh. I'm very sorry." As she spoke, Nerys placed a hand on Sophie's arm. A tingling warmth spread through her, immediately taking the edge off the pain brought on by the mention of her mother's passing.

"That's alright. You couldn't have known."

"Still, this must be very hard for you. A new city and school, and your dad far away."

"It could be worse."

She looked to her new friend, seeing a dark expression flicker across her face. For an instant her green eyes became cold and hard, her smile a grimace. Then the sunny expression returned, along with the calmness that seemed to follow her.

Sophie shivered. *That was weird.*

Several sets of footsteps approached, drawing the girls' attention. They looked up, finding themselves an audience before Carleen and three of her friends, the latter all standing slightly behind their obvious leader. She smiled at Sophie, a look as insincere as Nerys's was kind.

"Hi there. I'm Carleen Mansfield. You just moved here, right?"

"Yes, I came in the summer."

"What's your name?"

"Sophie James."

"Well Sophie James, it's nice to meet you." Her tone suggested it was anything but.

She moved her gaze to Nerys, eyes narrowing slightly. "Hi, Nerys. Have a nice summer?"

"Wonderful. Thanks for asking."

"Well, ok then. I just wanted to welcome you to St. Augustine's. I'm sure you'll fit in just fine."

One of the girls behind her giggled, a plump, cherubic-looking thing with an unbecoming haircut. Before Sophie could answer they all spun on their heels, almost as if the move had been choreographed, and sauntered off to a nearby table. Carleen sat with her back to them, the center of attention in her teenage kingdom.

"Look like you're on someone's radar."

"Why? I didn't do anything."

Nerys laughed. "You didn't have to. Just the way you look is enough to set a girl like Carleen off."

"What's that supposed to mean?"

"You're pretty, Sophie, and in Carleen's eyes that means competition."

Sophie felt her cheeks flame. She'd often been told she was pretty, but she never quite believed it. She wasn't one of those girls who knew how to wear their hair the right way, or what makeup looked best on her. She didn't follow fashion trends. A growth spurt in the eighth grade had put her just over the five foot ten mark, making her feel like a giant.

Nerys by comparison was lithe and of average height, with soft, ultra-feminine features. If anyone should be called a beauty, it was her.

"What are some good clubs to join here?" Sophie asked, hoping to steer the conversation in another direction.

Nerys rattled on for several minutes, giving her a list that put her old school to shame. The photography club sounded fun, and maybe she'd try out for field hockey or volley ball. As she spoke the sun settled into a gauzy halo behind her new friend, highlighting her strange beauty. The effect was lovely, and unsettling in a way that Sophie could not quite put her finger on.

All too soon it was time to head back to class. They had to separate for the next hour, as she had gym class and Nerys was scheduled for biology. They'd meet for the last period, an environmental science class Sophie had signed up for on a whim.

In gym she was partnered with a friendly girl named Marcy for a two-week segment of badminton. They joked and sweated their way through the class, the time passing quickly. Neither one was exceptionally gifted at the sport, but they both played with enthusiasm. It turned out Marcy lived right around the corner from her grandmother's house and she offered to walk to school with Sophie if she wanted the company. Being a little sparse in the friend department, she didn't see any reason to refuse.

Nerys waited in the classroom for their last period, again seated near the back of the space. She was speaking with another girl, but looked up and waved as Sophie started in her direction, almost as though she'd felt her presence. The room had been set up in typical lab style, with rows of two-person tables, complete with sinks and attachments for Bunsen burners.

"How was gym?" Nerys asked.

"Ok. We're playing badminton."

"Nice. This is Liza. Liza, this is Sophie."

"Hi, Sophie." The girl smiled, revealing a set of braces. She had a fine sprinkling of freckles across her nose and head full of unruly, dark curls.

They chatted for a few minutes, until the teacher made a sudden appearance in the doorway. His presence was so startling he could have materialized out of thin air. With determination he marched to the desk at the front of the room, depositing his carrier-type bag on the cluttered surface. He cast about the room, his gaze for a moment settling on Sophie and Nerys's table.

The man was so handsome Sophie was sure she had to be dreaming. She blinked several times, but his appearance didn't change. He looked to be in his mid-twenties, tall and broad-shouldered. Shaggy, dark hair framed strong, masculine features. His fair complexion made his blue eyes laser bright, impossible not to notice. While still looking at the girls he smiled, exposing slightly crooked, white teeth, a flaw that accentuated his attractiveness rather than detracted from it.

Twenty girls suddenly sat up straighter, giving the teacher their rapt attention.

"Hello, ladies. I'm Mr. Henry and I will be your teacher for this class. Why don't we go around the room and introduce ourselves."

Many of the girls giggled and stammered their way through introductions, to which Mr. Henry continued his charming and easy smile. At her turn, Nerys was uncharacteristically cool. She didn't meet his gaze. Sophie experienced an icy, prickly sensation along her side closest to Nerys, almost as though her reaction to the teacher had manifested itself physically. She couldn't help but shiver, catching Nerys's attention. When their gazes met, Nerys smiled and a sensation of warmth returned.

The rest of the class passed in a whirl of course overview and the explanation of their first assignment, due the end of the following week. Nerys was ready to leave the moment the bell sounded, and Sophie followed along. She gave Mr. Henry one last glance, catching him surrounded by a number of the girls in the class. He turned as though he felt her gaze, and gave Sophie a nod. For a split second something dark and frightening passed between them, like a sudden shadow cast only over the two of them. Her heart jumped into her throat, her blood ice.

She blinked, erasing the sensation. Mr. Henry was looking at her still, a quizzical expression on his face. She felt Nerys tugging at her sleeve and the next thing she knew they were out in the hallway.

"Are you alright, Sophie?"

"Yeah, sorry. Just got a weird feeling back there."

Nerys looked behind them, concern drawing her brows together. "Let's get going. I'll walk you home."

They stepped out into the waiting sunshine, leaving behind first-day worries and strange interactions. Out on the sidewalk they were nothing more than a couple of average teenage girls, glad to be free of the confines of high school drudgery.

Who knew stranger things were yet to come.

CHAPTER 2

Seven am arrived like a slap to the face. Sophie forced herself from the warm comfort of her bed, pushing aside the lingering ghost of the dream she'd been having right before the shrill bark of her alarm had interrupted. It had been something to do with an immense, velvet-green field, where flower grew as large as trees and the sky stretched in perfect, cloudless blue as far as the eye could see.

She showered and ate some toast with her grandmother's homemade jam, before collecting her stuff for school. Her grandmother also puttered around, sipping at a steaming mug of tea, her hair full of curlers. She worked in the opposite direction as Sophie's school, so driving her granddaughter was not convenient. Sophie didn't mind, the walk was not far, and she'd have some company at least. Like the day before, her lunch was waiting for her, carefully packed with her personal preferences in mind. She thanked her grandmother as she slipped it into her backpack.

She popped in her earphones, and found something upbeat on her iPod to accompany her final actions before heading out into the waiting sunshine. Marcy had agreed to meet her at the corner, which was roughly half-way between their respective houses.

Sophie's long, dark hair was still damp where it rested against her neck and blouse.

The warmth of the morning indicated an even hotter afternoon would be coming.

She was glad she'd chosen the skirt over the long pants to wear, appreciative that there was some choice in their required school uniform. Back home she'd been able to wear whatever she wanted, another difference she'd have to get accustomed to.

Marcy waved as she caught sight of Sophie. She removed her earphones and stepped in alongside the girl.

"Thanks for meeting me. It's nice to have someone to walk with."

"No problem," Marcy answered. "I feel the same way. None of my other friends live in this area, so it works out for both of us."

They chatted a bit about their classes and families, and what had brought Sophie to Knob's End. Marcy knew her grandmother, as she worked at the clinic of her family doctor, but she hadn't known about Sophie's mom's passing. Once out in the open, Sophie quickly steered the conversation in another direction.

"So, do you try out for any of the sports teams? I was thinking about field hockey or maybe volleyball."

"I play field hockey. We have an awesome team. You should definitely try out."

"Cool, be nice to know someone."

"Yeah. Say, I hear that the new science teacher is really hot. You're in his environmental class, right?"

"Mr. Henry you mean? Yeah, he's pretty cute alright. How'd you know I was in that class?"

"My friend Nancy's in it, too. She told me."

Sophie tried to picture who Nancy was. She was pretty sure she had shoulder-length red hair and sat on the opposite side of the room, but she wasn't positive. There'd been a lot of new names and faces the day before, and it would be a while before she had all the girls in her classes straight.

"Sophie! Wait up."

She turned at the sound of the voice, finding Nerys jogging up behind them. Despite the effort, she wasn't breathing hard and not one hair had been ruffled out of place. Her blouse was crisp and white, as though it had just been pulled from the package. If she wasn't so nice, Nerys's outward perfection would have been very off-putting.

"Hi, Nerys. Where'd you come from?"

"I told you I lived nearby. I was hoping I'd catch you at your place before you left, but you were already gone. Hi, Marcy."

Marcy smiled. "Hi, Nerys."

"You guys know each other then?"

Nerys nodded. "Marcy was in a couple of my classes last year."

"Yeah, she was in your boat last year, being the new girl."

The statement caught Sophie by surprise. In all the conversations they'd had the day before Nerys hadn't once mentioned she was new to town. Sophie had assumed she was a native resident.

"I didn't know that."

Nerys's smile faltered. "My dad took a position at the university in Carlisle, so we moved here. Sorry, I didn't even think to mention it."

Carlisle was a larger town about thirty kilometers away. Many people from Knob's End commuted there for work.

"No big deal. So what's he teach?"

"Celtic studies," Nerys answered a little too quickly.

"Cool. Is that your background then?" Sophie asked.

"My family has a Welsh heritage."

"Wow. Have you ever been there?"

"We used to live there," Nerys answered. "We moved when I was a kid. So did you get that math homework done?"

"Yeah. Nothing like a teacher who gives you homework on the first day of school." Marcy didn't seem to notice anything strange, but Sophie felt as though they'd been deliberately steered away from a touchy subject.

They'd continued walking as they chatted, and in short order St. Augustine's appeared before them. Once inside they parted ways with Marcy, whose locker was in a different area than theirs. She did agree to meet them for lunch, then disappeared into the mass of hurrying girls.

Mr. Sampson was already in the class when the girls arrived. Carleen gave Sophie a forced smile as she passed, which she returned so as to remain in her good graces, rather than out of any real desire to connect with the girl. The morning announcements played and the roll was called. As the bell rang

Nerys was already on her feet, a move so quick Sophie was sure she must have turned a way for a few seconds for her to have accomplished it. She grabbed her bag and started to follow her to the door.

Mr. Sampson suddenly cut between the two girls, his grey eyes serious. "Just a moment, Sophie. I'd like to speak with you for a minute."

"We need to get to English class, Mr. Sampson," Nerys said.

"Please tell Mrs. Gracen that Sophie will be few minutes late, Nerys."

Nerys hesitated for a few seconds, then seeming to realize she had no other option, relented. She gave Sophie a strange look before departing.

Mr. Sampson waited until the room had cleared before speaking. "Well, Sophie, I just wanted to take the time to touch base with you. Mrs. Blackstone has reviewed your situation with me, and I want you to know that if you have any problems, that I am more than happy to help you. You just need to ask."

Sophie felt like she was squirming inside her own skin. "Um, thanks, Mr. Sampson.
Everything's been fine so far. Nerys has been helping me out, you know showing me around and introducing me to people."

"That's great. I'm glad you've made some friends already. Just keep in mind what I said, no problem is too big or too small."

"Ok. Thanks again." Sophie adjusted the strap on her shoulder and started toward the door. She felt a hand touch her lower arm, a connection that sent a shock of tingles though her body. She stumbled as the room began to spin.

When she turned to look at Mr. Sampson his face looked— different. There was nothing she could clearly pinpoint, it was him and somehow not. Her tongue felt heavy, like the one time she'd had her mouth frozen at the dentist's office.

"Are you alright, Sophie," he asked, dispelling the sensation as though it had never happened.

"Yes, sorry. I'm fine. I really should get to class."

She could feel Mr. Sampson's eyes boring into her back until she turned into the hallway. She realized then that she was holding her breath, her lungs burning from the effort.

The class was busy reading Macbeth when Sophie arrived. Nerys looked up briefly when she took her seat, then returned her attention to her book. Mrs. Gracen came to hand Sophie a package of paper, which she realized was the instructions for their assignment.

With an inward groan, she retrieved her copy from her bag and started reading. She loved to read, but Shakespeare was not her thing.

Math class was even more tedious than English had been. The minutes ticked by like hours, making Sophie edgy and irritated. She could not concentrate at all on the lesson the teacher delivered. She hoped it made sense to her when she got home.

The bell for lunchtime finally sounded, heralding an hour of relative freedom. She and Nerys grabbed their lunches and headed to the elm tree where they'd arranged to meet Marcy. She was already there, sitting with the girl Sophie had pictured as Nancy, who as it turned out, she was. Carleen sat with her posse at the same table as the day before, again her back to the tree. If she'd noticed their arrival, she didn't acknowledge it.

It turned out that Nancy also played on the field hockey team, as the goalie. "There's a couple of spots open this year because of some seniors leaving. Tryouts are next week, Wednesday I think." Nancy looked to Marcy for confirmation.

"Just a sec. I wrote it down somewhere." She pulled a notebook from her bag, and scanned the front page. "Yeah, Wednesday at three."

"What about you, Nerys?" Sophie asked.

"Thanks, but I'm not much of a sports girl."

Nancy and Marcy shared a look that seemed to indicate they agreed with her statement. To Sophie she seemed more like a dancer with her grace and fluidity.

"Well, you can come and cheer us on," Marcy said.

"Sure." She smiled, in return bringing ear-to-ear grins to all the girls' faces.

Nerys's gaze wandered, settling on something or someone beyond Sophie's shoulder. Her delicate features pinched as though she'd smelled something bad. Sophie's curiosity got the better of her and she cast a look behind her. Mr. Henry sat at a table near the door to the cafeteria reading a book, oblivious to the stares from many of the girls in his vicinity. Absentmindedly he picked at a sandwich on the table.

Marcy giggled. "Is that the new teacher?"

"Yes," Nerys said.

"He's yummy."

"Sure is," Nancy agreed. "You should switch to our class."

The girls exchanged phone numbers and emails as they finished lunch. Sophie felt much happier than she had in months, sitting with her new friends and chatting about nothing in particular. When the bell rang she and Marcy headed off to gym class. Mr. Henry gave her a smile as she passed, which made her heart give an off-tempo shudder. Marcy poked her in the ribs with her elbow, and smirked. Out of the corner of her eye she saw that Mr. Sampson was also in the courtyard, standing near the doors to the cafeteria. He was watching the exchange between Sophie and Mr. Henry, a deep frown on his face.

The hour of badminton passed with ease. She and Marcy managed to get into a nice rhythm, much improved over the previous day's performance. One girl took a birdie to the eye, causing her to sit out the remainder of the class. The poor girl didn't seem to possess much in the way of coordination, managing to trip over her own feet as she left the court.

She found that Nancy had changed her seat when she entered her last period class. She now sat behind the table she shared with Nerys, with the same partner she'd already had. Nerys was chatting with the two girls as she sat down. Liza gave a little wave, which Sophie returned. She was still pulling her books from her bag when Mr. Henry swept in and began the lesson.

As it had in math class, her mind started to wander. She remembered the dream she'd woken from with sudden vividness, as though a switch had been flipped inside her mind. The classroom no longer existed. She'd been transplanted to an emerald field, where she followed a rugged path toward a crystal blue lake. There she came upon a young man.

He had led his horse to the same lake for a drink. When he heard her approach he turned. His face seemed so familiar, yet Sophie was certain he was no one she'd ever met. His lips parted as though he were about to speak to her.

"Sophie," Nerys whispered beside her.

She snapped back to reality, realizing she was staring off into space, her pen dangling from her fingers. Of course Mr. Henry was looking at her, but he didn't seem angry, more amused than anything. Sophie let her gaze drop back to her textbook, where she noticed she'd doodled a weird symbol in the margin, something she had no idea what it meant.

After class she and Nerys met up with Marcy to walk home, who they dropped off first as her house was the closest to the school. Nerys continued along with her, right until they were standing at Sophie's driveway.

"Do you want to come in?" Sophie asked.

"Maybe tomorrow. I have something I need to do today."

"Ok. See you in the morning then."

"I'll be on time, I promise."

Nerys continued down the street, and as she watched Sophie realized she hadn't asked where she lived. She figured it must be nearby, otherwise it didn't make sense for her to be walking with her and Marcy.

Inside she found her grandmother had left her a plate of home-baked cookies on the counter, her favourite oatmeal raisin. She grabbed two and a bottle of water, and spread her homework out on the kitchen table. The first bite made her whimper. No one baked cookies like Grandma Elinor.

After filling her fat and sugar cravings with the cookies she ploughed through her math homework. What had seemed like an exercise in futility in class was now clear. She closed her text book with a satisfactory thud, and returned it to her bag. She did have an English project she could be working on, but she didn't see the rush. She'd have plenty of time over the weekend.

Since Nerys had already told her she was busy, Sophie decided to give Marcy a call. As luck would have it, Marcy was also done with her homework and equally as bored. They decided to head over to the school and practice some shots to get ready for field hockey tryouts. It took fifteen minutes, but Sophie finally located her stick in the garage where it must have been dumped when she'd moved there in the summer. She'd about torn the house apart when suddenly a clear picture of where the stick was had popped into her head. It had fallen behind a rack of garden tools, unnoticeable until the whole unit was pulled away from the wall. She'd laughed when she found it, wondering why she'd ever thought to look there.

Her comfy shorts and a t-shirt mimicked the outfit she found Marcy in when they met at the corner. "Sorry, it took me a while to find my stick."

"No worries."

As they walked, Sophie found out that Marcy had a boyfriend named Jake, who attended the public high school. He played basketball, worked at a grocery store and got along with her parents. They'd been going out for two years. Thankfully when Sophie had left her hometown, a boyfriend wasn't one of the things she'd had to say goodbye to.

The girls cut through the parking lot, around the north side of the building, heading toward the immaculate sports field. They heard two male voices as they were about to turn the corner, and something about the tones being used stopped them both in their tracks.

Sophie crept up to the corner and gave a quick peek. She found Mr. Henry and Mr. Sampson engaged in a heated conversation. Though neither one was yelling they were both flushed, and Mr. Sampson's hand had curled into a fist at his side.

Without warning his attention flicked in Sophie's direction. His eyes were black and hard, full of an anger Sophie had never seen in anyone before. Mr. Henry also looked in her direction, and after a moment of surprise his easy-going smile slipped onto his face. She felt Mr. Sampson's gaze burning against her skin, and the air about her crackled with static electricity. Then as abruptly as he'd turned his attention to her, Mr. Sampson stormed away, got into a nearby car and drove out of the lot. Mr. Henry gave a half-hearted shrug and left on foot.

Marcy watched the car drive out of sight before looking to Sophie. "Was that Mr. Sampson?"

"Yeah, looked like he and Mr. Henry were having an argument."

"Weird. Mr. Sampson's such a reserved, quiet kind of guy."

They continued on the field, Mr. Henry nowhere to be seen. "Has he been here long?"

"Who? Mr. Sampson? No, he came last year."

Just like Nerys. The thought shot through her brain, bringing with it an uncomfortable chill, though she couldn't understand what one thing had to do with the other. People often moved for work or other personal reasons, there was nothing suspicious about that.

"You ready?"

"Huh?" Sophie realized she was standing in the field, leaning against her stick.

"Are we going to practice?"

"Yeah. I'm ready."

They played for about an hour before they decided to head home for dinner. Marcy didn't seem to think much of the incident between the teachers, so Sophie pushed it to the back of her mind. Grandma Elinor had brought home food from a Greek restaurant they both enjoyed, and she lost track of any troubling thoughts.

Sophie watched a bit of television with her grandma before turning in to bed. Her last though before slipping over the boundaries of sleep was of the dark look on Mr. Sampson's face, almost like he'd wanted to kill the other teacher.

CHAPTER 3

The next morning Sophie mentioned the strange incident to Nerys on the way to homeroom. Her friend arched one fine eyebrow, but didn't seem too concerned or particularly surprised. As they came into the room Mr. Sampson turned in their direction. He gave Sophie a neutral look, which unnerved her. Her stomach clenched.

Nerys noticed her reaction, and took Sophie by the arm. The apprehension that had latched on to her dissipated, leaving Sophie calm, yet slightly puzzled. They took their seats and listened to the morning announcements without further incident. Mr. Sampson did not attempt to speak to Sophie, but whether that was a good or bad thing, she wasn't certain.

The rest of the day passed uneventfully. At lunch, Liza also joined them, giving Sophie a much-needed sense of acceptance. Worries about making new friends and finding her place in an unfamiliar school had plagued her all summer long. Now there was the beginnings of their own clique, albeit a small one, and a group without a clear definition.

They had the unnaturally pretty (Nerys), jocks (Marcy and Nancy), a brain (Liza) and the new girl.

After school Sophie attacked her homework, determined to get her math and at least one page of her science assignment completed. Once field hockey started there would be less time for scholastic responsibilities, and she didn't want to get behind. Opening her science text, she spied the strange symbol she'd jotted in the margin. It brought with it a sharp sense of panic, her ribcage feeling as though it was putting too much pressure on her heart and lungs. She quickly turned the page, which in turn banished the sensation. When finished she had a fleeting thought of beginning her English project, but she felt as though she'd put in enough time for one afternoon.

Instead she grabbed a book and a cookie and went out to the front porch to read. It was only four o'clock and she didn't expect her grandmother home until at least five-thirty, later if she decided to run errands after the clinic closed. The air outside was warm and heavy with the fragrance of the flowers blooming in the well-tended garden. Several kids were outside biking, and the two young boys across the streets were decorating their driveway with a bucket full of chalk.

The story was just getting good when a figure raced by the house. The movement was so quick and sudden it startled Sophie out of her reading-induced oblivion. She jumped to her feet, staring at the receding figure with the long stream of golden hair billowing out behind. Only one person she'd ever seen had hair like that.

Nerys.

Without thinking she dropped her book and gave chase, the figure moving with impossible speed. Several times she lost sight, only to turn a corner to pick up the trail again. Their progress moved them from the suburbs to a more rural, sparsely populated area of the city. When her friend passed through the gates of a small cemetery, Sophie couldn't have been more surprised at her destination.

She followed along the twisting pathways, to an area that seemed particularly untended, the plant life threatening to overtake the haphazard grouping of ancient headstones. Nerys moved along with remarkable grace, whereas Sophie stumbled and tripped on a number of occasions, once smashing her shin against a moss covered marker.

A thick grouping of trees crowded along the back end of this particular section, leaning toward the grave markers like a menacing sentry line. The air became thicker there, noticeably colder. The bare skin on Sophie's arms prickled in protest. Fear hit her as abruptly as slap to the face, sweat trickling down her back. A tiny voice inside her mind said, *Don't go in there.*

She forced herself to take a deep breath and then plunged

into the thicket. The branches and roots snatched at her, impeding her every step. If she didn't know any better she'd have been tempted to believe the trees were actually trying to prevent her movement. As if such a thing could actually happen.

A flash of golden hair ahead let her know that she was on the right track. She picked up her pace, pushing until her lungs burned. The ground became increasingly spongy, the muck pulling at her shoes like hungry mouths.

At last she escaped the claustrophobic atmosphere in the mini forest, bursting into a field where the colours were so bright they stung her unsuspecting eyes. A small slope of green led to an s-shaped pond, where she could see Nerys had waded in. The water swirled about her small frame, sending a hypnotizing series of ripples back to the shore. Without warning Nerys dived below the surface.

Sophie waited for what seemed like a very long time, but Nerys did not reappear. She walked the perimeter of the pond, looking for somewhere she could have come out without her noticing, but didn't find anywhere that seemed likely. Then she waded into the pond, panicked that she might have let her friend drown, only to discover the body of water was no more than chest deep in any one place. In fact she could see clear through to the bottom, where there was nothing more sinister than some rocks, bits of garbage and the odd shoe. She walked out again, sure she must have missed something. The sun was warm against her damp clothing.

A second lap didn't make the situation any clearer. What she did discover though was a large stone, positioned at the narrowest end of the pond, where the sun was unable to touch it. On the surface of the rock that faced the water was a small symbol.

The same one she had drawn in her science book. Her breath caught in her throat.

What was going on?

Sophie had waited for almost an hour before she finally gave up and returned home.

Basically her friend had vanished right before her eyes. *Ri-ight.*

Her grandmother hadn't returned home yet, so she hadn't

needed to explain why she was wet from head to toe. She put her clothes into the washing machine and headed to the shower. A slightly sour smell clung to her from her dip in the pond, which she didn't enjoy. Once clean she pulled on some pajamas and went to the kitchen to start supper.

In the fridge she found some thawed chicken breasts, which she put in the oven to bake, along with a couple of potatoes. There was left over salad from the dinner the night before which she'd use up. Some grated cheddar and sour cream would top the potatoes, making her mouth water at the thought. Her expedition had left her ravenous.

Dinner was just coming together when she heard her grandmother's car in the driveway. She pulled down two plates form the cupboard and started fixing their meal.

"Hi, pumpkin. How was school?" Grandma Elinor asked as she dropped her enormous purse on the counter. It made a strange clatter as it connected with the tile, making Sophie wonder what she was carrying around with her.

"Great. I've made a couple of friends and I'm going to try out for the field hockey team."

"Well then, sounds like you're off to a good start."

Grandma Elinor was a kind-hearted woman, but not the most observant. Sophie imagined she could run a number of things past her without tickling any kind of suspicion on her part. Not that she was that kind of kid; it was something she'd simply noticed in the months they'd been living together. Actually she'd have felt really bad pulling something like that on her, when all the woman wanted was Sophie's happiness.

They chatted over dinner, her grandmother telling her a funny story about a young boy who'd managed to get a marble stuck up his nose. The mother had been horrified, sure the doctor would think she was a terrible parent, but Grandma Elinor had assured her it wasn't the first child they'd seen in such a predicament. This led to a series of hilarious stories about the escapades of her father and his siblings as young children.

After the dinner dishes had been rinsed and placed in the dishwasher the ladies went their separate ways. Grandma Elinor had her book club meeting, and Sophie decided to watch some television. She found a sitcom she liked and settled down on the couch.

Several shows followed, none that stayed with her longer than the time they played on the screen.

A number of times she'd thought about calling Nerys. Hers was one of the numbers she'd collected over the lunch hour. She was dying to find out what had actually happened earlier and she didn't know if she could wait until the following morning. At last her curiosity got the better of her and she grabbed the phone. She retrieved the book from her bag and found the right number.

It rang several times, long enough that Sophie was about to hang up when a female suddenly answered. "Hello."

"Hello, can I speak with Nerys please?"

There was a small pause. "I'm sorry, Nerys isn't available at the moment. Can I take a message for her?" The voice had a distinct accent, Welsh, Sophie assumed.

"Ah, sure. Just tell her that Sophie called."

"Will do, dear. Good-night."

"Bye." The phone disconnected with a soft click.

Like it or not, she'd have to wait till morning for an explanation. She tried to read herself into exhaustion, but her mind was too keyed up to concentrate, and also too busy to settle down enough for sleep. She was tossing and turning long after her grandmother had returned home. The last time she looked at her clock it was nearly three am.

The alarm felt like a buzz saw inside her brain when it went off a few hours later. She slapped at it angrily, managing to knock the clock to the floor. She felt slightly ill when she sat up, as she often did with too little sleep. Her eyes burned and itched, protesting having to open. The warm sun in the bathroom made her recoil.

Once dressed, she shuffled downstairs and put on a pot of coffee. It was not a regular habit, but she definitely needed a boost to get her going. As the tantalizing aroma filled the kitchen she popped a bagel in the toaster. In one of the cupboards she located a travel mug big enough to hold two cups of coffee, to which she added a generous dose of cream and several spoonfuls of sugar. She was sliding the lid into place when her grandmother appeared.

"You feel like catching a movie tonight? My treat."

"Sure."

"Ok, well you find something you want to see."

"Sounds good. See you later."

She stayed long enough to eat her breakfast, then with mug in hand she grabbed her bag and marched outside. She was at the driveway before she realized a figure was standing on the sidewalk before her house. Nerys smiled as Sophie came to a sudden standstill. The sun made her golden hair gleam, and highlighted the unnatural perfection of the girl's ivory skin.

"Well, after yesterday I wasn't sure if you'd be here," Sophie said, joining the girl. "Yesterday?" Nerys's smile didn't even falter.

"Yes, yesterday. You know when you ran by my house and I followed you out to that weird cemetery where you dived into a very shallow pond and disappeared."

"Well, you make it sound so dramatic."

Sophie took a misstep. "Wait, so you're not denying it."

"No, I did go in the pond. I know it's weird, but it reminds me of another place and I like to do it sometimes. But I didn't disappear. I'm not a magician. I came out in a spot where you couldn't see me and I left."

"I looked around, and I didn't see anywhere you could have come out where I couldn't see you."

"Well obviously I did, 'cause here I am." Her tone was so mild it made Sophie feel foolish.

"Why did you leave?"

"I don't know. I felt weird with you watching me. It's a private thing."

Sophie didn't know how she felt about the explanation. It sounded logical, even probable, but something didn't sit right with her. Why hadn't she just asked Sophie not to follow her?

She kept the question to herself as she could see Marcy had come to the corner. She was watching them, probably wondering why they were still standing in front of Sophie's house talking , instead of coming to meet her. She fell into step alongside Nerys, and they headed down the block to their waiting friend.

A routine had been firmly established; homeroom under Mr. Sampson's endless scrutiny, English and math which passed with tolerable monotony, lunch, gym, and Mr. Henry's science class. It was in last period that Sophie noticed the most change in Nerys's disposition. She seemed very affected by Mr. Henry's presence, though she never spoke of any reasons for why he might have made her uncomfortable. She also noticed that as much as Nerys avoided eye contact with the man, he let his gaze settle on their table throughout the duration of class. Whenever Sophie caught him looking their way he simply smiled.

The next couple of weeks passed in such a fashion. Sophie did spend some time with Marcy and Nancy outside of school, shopping and going to movies, normal teenage girl stuff. She also made the field hockey team, which meant several practices a week. Nerys accompanied them a few times, but more often than not she had something else to do.

Sophie rode her bike to the cemetery a few times to look around, but she never saw Nerys there again. The strange symbol continued to bother her. She'd tried to research it a number of times, but could find no information about it anywhere.

One particular afternoon, with a cool wind blowing that indicated Mother Nature had finally decided it was time for fall, Sophie found herself pedaling her bike through the gates of the now familiar cemetery. She jumped off and popped it up on its kickstand once she hit the area where she would have to continue on foot. She trudged through the tangle of grass and vines, and overhanging limbs, a voyage that seemed particularly difficult that day. Once near the edge of the forest a pair of voices touched her, engaged in a heated conversation. She crept forward until she could see, careful to stay within the natural camouflage.

When Nerys came into view she wasn't surprised, but her friend's verbal sparring partner came as a shock. Mr. Henry, dressed in casual jeans and t-shirt and looking more handsome than he ever had, was standing very close to Nerys. Nerys's aggressive hand gestures and tense body showed an anger Sophie had never witnessed before. Mr. Henry simply looked upset.

"You need to stay away from me! And Sophie, too!"

Her name made her gulp, and for a few painful seconds she thought they might have heard her.

"Nerys, you have this all wrong. I'm here to help you."

"Right. Help me right into marriage you mean. Who sent you?"

"No one sent me."

"You must be one of Idris's men. How did you find me?"

"Calm down. I'm not anyone's man."

Nerys backed away, eyes black and hard, reminding Sophie of another person's similar reaction to Mr. Henry. "I'm on to you."

Then she turned and fled, a movement so fast Sophie's eyes couldn't track it. Mr. Sampson remained, staring off in the direction that she'd left in. Sophie held her breath, waiting. His gaze turned, gorgeous blue eyes staring at the exact spot in which she stood. She forced herself to be silent and stay as still as possible. The forest was so dense and dark there was no way her could see her. *Could he?* At last he began to walk away, thankfully in the opposite direction from her.

The entire ride home Sophie replayed the conversation over and over in her mind. It made absolutely no sense. *Marriage?* It was strange enough that Nerys liked to visit such a place, but Mr. Henry, too?

For the remainder of the week Nerys didn't walk to or from school with Sophie and Marcy. At lunch she begged off eating with them with excuses of needing to do homework. In class she was unusually quiet, only talking about school-related topics. She and Mr. Henry both avoided eye contact with each other, a circumstance no one else seemed to find strange except Sophie.

When she appeared at her side on Friday afternoon after environmental science class wanting to walk home with her, Sophie couldn't have been more surprised. She accepted, acting as though nothing odd was going on, yet silently hoping there'd be a way to pry some information from the girl. It seemed Nerys had an agenda of her own.

"Do you want to come to my house tonight? You could have dinner," she said, less than a minute after Marcy had left them.

Sophie was so surprised she skidded to a stop. "Really? Sure. Like right now?"

"Sure. Why don't we stop by your place so you can change out of your uniform and then we can go to my place?"

So fifteen minutes later the girls were walking to Nerys's house. Sophie had left a note for her grandmother, letting her know about her plans. They continued on for several blocks, much farther than seemed logical for Nerys to walk with the girls to school as she did. Soon the houses became larger, more opulent, and spaced farther apart. Nerys directed them to a small cul-de-sac that contained only three homes. She walked toward the one in the center, a massive structure set at least an acre back from the street. The property was encircled by ten-foot privacy fences, which required a code to be punched into the security system for the gates to open. Obviously Nerys's family was wealthy, but Sophie had to wonder about the need for such safety measures.

Inside the gates the property had a number of cameras watching like silent, electronic eyes. Nerys paid them no mind, but Sophie felt uncomfortable under their inspection. Once inside the fence she could see that the house backed up against a large hill, covered with dense foliage and old-growth trees. It could be accurately described as a private forest in their backyard.

Nerys pulled a key from her pocket as they ascended the massive front steps. A ten- foot door accessed the front of the structure. Nerys let them in and quickly punched in a code on the keypad beside the door.

"Come on. Mom and Dad are probably in the study."

They passed through a long corridor lined in tight succession with portraits of a number of startling beautiful and odd-looking people. A number of times Sophie wanted to stop for a better look, but Nerys moved along at a quick pace. The corridor curved to the right, becoming wider and taller as they passed the bend. The portraits were replaced with a series of intricately carved doors, all closed to prying eyes.

At last an open doorway appeared, where Nerys stopped and indicated with a sweep of her hand that Sophie should enter. She felt a flock of butterflies take flight in her stomach, but she continued on as expected of her. Inside, a middle-aged man and woman sat at an enormous table, examining some kind of map that had been laid out on its surface. A number of books, scrolls, and other documents were scattered over the table, and the room was lined with floor-to-ceiling shelves filled with more volumes than most libraries owned.

Two sets of eyes popped up, peering with undisguised curiosity as Sophie entered the room. Nerys appeared at her side and led her to where the two were now standing. The woman came around the table to greet her, stiffly offering her hand as though unaccustomed to the gesture. Like Nerys's, her touch was warm, somehow managing to knock aside her apprehension. The man followed suit, shaking hands with a quick, small movement.

"Mom, Dad, this is Sophie," Nerys said.

"Hello, dear. We're so pleased to meet you at last." The woman smiled just like her daughter.

"Yes, yes. We've heard so much about you," the man said.

"Sophie, these are my parents, Gruddyeu and Talar."

The names were strange and prickly. Sophie hoped she wasn't expected to repeat them. She didn't know if she was capable of producing such a sound.

"*Bendith y Mamau.*" The woman gave her daughter a conspiratorial look.

"Sorry? I don't understand."

"Excuse me, dear. I was just saying I think you have a touch of the...Welsh in you."

"I don't know. I suppose there could be somewhere along my family line."

All three smiled as though her suggestion were absolute truth. Sophie let the matter pass, not only because it wasn't something worth disagreeing over, but also because she couldn't be sure about the validity or not. Her family simply wasn't big on roots or heritage. They fell into that neat grouping of middle-class, several generations-born, non-denominational North Americans, whose identity was shaped by schooling, work, and ever-changing societal attitudes. Judging by the decorum of the

room she now stood in, Sophie would safely guess that history
and cultural heritage played a big part in Nerys's family's life.
She let her eyes travel over the strange tapestries and what
appeared to be a coat of arms.

"Have a seat, girl. Let me get us some tea."

Talar disappeared before a sound could leave Sophie's
mouth. She gathered speed and agility were also family traits,
as Nerys often moved in ways that didn't seem natural, just
like her mother's sudden departure from the room. Gruddyeu
resumed his seat, and openly stared at Sophie. When she
couldn't stand him looking at her any longer she tapped the
map between them.

"What's this you were looking at?" she asked.

Gruddyeu's gaze dropped to map, eyes wide as though it
were the first time he'd seen it. "Oh, this old thing. It's a map
of Wales from back in the early part of the 900's AD." The
words rolled off his tongue with a pleasing lilt, adding to the
strangeness of the comment.

"The 900's? Like more than a thousand years ago?"

"Yes, dear. That's what I said. You're not hard of hearing, are
you?" He peered at from under thick, brushy brows.

"What? No, I can hear fine. I just can't believe you have such
a thing lying around your home. It must be worth a fortune.
Shouldn't it be in a museum or something?"

"Worth, like beauty, is often in the eye of the beholder. To
most this is nothing more than an old scrap of paper, with
places and borders scribbled on it that don't even exist anymore.
To some it's a genuine piece of history." His eyes twinkled, a
distracting effect that momentarily made Sophie's response flee
from her head.

"Here we are," Talar sang, charging into the room with a
tray piled high with china and cookies. "Tea is served."

Nerys and Gruddyeu accepted their cups like nothing out
of the ordinary was happening, while Sophie's brain began to
spin from the combination of outright weirdness and quaint
traditionalism. She had never met people like the Cadwaladers
before. She didn't feel uncomfortable exactly, more confused,
like she somehow wasn't getting the joke.

While the three fussed about with fixing their tea and selecting sweets, Sophie took the opportunity to look Nerys's parents over more closely. Both were thin, almost the same height, which was neither tall nor short, about average. They both had pale hair and yellow-green eyes like their daughter, possessing an ethereal attractiveness that was somehow both similar to and different from their offspring. While she had guessed them to be middle-aged upon first glance, up close their age was hard to discern. They shared smooth, unlined faces, their skin the colour of fresh cream. Something about the way they moved was magical and wonderful to watch.

"How'd you take your tea, dear?" Talar asked, while Gruddyeu held out plate of sweets.

"Milk and sugar, please," she answered and snatched what she thought was a peanut butter cookie. It was, and perfectly baked, so the outside was crispy and the inside soft.

They chatted about school and Sophie's life over their snack, before Talar indicated that's she'd better begin supper if they wanted to eat before bedtime. Nerys took the hint and walked Sophie out to the backyard, where the girls sat on a wooden bench-swing, tethered to the limb of an enormous tree. The air moved about them with a vibrant, electric quality, almost like its own entity. Sophie felt a soft caressing sensation about her body, the whole of the outside seemed to be testing her energy, perhaps gauging her worthiness of being in its presence.

The strange thoughts whirling about in her brain came with surprising ease, shocking Sophie. *Nature is not alive in the sense that it cares who you are,* she silently admonished herself. As though she'd understand what had just crossed her mind Nerys patted her hand.

"So your parents are very interesting," Sophie said.

"Yes, aren't they?"

"So why is your mother so sure I have a Welsh heritage?"

"Just a feeling she gets. Mom's very good about those things," she said as though her statement in any way explained how her mother could know such a thing.

"Does you dad often bring home things like that map? I have to tell you it blew my mind to think that I was seeing such an ancient document with my own eyes."

Nerys shrugged. "He's always digging up old bits of this and that."

"Because of his job? You said he teaches Celtic studies, right?"

"Yes, it's like history and geography and culture all rolled into one."

"That's very cool."

"I guess."

Since she didn't seem to be making any headway in other areas she took a chance. "Been out to the cemetery lately?"

Nerys looked startled, then quickly recovered herself. "Once or twice. Should we go watch a movie or something?"

"Sure." Sophie had no choice but to let the matter go.

Nerys glanced at the woods behind them, a wistful expression passing over her face.

Back inside, she retraced her steps to the front of the house to a large family room. While the den possessed an old-fashioned feel, the family room was clearly modern. The furniture was all clean lines and a massive flat-screen with surround sound dominated one wall. It was like stepping from one world to another. Sophie had to wonder what all the unseen rooms between the one she was in and the den looked like.

They decided to watch the music channel, a normal teenage thing to do that had Sophie second guessing her earlier reaction. The Cadwaladers were certainly quirky, the house was filled with strange portraits and historical artifacts, which could all be traced back to Gruddyeu's professional endeavors and good old-fashioned cultural pride. Soon the images filling the screen sucked in Sophie's attention, leaving the silent debate to rest.

Dinner was a wonderful roast beef with all the trimmings. All four ate with gusto, keeping conversation light and to a minimum. When they couldn't possible eat another bite and Talar had firmly declined their offer to clear the table, the girls went to Nerys's room.

The space was easily three times larger than Sophie's. The walls had been painted a soft blue-grey, with wide white floor trim and crown molding. A large bay window overlooked the backyard, with the forest a majestic natural backdrop. Sophie took her time looking at the beautiful furniture, all heavy, dark wood pieces with beautifully intricate designs. The carvings almost seemed to tell a tale, with the same symbols and figures cropping up numerous times. Nerys watched Sophie for her reaction, but didn't offer an explanation as to the origin of the pieces. That they were old there was no doubt, but placing such items was far beyond Sophie's experience.

Besides the furniture, the rest of the items accumulated in the space were traditional teenage girl. There were stuffed animals, books, posters, and CDs. A laptop sat on a desk pushed into one corner. Near the window was a delicate vanity covered with cosmetics, perfumes, and boxes for jewelry. One piece caught Sophie's attention and she moved in for a closer look.

It was a charm of some kind, hung on a delicate silver chain. When Sophie touched it she heard a sharp snap, like a powerful electrical shock. She pulled her hand back, sure she'd find a burn on the tips of her fingers, but the skin was untouched. She reached out again, and this time the contact brought with it an image so clear the room about her disappeared.

Similar to the dream she'd had, she found herself standing in an immense green field, with the sound of running water tickling at her ear. The sky was psychotic in its blueness, so clear. A towering forest lined the farthest edge of the green space in which she stood, all trunks unnaturally straight and similar in width. A gentle slope to her right was covered with blooms the exact shade of a fresh tangerine, the circumference of the outermost petals larger than a basketball. The breeze tasted of honey and rosemary.

Then it was gone. After a sensation akin to being sucked through a giant straw, Nerys's room reappeared. She looked about, shaken and her stomach drawn into a tight knot. Nerys was at her side, a warm hand on her arm. The charm lay on the vanity top, where it had apparently fallen from her grasp. As she turned to question her friend about the impossible event that had just happened to her, a small piece of paper tucked into the upper right corner of the vanity's mirror grabbed her attention.

She snatched it down, the most amazing image held before her. It was a small, yet very detailed sketch of three young women who all shared a striking resemblance to Nerys. In fact, Sophie believed the girl on the right side of the small grouping was Nerys, but she was dressed in a manner foreign to anything Sophie had even seen before. All three wore long, flowing gowns, their long tresses adorned with ribbons and flowers. About their necks were identical charms; the same as the one now in Sophie's presence.

"What is going on here, Nerys?" Sophie demanded when she finally found her voice.

"I think the truth is due, Nerys," Talar said from the doorway, startling both girls. "Yes, I suppose its unavoidable now."

"Ok, seriously, you need to stop speaking in riddles," Sophie said. She felt as though she'd had the wind knocked out of her.

"I haven't been entirely honest with you, Sophie," Nerys said.

"So I gathered."

"Well, I guess the best way to proceed is just to say it." Talar nodded. "Well, first of all, this is not my mother, but my aunt. My mother and father are back home, engaged in a search for something that is very important to our family."

"In Wales you mean?"

Nerys smiled. "Sort of. We are from a part of Wales that few living creatures ever see, especially humans."

"Humans?"

Talar stepped into the room, taking over from Nerys. "Yes, dear. You see we are from what many call the Otherworld. We are *Tylwyth Teg*, the fair folk. What you would know as faeries. Though that's not a very accurate label."

"Talar," Nerys urged.

"You see, Nerys, along with her two sisters, are in hiding here in the human world, while her parents are fighting for control over our land. My husband and I are here to protect her."

The two were watching for Sophie's reaction with the

grimmest expressions. Both were taken aback when she burst out laughing. "You're kidding."

"Not at all, dear."

The laughter dried up in her throat. "Why are you telling me this?"

"Because I believe you are meant to help us."

"Help you what?"

Talar came to kneel before Sophie. "Find the Dagger of Everlasting Truth, of course.

This is the only way to end this challenge once and for all."

CHAPTER 4

An hour later Sophie was walking home. Her head swam with an unbelievable amount of knowledge, none of which seemed to have any basis in reality. Not any reality that she'd ever known anyway. Yet Nerys and Talar had imparted a tale of such vividness, of such extremes, that she was inclined to believe them. The only other explanation would be that both were completely mad.

"What is the Dagger of Everlasting Truth?" she of course had asked.

"One thousand years ago it was the weapon our descendent used to make a blood pact with the King of the *Coraniaids* to help end a great battle. The *Coraniaids* land lay between that of the *Tylwyth Teg* and the *Si of Gaidheal*, our enemies to the north. If they could gain access to the *Coraniaid's* land, and be allowed to pass through, the *Tylwyth Teg* would be able to engage in a surprise attack on the *Si*, thus gaining the upper hand in a war that had been raging for years. In exchange for their help, our then King agreed to betroth Nerys and her sisters to the three sons of their future leader, births which were prophesized by Eirianwen, a *Gwiddonod*, or what your world would call a seer or a witch." Talar keep her gaze steady and delivered her response as if it were the most natural story one could expect to hear.

"OK. Why would this guy want to have these marriages happen?"

"In addition to the triple births, the *Gwiddonod* also saw how powerful and far- reaching the lands of the Annwn would become by this time. The King of the *Coraniaids* wanted to align his people with ours, thereby gaining access to our riches, and hopefully breed our *Tylwyth Teg* powers into his bloodline."

"Considering you have gone to great length to hide Nerys to prevent this from happening, I'm assuming that marrying these guys would not be a good thing?"

"Not at all. The *Coraniaids*, though gifted supernatural beings in their own right, they are driven solely by material gains, and have no capacity for compassion. They would as soon stab their own mother in the back as a most fearsome enemy. It has been foreseen that any union between our two races would lead to the destruction of our way of life, and of all that reside in the Otherworld. The *Coraniaids* would not be content with equal status, they will want to overtake and control us, and they would be more than happy to double-cross us and align with the Si to make it happen. We cannot let this happen."

"How will finding this dagger help us?"

"If we find the dagger, we can destroy it, thus breaking the contract. At least that's what little information left indicates. The whole truth of what happened all those years ago has been twisted over time."

"How will breaking the contract help?"

"With it broken, the magic surrounding this agreement will be eliminated, and the *Coraniaids* will not be able to enter our lands. If it remains lost, or worse yet falls into the hands of the *Coraniaids*, the magic will allow them to enter the Otherworld. There will be no way to stop them."

"How do we find the dagger?"

"We do not know. It has been lost for hundreds of years. In fact knowledge of the very pact itself had also been lost by our people. It was only rediscovered when Idris, the current King of *Coranis* sent a message to Nerys's father last year, asking for a meeting to discuss the upcoming nuptials."

"My father about lost his mind at receiving the letter. The *Tylwyth Teg* and the *Coraniaids* have had a hostile tolerance of each other at best. The thought of giving his daughters over to them was unfathomable," Nerys said, having taken a seat on the edge of the vanity.

"So you're hiding as a high school student?"

"Yes, the *Coraniaids* do not possess strong enough magic to perform well in this world. If they are able to enter at all, they will be weak," Nerys answered.

"Where are your sisters?"

"Hiding at other schools in different places in the world. I don't know their exact location, as my father thought it best for our safety."

"So why me? I mean why are you telling me this?"

"Like Talar said, Sophie, you have a touch of the *Tylwyth Teg* in your blood. If given the right conditions you will have strengths and talents you would never have imagined."

Sophie looked at the two women, thinking carefully before speaking again. She had always been good at finding things, somehow just knowing where they would be.

Sometimes it wasn't just objects, but people she knew things about that she shouldn't. Her mother had often teased her about being psychic, an idea she used to laugh off. She then had to wonder if there hadn't been some truth to it.

The two were staring at her so intently she broke out in a sweat. Her skin became itchy and tight. "What else?"

Nerys dropped her gaze, but Talar offered a tight smile. "There have been stories of a human girl who would appear to one of the sisters. A human who could help make things right for our kind."

Sophie inhaled her next breath with an awkward gulp. "You think that's me?" Both nodded, eyes solemn.

"This is crazy!"

"We can prove it," Talar offered. "How?"

"We can take you to the Otherworld."

That stopped Sophie cold. Whatever response she'd formed fled from her brain faster than a rat from a sinking ship. Then she suddenly understood.

"Through the pond, right? At the cemetery."

"Yes, the *Tylwyth Teg* have a natural affinity with water, it does not harm us. That particular spot has been enchanted, now acting as a portal to our homeland," Talar said.

"So that's why you seemed to just disappear. Because you actually had."

"Yes," Nerys admitted. "Humans are not supposed to be able move through the forest that surrounds the pond. A spell has been put in place to keep the spot secret, but you somehow passed. That's another reason we feel that you are the one to help us."

Sophie remembered the strange sensation she'd experienced when moving through the area, as though nature itself had been trying to prevent her from getting through. She remembered something else.

"What about Mr. Henry? I saw you arguing with him there one day." Talar and Nerys passed a strained look.

"We're not sure about him. He has some magical ability, we're just not exactly sure what. Father is away looking for the dagger and we cannot contact him to discuss the issue."

For the first time Nerys looked upset.

"Has he tried to harm you?"

"Quite the opposite. He has been nothing but nice, even offering to help me. I can't explain it, but I just feel like something's not right with him."

"That's how I feel about Mr. Sampson," Sophie mumbled, then immediately wanted to take it back. What was a nosy teacher compared to the situation Nerys and her family was in?

"What do you mean, Sophie?" Talar asked.

"Nothing. Forget it."

"No, please tell me." She placed a hand on Sophie's arm, causing a sensation like a warm, painless current of electricity to race along her skin.

"I can't explain, really. He makes me feel…strange. Not bad exactly, more like nervous."

"That's interesting."

"And remember the time I saw him arguing with Mr. Henry? This was after I'd seen him with you at the pond. It just all seems weird, doesn't it?"

"It does seem suspect, what with Henry's affinity with magic."

All three were quiet for a pause, thinking about what role the two men might have in the situation, that is if there was a situation to be involved in. Sophie wasn't entirely certain that Nerys and Talar were on the level.

"Remember the symbol you doodled in your math book a few weeks back?" Nerys asked.

"Yes," Sophie answered, feeling oddly defensive.

"That's a *Tylwyth Teg* symbol meaning truth. It's from the distant past, from ancestors even farther removed then this situation with the *Coraniaids*. The first moment I laid eyes on you, standing outside the gates of St. Augustine's, I felt an unexplainable connection to you. When I saw that symbol come from your hands, I knew I was meant to be close to you."

The thoughtful silence settled in again. Sophie wondered if her brain might actually explode if pushed even further past the boundaries of believability. Though for the life of her, she could not figure out why they would be lying.

"I need some time to think about this," Sophie said.

Neither woman seemed surprised. Sophie half-expected them to try and stop her as she made her way to the door, but both remained where they were. The door made a thunderous clang behind her, and she had to fight the urge to bolt down the stairs.

Outside, night was just starting to fall, casting the sky in a soft, purplish haze. Sophie took her time making her way home. She let her footsteps act as a metronome, keeping the tempo of her jumbled thoughts steady. As her street came into view it started to rain, the fall so gentle it was little more than mist.

She crossed the street, which was silent and clinging to a feeling of desertion. Several homes had lights on and cars in the driveway, but no one was visible. Her shoe caught in a crack in the sidewalk, making her stumble and almost fall to the ground. As her vision lowered with her body a blur of motion caught her eye, yet she couldn't give it her attention and prevent herself from injury at the same time. When she'd regained her balance she scanned the area in front of her, seeing nothing out of place. A chill whispered along her spine.

"Are you alright then?" came a male voice from her right side.

"Holy crap!" she blurted out, and jumped about a foot in the air.

Mr. Henry stood on the sidewalk, looking at her quizzically. He held a black umbrella over his head and waited for her to calm down.

"You scared me to death," she said, feeling rather sheepish.

"I'm sorry, I thought you saw me before you stumbled. I just wanted to make sure you hadn't twisted your ankle or something."

Sophie remembered the discussion she'd had about Mr. Henry with Nerys and Talar. Looking into his eyes she felt— something. Her heart was pounding, her breath tight in her chest, yet she was drawn to him. It was the first time she'd ever been alone with the man, or so close in proximity. There was an aura about him, which made it hard to think clearly, but also made her happy. She heard Nerys's voice in her head: *Stay away from Sophie.*

And the spell was broken. Mr. Henry picked up on it also, ascertained by a subtle dimming of his ever-present smile.

"I'm good. See you Monday." Then she continued on, not giving him the chance to prolong the exchange. She had the idea that she might not be able to break away so easily a second time.

When she reached her driveway she chanced a quick look back, finding the street as deserted as it was before Mr. Henry's appearance. Sophie all but leapt up the stairs, never having been so happy to be home as she was at that moment.

Grandma Elinor was in the family room, watching a movie and munching on a huge bowl of popcorn. Sophie plopped down beside her, happy to have a distraction from all the weirdness that had been her life recently.

"Whatcha watching?"

"The Proposal. I just love that Ryan Reynolds." There was a mischievous twinkle in her eye.

Sophie had to laugh. She happened to like the actor herself. Cute and funny is a hard combination to beat. She grabbed a handful of popcorn and watched the rest of the movie before retiring to bed. It had been a long time since she'd laughed so hard and it had felt good, but once alone again the strange musings crept back in.

A storm blossomed from the soft rain, with accompanying thunder and bright flashes of lightning. The rain pounding against her window kept her awake, and seemed to whisper warnings of lurking danger. The intermittent episodes of thunder startled Sophie to a hyperactive degree. Even after the storm has subsided she lay in the dark, listening, and waiting for sleep to come.

When it did she returned to the same green field where the young man from her previous episode still stood, waiting for his horse to finish its drink. This time he acknowledged her presence, turning a hesitant smile in her direction. The horse also looked her way, briefly, then returned to its previous activity.

Sophie walked down the slope, toward the small pocket of pristine water. The air was warm and heavy, moving gently through the vast expanse of countryside. On the far bank of the pond, flowers the size of transport tires bloomed in every conceivable colour, a garish and utterly delightful display. Tall, uniform trees lined the edge of the green field as far as Sophie could see. The horse's hooves had left brownish indents in the grass, a series of half-moons leading to its present position.

"Hello there, miss. Lost, are you?" The young man's voice was honey and velvet, each word ending in a soft lilt.

"I guess I am," Sophie agreed.

He offered his hand in greeting. Sophie hesitated long enough to elicit a frown before taking his hand in her own. Like Nerys, the touch was warm and energizing, whispering an overflow of power up her bare arm. She lingered in his touch, turning the frown into a curious grin.

"The name is Cadoc. May I ask what you are called?"

"Sophie."

"A lovely name, Mistress Sophie." He made a sort of sweeping bow in her direction, which left her completely puzzled as to how she should respond.

"Ah, thank you. Now about the lost thing. Can you tell me where I am?"

"You have found yourself in *Blodeuwedd*, land of the ever-blooming flowers. Over the hill is the territory of Rhiannon, and farther beyond that the location of *Llyn y Fan Fach* and the home of *Gwyn ap Nudd*, our reigning King. You are not *Tylwyth Teg*, are you?" A note of concern had crept into his words.

"No, but I am a friend." His cadence and odd manner of speaking was throwing her off, yet she found the sound a pleasure to her ear.

"A friend? As often an enemy will insist."

"Quite true."

A strange sound came from off in the unseen distance, growing louder with each passing second. A combination of screech and wail the sound closed in, accompanied by an ominous shadow cast down upon them by a large and fast-moving object in the sky. Cadoc shaded his eyes with one hand and looked up. Sophie's gaze followed, taking in a sight she could never in her wildest dreams have imagined.

Three giant bird-like creatures were flying overhead, their wing-span equal to that of a small plane. Their flapping caused the flowers to sway and sent a ripple of movement across the otherwise still pond. For a few moments their presence blocked the brightness of the sun, which sat high in the sky. Cadoc's horse gave a soft whine.

"Ah, the *Adar Llwch Gwin* have been quite active lately." He returned he gaze to Sophie's face. When he saw her fear he took a step closer. "No need to be afraid. They are assisting the King and his men on their quest."

Cadoc seemed to assume that Sophie would be satisfied with his explanation, but she had no idea what he was talking about. He would definitely know she didn't belong there if she had such a strong reaction to everything she saw, or asked too many questions. Better to keep her eyes and ears open, and try to figure things out for herself.

"Right. I'd forgotten about that. I just find their appearance a bit unsettling."

Truth be told, they'd passed so quickly Sophie had little more than an impression of black feathers and large, hooked beaks.

"Can I help you find your way to wherever it is that you're going? I'm a most excellent navigator. I've been riding since a wee boy, and I figure I've seen just about every part of *Annwn*. Many several times over." He didn't seem to be bragging, just sure of himself.

"*Annwn*?" she asked.

"Yes, *Annwn*. The land you are now in." His nose crinkled and his fine, dark brows pulled together. "Are you quite alright, Mistress Sophie?"

They were now standing very close together, giving Sophie a better look at him. He was taller than her, slight, but had a presence of strength in the way he held himself. Shaggy dark hair surrounded a narrow face, which contained a patrician nose and full lips. His eyes were the colour of ripe celery, and twinkled in the most engaging way. The long tunic draped over his frame was dark, made from a rough material. Underneath this he wore what Sophie would have called 'leggings," but she assumed they had a different name there. Heavy leather boots laced up the front covered his legs to just below the knee, and he had a short dagger tucked into the strip of leather about his waist.

She was staring at him she suddenly realized. "Yes, I'm fine. Sorry. I'm just a bit disoriented. Not sure how I ended up here."

"Perhaps we can figure that out if you would be so kind as to give me the name of your destination?"

Now that was a stumper.

Luckily, an interruption saved Sophie from having to conceive a plausible lie. A voice, belonging to an older female, called her name. Both she and Cadoc turned at the sound. Where once had been forest, now existed a veil of darkness. Her name was called again, draining away the carpet of emerald grass beneath her feet.

"Sophie!"

She shot awake, her heart hammering and sweat dripping down the side of her face.

It took a full minute before she realized she was in her own bedroom, and it had been her grandmother Elinor calling her name.

"What?"

"Are you planning on getting up sometime today? It's nearly one o'clock."

"What?" It seemed to be the only thing she could say.

Her grandmother bustled about her room, snatching the overflowing basket of dirty clothes from the corner. She paused at the door. "I'll put the first load through for you, then you're on your own. Are you feeling alright, dear?"

Sophie wasn't sure that she was, but she forced herself to smile and nod. Her grandmother pulled the door closed behind her, leaving Sophie to the solitude of her room. A glance at her clock radio confirmed the time. Her mouth was fuzzy, and her limbs like lead, as though they hadn't gotten the memo that it was time to be awake. She lay on her bed for a few more minutes before trudging down the hall for a long, hot shower.

She felt almost human as she toweled off and dressed in some comfortable clothing.

Her book bag sat on the floor beside her desk, where she'd dropped it the day before. She needed to work on her science project and her Macbeth paper, though neither activity thrilled her. A grumble from her stomach reminded her it had been many hours since she'd last eaten, and she figured some food might help her energy level and ability to focus. Somewhere in the background of her mind, the image of Cadoc continued to flitter about.

She found her grandmother had been busy making a pot of homemade chicken soup while she'd been slumbering away the day. She filled a bowl, and grabbed a couple of rolls with butter. As an afterthought she started a pot of coffee brewing.

With her belly full of warmth and her carbohydrate craving satisfied, Sophie poured herself a cup of coffee and reluctantly returned to her room for a serious homework session. With the radio playing softly, she pulled her science text from the bag and flipped through the pages to find the information she needed. As though moving on its own accord the pages fell open to reveal the symbol she'd doodled in one of the margins. She traced her fingertip along the lines and thought about what Nerys had said.

It's a Tylwyth Teg symbol meaning truth.

The phone rang, startling her reverie. "Hello."

"Sophie? It's Nerys."

"What a coincidence. I was just thinking about you."

Silence. "It's not a coincidence. Talar invoked a connection spell on you last night, to make us aware of any time you might think of us...and our situation."

"Like reading my mind?" Sophie shifted in her chair. She didn't like the thought of that.

"No, nothing so sinister. It's much more vague than any kind of telepathic connection. I just get a sensation, like a reaction to a change in temperature when your thoughts shift. Be glad I don't have the ability to affect the elements or transform into an animal like my sisters."

"You're kidding?"

"Not at all."

"I've been having strange dreams lately. Are you responsible for those, too?"

"You're giving me too much credit. Dream manipulation isn't one of my talents."
What are the dreams about?"

"I keep finding myself in this beautiful field where the grass is greener than anything I have ever seen before. There is a young man down at a small pond, where he's letting his horse have a drink. In the background are these giant flowers..."

"*Blodeuwedd,*" Nerys said.

"Yes, that's what he called it."

"Who's he?"

"The young man. He said his name is Cadoc."

Nerys took a sharp intake of breath. "Cadoc the Wanderer? I don't understand how you could be dreaming of these things."

"Every conversation I have with you just gets weirder and weirder. Cadoc the Wanderer? Really? Don't you people have any normal kind of names? All these titles and words I wouldn't even try to pronounce."

"This is another world you're talking about."

"Yeah, and about that. Where exactly is this Otherworld? Or, wait...Annwn, that's what Cadoc called it."

"Yes, the true name is Annwn, though most outsiders seem to prefer Otherworld. Just how long was this dream anyway?"

"Not very long, but it was so real."

"Like a memory?"

"Sorta, yeah."

"Well, maybe it was. Or a premonition."

"You've lost me again."

"This is not a matter to discuss over the phone. Can we meet later?"

"Sure. I need a few hours to get my homework done."

"Alright. How about five. You know where." She did. "See you then."

CHAPTER 5

The rain had left the air cool and moist. Sophie walked along the damp sidewalk at a brisk pace, oblivious to anything going on around her. Her mind was firmly set on the matter at hand; getting to the truth of the situation with Nerys. When the gates to the cemetery appeared in the distance her heart gave a series of sharp, off-tempo thumps.

Either Nerys was a complete nut or everything she'd told her would prove true. She didn't know which scenario gave her more worry.

The dirt trails had turned into a sloppy, sliding mess with the rain, making Sophie glad she'd chosen to wear her unfashionable rain boots. They were keeping her feet dry and offered some traction against the soft ground. Through the overcast sky the sun attempted to be seen, breaking through in intermittent bursts of warmth.

The jumbled grouping of headstones, like a mouth full of broken teeth, came into view. This time Sophie focused on the sensations the place brought to her. The air was denser than near the gates, and held a hint of honey and rosemary, the same scent she'd been touched by during the incident in Nerys's room. Everything she looked at gave her the impression of being slightly more than what her eyes were taking in, like something caught in one's peripheral vision.

A rustle of wind through the trees to her left stole her attention. As she walked toward them the image began to shimmer, fading in and out like a channel losing its reception. When the incident finally subsided, settling into a state of stability, Sophie could see that the forest was only half as dense as she'd thought it to be. Most of the trees were aged and damaged, and the ravage of underbrush that had seemed to grab at her person, making her previous treks through the space that much more difficult, didn't actually exist at all.

Magic, she thought with annoyance.

As she stepped into the trees a shiver danced up her spine, making her stop in her tracks. Sophie took a nervous look about her, finding no one. The sensation clung to her, making her skin crawl. She forced herself to look straight ahead and she moved through the area as fast as she could without falling, while the odd panic scurried about in her brain.

When the pond appeared she upped her movement to a jog, bursting out of the woods with a gasp. She hadn't realized she'd been holding her breath.

Nerys stood at the pond's edge. She smirked as Sophie marched toward her.

"Creepy, isn't it?"

"Huh? Yeah, what's going on?" Sophie asked. She had the urge to shake like a dog, as though the sensation had a physical substance that clung to her like the tendrils of a spider web.

"I removed the glamour so you could pass easily, but the icky feeling you're experiencing is the layers of death attached to this place. It's thick here, enhanced by the connection I've made to the Otherworld."

Sophie still had the heebie-jeebies, and she couldn't help but look about as though there was something lurking in the shadows that might attempt to harm her.

"I think with you forcing yourself to be so aware of what's going on here that your natural sensitivity or psychic abilities, whatever you want to call it, has been upped."

"You're really convinced that I have some kind of special powers, aren't you?"

"You said yourself that you have a talent for finding things and I can tell by the way you're acting that you feel something here that most people wouldn't notice."

"Ok, sure. I do feel something, but that doesn't mean I have a fairy relative in my history somewhere."

"We prefer *Tylwyth Teg*. We're not little creatures with wings that fly about granting wishes or whatever humans think we do."

"So none of you have wings?"

"No," she said, clearly aggrieved at the thought. "I think somewhere along the way a human has mixed us up with a pixie or some other such creature."

"Pixies?"

"Yes, little creatures with wings who can be most annoying and are not altogether bright! Now you're getting me off topic. Are you prepared to go?"

Sophie had been so distracted she hadn't noticed before how Nerys was dressed.

She wore a floaty, draped garment, cinched at the waist with a thin leather strap. About her neck was the charm from her bedroom vanity.

"Sure."

Nerys gave her once-over, displeasure scrunching her fine features together. "You are going to stick out like a sore thumb."

"Can't you cast some kind of spell over me?"

"I could, but not here. Using magic leaves a residual trace of energy, and since people are trying to find me and my sisters, that's the kind of thing they'll be looking for."

"What about the spell used to make this pond a portal to the Otherworld? Can't that be traced?"

"Exactly my point. Too much magic used in one place is going to attract notice. And even if the Coraniaids can't function in this world themselves, they may have found someone or something that will come for them."

"I don't like the sound of that," Sophie said.

"Me either." She took Sophie's hand, sending a shock of heat up her arm. "You are thinking as a human. You have no idea about the creatures that could and do reside in my world. Things I might not even be aware of."

"Geez, now you're scaring me. Aren't you like royalty or something in the Otherworld? Shouldn't you guys have lots of people working for you trying to figure this stuff out?" In addition to what felt like a ten-pound rock in her stomach, Sophie's hands began to tremble.

"In many ways *Annwn* is far superior to this world, but in others it is still a primitive place, ruled by force and fear. The *Tylwyth Teg* are but one of many life forms that call it home. Like earth there are many territories and clashing ideals, with many groups vying for some slice of control."

"I'm confused. Is *Annwn* the world, or like your country?" Sophie's head was spinning, and the more Nerys spoke the worse it became.

"The Otherworld is the whole, and *Annwn* our small part in it. But we are wasting time talking when we should be seeing." A buzzing, current-coloured haze appeared about Nerys's form as her irritation took substance. Taking notice of it she gave a backward swipe and the phenomena evaporated as quickly as it had come.

Foregoing another delay by conversation Nerys gave Sophie's hand a tug and starting wading into the pond's cool water. It was like no experience Sophie had ever had, the water didn't so much touch her as envelope her, as though some invisible barrier was preventing the liquid from making actual contact with her person. The deeper they waded into the cool liquid the more intense the pressure pushing against her. As she was beginning to get used to the odd sensation the bottom of the pond seemed to fall out beneath her feet, sucking her downward like water being released from a bath. Where once had been a background of damp grass and cloudy skies was darkness; a swirling, bubbling darkness drinking her down and far away.

She struggled at first, until realizing that the effect wasn't hurting her. It was a vibrating, hurtling sensation moving along her skin as though she floated in a glass of cool ginger ale. The association made her giggle, the sound distorted by their close confinement and the speed at which they travelled. At last they neared their destination. A light began to shine through the liquid blackness, and Sophie felt the pressure subside. Her head emerged, her form breaking the surface of a calm expanse of water until she found herself standing knee deep in a small lake.

She was still holding Nerys's hand, who led her to the shore.

Looking down she realized she wasn't the least bit wet, and further still her sweatpants and t-shirt had been replaced by a weird, toga-dress thing, a replica of what Nerys was wearing. Her clunky rain boots had been replaced with delicate sandals.

"Wait! What? How'd you do that?"

"This?" Nerys teased, and in the blink of an eye the garment was replaced by one of a different colour.

"Stop that!"

Nerys burst into laughter, a sound immediately mimicked by a chorus of voices behind where the girls were standing. Sophie whirled about in surprise, further shocked by the source of the sound. About ten feet off, floating in a tightly gathered group in the calm, blue water, was a group of creatures like nothing she had ever laid eyes on before. Seven angelic faces framed with golden curls watched from where they floated at the lake's surface. Their limbs were long and supple, which Sophie assumed made them more streamlined for a life spent in the water. Under her scrutiny one creature dove into the lake's depths, feet with a fin-like appearance popping briefly into view before disappearing with the rest of its body. It reappeared an impressive distance from the rest of its group.

"Those are Morgens. Water sprites," Nerys said, waving at the rest of the flock before they disappeared beneath the water's surface. "They're harmless. Well, to me anyway. They know better."

"Are you sure?" she asked, watching as they group resurfaced about a hundred yards down the length of the lake.

"Of course. I used to swim with them all the time when I was a young girl. Now the *Llamhigyn y Dwr*, those you have to watch out for. They bite."

Before Sophie could ask her friend to explain what she should be on the look-out for she marched off, leaving Sophie to follow or be left behind. She scurried after her, not as sure-footed in the thin sandals as Nerys. The rocky, moss-coated shore gave way to softly rolling hills of green. One such hill led to a plateau, a pasture-like space of tangled grass and wildflowers stretching as far as Sophie could see. One edge was bordered by the body of water they had just emerged from, flowing for several miles as a liquid serpent through the endless expanse of green. Dense forest lined the other side, too crowded to let but the smallest stream of light pass through.

Nerys followed a well-worn path that copied the curving flow of the lake. She seemed to know the area well, giving the space about her nothing more than a cursory glance. The group of Morgens swam along, keeping pace as the girls walked. They dove and jumped, playfully nudging each other. Nerys smiled at their lively behaviour, shouting out encouragement to stay with them from time to time. Sophie wasn't sure if they could talk, but they could certainly laugh. The sound of their merriment danced on the air, sweet and infectious. Despite her uncertainty with her new surroundings, Sophie found herself smiling.

Unlike Nerys, who seemed oblivious, Sophie couldn't keep her eyes focused on any one thing. Her gaze jumped about, from the Morgens to the strange foliage and menacing line of trees. When a patch of darkness materialized overhead she knew before looking up that an Adar Llwch Gwin was passing by. Like in her dream of Cadoc, the giant birds flew by in a small flock, an occurrence that gave Nerys pause. She actually stopped walking for a few moments, and with a delicate hand shielding her eyes watched their flight across the cloudless sky. Sophie also watched as they continued on their way, taking in more details of their appearance than the last time she'd had occasion to witness their movement. In addition to the sharp, hooked beak, the faces had large, onyx eyes and a peeked ridge running along the top of the skull into the spine, where it disappeared in a mass of feathers. The talons on the feet looked to be the length of Sophie's forearm, able to snatch whatever prey their sights might be set on.

"Adar Llwch Gwin. Right?" Sophie asked as the massive forms gradually became nothing more than a tiny speck on the horizon.

Nerys seemed startled that she had spoken. "How did you know that?"

"Cadoc told me. Or at least I dreamed that he told me. Is that what they're called?"

"Yes. A rare sight in truth. They are a shy creature by nature, but my father keeps a few, training them to assist in the odd search. As you can surmise they are capable or travelling vast distances with ease, and can access even the most remote or seemingly inaccessible location."

"I can get how they'd be helpful. Though they're kind of scary-looking."

"Another benefit. My father's man Drudwas was given a set of these birds by his wife, a *Tylwyth Teg*. Drudwas himself is human, though none are sure of his true origin. He was found by servants one morning as they went to do washing at *Llyn y Fan Fach*, near my family home. He was taken in and raised by a group of women, training at an early age to be the carer of my father's horses. As time went on he took on many important duties, and eventually married one of our kind. My father trusts him above most. He has never let my family down."

"You never found out where he came from?"

"Never. The odd time humans slip in, or we slip out. Sometimes to never be seen again."

Sophie let the comment sink in. The Morgens had stopped swimming, the group now perched on a grouping of rocks. Their torsos were wrapped with something that looked suspiciously like seaweed, hiding whether they were male or female. Each had the same mane of hair, and slanted crystalline eyes, the body shape decidedly androgynous. Nerys offered a parting wave as she began walking again, met by a group titter that caused the hair on Sophie's arm to stand at attention.

After walking for what seemed like miles, and leaving the winding body of water far behind, Sophie spotted a few of the gigantic flowers from her dream dotting the horizon.

She inhaled deeply, letting the sweetness of the air fill her lungs. Soon the random clusters became a field of flowers, most standing twice her height. A wayward petal the size of a large pizza caught about her arm, its texture lighter and smoother than silk. She laughed at the wonder of it. Even Nerys seemed delighted, as though her familiarity with the place couldn't take away from the pleasure it offered to the senses.

"Are we in Blodeuwedd?" Sophie asked.

"Yes, at the western edge."

"Maybe we'll meet up with Cadoc, like in my dream."

"Don't know, Sophie. From what you described it sounds as though you were in the area to the east, on the shore of Lyn Barfog, some twenty miles from here." She pointed in the direction opposite to the way they were travelling. "We need to get to my family's home, at Rhiannon."

"Why the heck didn't you just bring us out there then, instead of making us walk all this way?"

"Because transporting is not an exact science and Rhiannon is not especially close to a suitable body of water. I would also think that the Coraniaids would have spies close to the places they'd be expecting me to turn up."

"They do, Mistress Nerys," said a breathy, soft voice quite close to Sophie's right side.

Sophie looked about, seeing nothing but endless flowers. A tap on her shoulder made her knees knock together like maracas. She looked, again finding no one in proximity. Nerys started to laugh.

"Did you do that?" Sophie demanded.

"No, Blodeuwedd did."

"Yes, I did," said the same voice.

This time Sophie found herself face-to face with the speaker, if a walking talking flower could have a face that is. Blodeuwedd turned out to be a gangly, vaguely humanoid creature, with leaves for limbs and a pale violet petals for hair. The bloom resembled a daisy, where the outermost petals fanned a white, circular center. Under close scrutiny a set of facial features became discernible amongst the snowy centre, an easy to miss face. It was more a distinction in the way the shorter petals aligned, their orientation taking on the outline of two eyes, a nose, and mouth. If you weren't prepared to see such a thing, you would most likely miss it.

The mouth opened, causing a wave of movement across the layers of shorter petals. "I am pleased to make the acquaintance of any friend of Nerys."

Sophie felt her own mouth hanging open, but she could not make any sound emerge. The creature offered one leafy limb in her direction, as though to shake. Nerys nodded her encouragement. Her own hand met it, finding the appendage had heft and the ability to grip like a human hand.

"This is my friend Sophie," Nerys offered when Sophie still hadn't spoken.

"A pleasure, Sophie. It is good to see you safe and well, Nerys. Have matters been settled then?"

"Not at all. This is merely a visit. I need to bring Sophie to my mother. I believe she will be able to help us."

"I hope so, my dear. The sooner this is over the better for all of Annwn."

"Agreed," Nerys looked to Sophie, whose hand was still held out before her. "Are you well, Sophie?"

"Yes, sorry. I beg your pardon, Blodeuwedd. I've never seen anything like you before."

"Nor will you again. She is one of a kind, and a careful observer of all that passes through her land."

She smiled at Nerys's compliment. "I do my best, Mistress. All has been quiet for many weeks now."

"Good news in its way. Though it would be nice to know what plans the Coraniaids have made."

Blodeuwedd shuddered at the mention of the name, causing her petals to flap. "Is it true they hear everything?"

"That is the legend."

"Then how can one fight such an enemy?"

"We have our ways. And without access to Annwn, nothing they overhear can be put into action."

"So true. Now I must be going, Nerys."

A gentle sweet-smelling wind ruffled Sophie's hair, and then Blodeuwedd was gone. She searched the never-ending expanse of blooms, realizing that Blodeuwedd's appearance was the perfect camouflage for such a place. She could hide in plain sight, and have one none the wiser.

Nerys gave a hint of a smile at her seamless departure, then continued on her way. "Be careful," the whispery voice of the land of flowers called after them.

The land of Rhiannon, and Nerys's mother awaited them. What they'd encounter before they reached their destination was yet to be seen.

CHAPTER 6

The pockets of oversized flowers soon began to thin, giving way to lush fields where cattle-like creatures grazed, and tidy hamlets filled with the most curious assortment of dwellings. Many times people greeted Nerys, or watched her pass with a quiet reverence.

Sophie soon understood that Nerys was an important figure in her land, the off-spring of *Annwn* royalty, and perhaps a leader in her own right one day. That understanding settled heavily on her mind, pushing aside any question of believability to her friend's claims. She was breathing the air in this alien world, feeling the dirt crunch beneath her feet. Truth wasn't in question any longer, it was what the revelation of such a truth would mean to her life.

The girls passed several lakes, which Sophie came to understand were called *llyns*, a word that seemed to require copious amounts of mucus to pronounce properly.

Congregated about these bodies of water were various species that either brought a smile to Sophie's face, or left her cringing. In one Nerys pointed out a pair of creatures, resembling small, sturdy horses. She brought a finger to her lips, warning Sophie to be quiet.

The creature's face was narrow, with a short mane like a janitor's push broom. They swam with grace and tremendous speed, and when one wandered onto an adjacent bank to graze, Sophie noticed that it had flat, webbed feet instead of hooves. When it realized it was being watched it gave an indignant snort in the girls' direction, then returned to the water.

"What are they?" Sophie asked.

"*Ceffyl Dwr.* A most powerful and magical creature. Almost impossible to catch."

"Like a horse?"

"Yes, and if you think their swimming is impressive, you should see them fly!"

"You're kidding me."

Nerys shook her head, laughing. "C'mon, we're almost there and I'm dying to see my mother."

Sophie stole one last look, but the two *Ceffyl Dwr* were nowhere to be seen. The narrow dirt path continued to follow the curving expanse of water, bringing them to a narrow, slightly off-kilter bridge built from piled rocks and long wooden planks. The lake had thinned, passing underneath at barely more than a trickle. The sound of their sandals against the wood ricocheted off the small thicket of trees to either side of the path, a denseness only interrupted briefly by the water's presence. A startling coldness filled Sophie's body as they walked the length of the bridge. Nerys also tensed and her tempo slowed. Just before the end she came to an abrupt stop.

"What's going on? This place gives me the willies, just like at the cemetery." As if in emphasis a large shudder rode up her spine.

Nerys didn't answer, instead closed her eyes. All about them, as though produced from the very air, a terrible wail sounded. Sophie jumped, stumbling against Nerys' back. She grabbed her friend's hand, eyes darting back and forth in search of the source of the sound.

A translucent, spectral being emerged from the trees to the girls' right, propelled by a frigid breeze that nipped at their skin. The being was female, with limp, grey tresses and the remains of a long dress draped over its skeletal frame. The eyes that regarded them were pools of darkness, wanting to drown them in the depths of the creature's despair.

"Don't look at it," Nerys said. Then she emitted a series of words, in conjunction with an elaborate set of hand gestures that stopped the creature in its tracks. It hung in the air, monstrous and hungry, yet forced to wait.

Nerys turned back to the end of the bridge, where a door had suddenly appeared.

The woods to either side of the door were still visible, leaving the barricade standing free of support, yet Sophie just knew there was no way they would be able to go around it. They would have to pass through it.

"*Bendith y Mamau*," Nerys said, to which the door swung open.

The coldness began to dissipate, and a quick glance in the creature's direction showed it retreating back to whatever terrible place it had come from. She followed Nerys through the doorway, finding them on the outskirts of a small village. The place smell of damp earth, smoke, and honey, making her brain light up in excited recognition of each distinctive aroma. A large, castle-like structure was a formidable presence in the background, a scarlet flag riding on a pole at the highest turret. Her friend giggled and clasped her hands together, before setting off again at a brisk pace.

"Are you going to explain to me what happened back there?" Sophie asked, jogging to keep up.

"Mother must have put an enchantment on the village to protect it."

"What was that thing?"

"Have you ever heard of a banshee?"

Surprisingly, she had. "Yes, it's like a ghost or spirit."

"Right. That's what that was, only we call them *cyhyraeth*. It recognized me as blood of this village, and allowed us to pass."

"*Bendith y Mamau*. Your aunt said that when I came for dinner."

"That's right. Good memory. Now let's go. Mother will be aware that I'm here by now." Her pace picked up even more, forcing Sophie to break into an awkward trot to keep up.

Many people of all respective ages milled about the village, a similar look to their features and golden hair the predominant attribute. Even when in the midst of menial chores like feeding horses or hanging laundry all moved with a not-to-be-missed grace. Several came to greet Nerys with affectionate hugs and groups broke into cheers of happiness at the sight of her.

Sophie found herself swept up in the merriment. She absorbed the outpouring of emotion from the village's inhabitants, an overwhelming and chaotic experience that left it difficult to think straight. Only when they at last passed through, progressing along the defined trail to the waiting castle, did the phenomena recede.

"This is your home I take it?" Sophie asked, though she already knew the answer. "Yes. It's a bit foreboding on the outside, but it really is lovely within."

"You're really important here, aren't you?"

Nerys gave her a serious look. "My family is. Of the twelve house of Annwn, Rhiannon is second only to Arawn, the homeland of our current king. Ruling of this area will fall to me or one of my sisters someday."

"Which is why it's so important to stop these marriages, right? You'd be essentially handing over your power base to outsiders."

"Right. The Land of Coranis is nowhere near as powerful as Annwn, though they are believed to possess a strange power allowing them to hear anything they wish to turn their attention to. We have been civil because we share a common border, and often travel and work the same area of the sea, but we do not wish to invite them inside our lands with any permanence."

"Yeah, I get that. You don't want to unnecessarily start any trouble, but you also don't want to hand over the keys to the kingdom. So to speak. So how did they ever get anyone to agree to this in the first place?"

"That's a story best left to mother's telling. I've heard only bits and pieces, but I'm sure she's become well-versed in all the details in my absence."

"You know, you're talking really weird since we've come here."

Nerys grinned. "I fall back on my natural ways, I confess. At least I'm not speaking my native tongue. Be glad of that."

"I am. There is no way I could ever produce some of the sounds I've heard in this place. It's not just another language, it's a physical ability I just don't have."

"Oh, everyone says that about the poor Welsh. Even in your

version of the place. It just takes some effort."

The towering doors to the castle's courtyard set in the protective stone gates were now right before them. Nerys gave a series of knocks against the wood, then stepped back to wait. After an agonizing two minutes the doors began to open inward, offering a glimpse of what lay within. Sophie followed Nerys through the entrance, not surprised when the doors came to a sharp close behind her. The space was like something she had only seen in movies, where people tended to animals, used strange machinery, and were generally hard at work at varied tasks needed to keep the castle and those who resided within its walls in tip-top shape.

Many lowered their eyes or gave a bowing nod of respect in Nerys's direction as she moved toward a small doorway set in the eastern wall of the castle's main structure. Two young men dressed in protective leather and metal stood guard, ready to draw the swords hanging at their sides. One flicked his gaze in Nerys's direction, to which she gave the barest of smiles. He was a handsome man, with darker than the norm hair and eyes like spring skies. If Sophie didn't know any better she'd have thought there might have been some attraction between the two.

The second guard pulled a large key from his belt and opened the door, allowing the girls to pass inside. Sophie experienced a flash of heat upon passing the darker-haired man, she assumed a cast-off of Nerys's reaction to his presence. She really needed to ask her friend about those weird emotional flare-ups she was having.

"So, he was cute," she said after the door had shut behind them.

"Who?" Nerys asked in a not entirely convincing tone.

"The guard back there. Don't pretend you don't know what I'm talking about."

She gave a self-conscious shrug, avoiding Sophie's gaze. "His name's Gethen. Son of one of my father's best men. He just took his position a few years ago."

"How nice to have him so close by."

"Yes, if I were still living here anyway." She started up a

curving flight of stone stairs. "He is cute, isn't he?"

"Very."

The stairs continued upward for a lengthy distance, to which Nerys did not seem the least bit affected. Sophie felt the travel in her lungs and calves, more than pleased when they came to the desired level of the dwelling. They entered a spacious hallway, lined with portraits and tapestries that depicted various battles and interactions with numerous strange beings and beasts. Sophie recognized Gruddyeu and Talar in one, captured in formal dress and impressive adornments.

The hallway opened up onto a grand space with a ceiling easily twenty feet high. To one side a pair of gold-painted double doors concealed a space beyond, and to the other a grand staircase rose to a wide balcony where a glorious multi-coloured window cast sweeping rainbows across the gleaming floor. Beyond were several doors and a long passage to the northern part of the building. A young woman stood at the rail, watching their approach with cautious eyes.

"Brynmor!" Nerys called out, obviously pleased to see her.

The woman kept her gaze steady, and did not immediately respond. "What brings you here, Mistress Nerys?"

The coolness of her tone seemed to catch Nerys by surprise. "I wish to speak with mother. I bring someone she needs to meet."

Brynmor gave Sophie her attention, looking her over from head to toe. "She did not inform me of your visit."

"I came without plan, Brynmor. What's wrong?"

"Many distressing incidents have occurred these past weeks, Nerys. I need to be certain you are in fact—you."

"The *cyhyraeth* allowed my entrance."

"True, but perhaps some unknown magic made this so."

The comment brought Nerys to a standstill. "How would you wish me to prove my identity?"

"Tell me what happened on Aderyn's fifth birthday."

Nerys grinned. "She transformed herself into a *Gwyllgi* to frighten Eira and myself, then couldn't figure out how to transform herself back for near three weeks. Father made her sleep with the other dogs until she regained her true form."

The response made Brynmor's face flush with happiness. She rushed down the stairs and flung herself into Nerys's arms. After much shrieking and gigging, which in turn induced a wave of giddy nausea in Sophie, the two settled down enough for introductions to be made.

"Brynmor, may I introduce my friend Sophie."

"A human?" she asked with some apparent trepidation.

"Yes, but a firm friend. I believe she is the one we have been told of."

Brynmor inhaled sharply. "Be truth?"

Nerys nodded. "Sophie, this is Brynmor. She is the daughter of my mother's lady.
We've grown up together."

Brynmor gave a quick curtsy. "Pleasure, Mistress Sophie."

"Ah, you too." She couldn't quite wrap her head around the expectations of her behaviour, so she continued to do her best to muddle through.

Brynmor and Nerys exchanged a private look, before bursting into laughter. Sophie wasn't sure if she was the source of their amusement or not, but she pretended indifference.

"Come with. She's waiting in her room," Brynmor said before starting back up the staircase.

Nerys took her hand, the touch sending a warm scurry up her arm. She wondered if Nerys was even aware of the physical effects she had on others. She seemed to take no notice of how the overflow of her emotional states transferred onto those about her. Maybe she was only as aware because she was not a *Tylwyth Teg*? Or maybe this is the sensitivity that Talar spoke of?

Soon the balcony was reached and Brynmor continued on, leading them down the passageway to the rear of the landing. Sophie let her fingertips brush along the uncovered area of stone wall, the texture rough and slightly cool. Several high-set windows looked through the thick stone walls down upon various areas of the castle's inner courtyard, where Sophie took in an impressive number of people, including many armed guards. One caught their movement past a particularly large pane of glass, meeting her perusal with stern eyes. The seriousness of the situation could not be missed.

Brynmor gave the chocolate brown door at the end of the hallway a light rap with her knuckles, which was answered by the sweetest of voices from inside. "Enter, Brynmor. I'm can wait no longer to see my daughter."

CHAPTER 7

The physical appearance of the woman far surpassed the beauty of her voice. In fact, if Sophie had not been viewing her with her own eyes she would not have believed that anyone could have been that stunning. Her hair matched Nerys's in colour and length, but possessed a fullness and curl. She was of a slender build, yet at the same time projected a voluptuousness that her offspring could not compete with. Her lips were tinged a peachy-pink, her skin a flawless ivory. The smile that appeared at the sight of her daughter dazzled.

"Mother!"

Sophie's breath caught in her throat as the two embraced. Their happiness could not be disguised, radiating about the room as a physical presence and making her painfully aware of how much she missed her own mother. As the thought filled her mind Nerys and her mother hastily pulled apart, casting troubled expressions in her direction. Nerys's mother walked toward her, placing a hand to each side of her face.

"So much pain for one so young," she said.

The lump in her throat seemed to quadruple at her words. The woman's eyes were searching, sympathetic.

"Mother, this is Sophie. I believe Talar has spoken to you about her."

"Yes, in depth."

Nerys came to stand with them. "Sophie this is my mother, *Tywysoges* Mairwen."

Out of the corner of her eye she saw Brynmor give a curtsy, an action she quickly mimicked. The servant nodded her approval.

"You may simply call me Mairwen. I know many have a difficult time with our native words."

"It's her title, like princess," Nerys said as an explanation.

"I am very honoured to meet you, Mairwen." Sophie curtsied again because she wasn't sure what else to do.

Mairwen smiled graciously, and taking Sophie's hand led her to a nearby table, sitting in the stream of light coming through one uncovered window. As the three sat, Brynmor scurried off as though some type of order had been given. Sophie settled onto a high-back dark wood chair, with a cushion so soft it was like sitting on a cloud.

A thought jumped into her mind, which must have been reflected on the change in her expression as Nerys and Mairwen both gave her their undivided attention. "Sorry, I was just thinking that we must have been here for quite a while now and I didn't exactly tell my grandmother when I'd be back. I don't want her to worry."

"She will not worry, dear. Hours passed in Annwn are but minutes in your reality."

"Really? Cool."

"Yes, an anomaly that has no explanation, yet is extremely useful."

"There's a lot of things here that I don't understand," Sophie said, her honesty turning watchful reticence into delight.

"It can be overwhelming for your kind, dear. The only cure is perseverance."

Mairwen's kind words lifted the cloud of unease that had settled about Sophie's person. Looking at the beautiful woman before her, Sophie couldn't image being able to stay afraid or angry in her presence for any period of time. She positively reeked of goodness and compassion, and her smile could melt the hardest of hearts. No wonder Nerys's father had fallen for her.

"Do you feel it, mother?" Nerys asked.

"I do. It's subtle, but not to be dismissed. She does have *Tylwyth Teg* blood, from somewhere in her past. It would be interesting to find the source." To Sophie she said, "Have you always possessed the gift of foresight?"

"I tried to explain to Nerys, it's not like I'm psychic. I just sometimes know where things are, how things happen, and once and a while I get a snippit of what people are thinking. But it's not something I can control. At least I don't think it is. I've never given it any real consideration before." Sophie realized she was babbling and promptly shut her mouth.

"I suspect it has been with you since birth, so as not to even be noticed. Often individual gifts strengthen with time, and many are kicked into overtime when puberty strikes," Mairwen said.

"This gift may lead us to the dagger."

"Perhaps. Though we must proceed with caution, Nerys. Much has happened while you have been away. There are whispers of uprisings against the King, and of enemies within the twelve houses."

"But why would any of the twelve want to align with the Coraniaids?"

"Control is always a powerful motivator, my love. Some find Gwyn ap Nudd too understated. There are those who think his age has made him soft, and perhaps it is his time to step down." Worry manifested as a tidy crease between Mairwen's golden brows.

"I don't like the sound of this, mother. Especially with you here without father."

"Do not worry, Nerys. The guards are always on hand."

"Yes, like that handsome Gethen," Sophie said before she could stop herself.

Nerys shot her look that should have dropped her dead on the spot. "Of course the guards are here, mother. I know daddy left you well attended. It will not stop my worry though."

"I think we should turn our minds away from needless apprehension. If Sophie is the one, she should be able to give direction for where the dagger lies."

Mairwen rose from the table, moving across the length of the room with a seamless, gliding walk. She stopped before a tall wardrobe, pulling a delicate key from the folds of her long dress to unlock it. Inside she reached for a rolled bit of parchment. Back at the table she laid the piece flat to reveal a crude map, which after a few moments of scrutiny Sophie recognized as the Islands of Great Britain. Yet the boundaries and place names dotting the yellowed parchment were none that she recognized from her modern day knowledge of the area. Save for the large Annwn scrawled across the lower portion of the main land mass she could have been viewing a completely foreign land. In some ways, she was.

In no conceivable way the map suddenly changed, drawing her attention with such force that once locked on it, she didn't know if it would be possible to draw her gaze away. Its presence called to her, demanding her focus. Her eyes followed the hand-drawn lines, taking names into her brain that should not have made sense, yet somehow sparked a deep sense of recognition. A phantom touch scurried across her arm, drawing a shudder. Her mouth lost all moisture, her throat constricting as though the invisible presence had its hands about her throat.

Her hands crept forward, but Sophie did not feel in control of the action. They came to rest at the section of the map where the border between Annwn and Coranis was clearly defined. Her fingers trembled. Hot tears filled her eyes, blurring the spiky script and the strange symbols dancing along the border between the respective areas.

"Llud LLaw Eraint." The uncomfortable words emerged from Sophie's throat, leaving a bitter taste behind.

Mother and daughter regarded each other with surprise, mixed with an undercurrent of alarm. The temperature of the room seemed to drop ten degrees in the blink of an eye, causing a startling chill.

"The name of the original King." Mairwen's voice was little more than a whisper.

"How could she know such a thing?" Nerys asked.

"There is no way I can fathom, my love. Perhaps she is the one."

Mairwen's touch to her outstretched hand broke the moment, effectively dispelling the strange phenomena. Yet even without the odd, intrusive pressure, she remained captivated by the document. Defying explanation, Sophie knew that it was an important piece to solving the puzzle of the lost dagger.

"This is the map that Llud LLaw Eraint used when making his way to the land of Coranis, isn't it?" Sophie asked, already knowing the answer.

"Yes," Mairwen answered.

Sophie reached down, tracing her fingertip along various locations and notes made on the map. A spark of electricity accompanied each touch. The physical shock parlayed into a mental one, giving Sophie glimpses of several distinct and vivid memories, all belonging to a man who had been dead for several centuries before her own birth. For a few, paralyzing seconds she saw what he had seen, felt the motion of his hands bringing ink to the paper now on display. The sensation exhilarated her, the vision clarifying as she forced herself to remain calm and embrace the manifestation.

"He was attempting to secure permission to pass through the land of the Coraniaids, to gain a surprise attack on Loarn, leader of Dal Riata in Gaidheal."

"Yes, this is all truth."

"Llud LLaw Eraint wanted to end a battle that had been waging for years, and felt it would only be a matter of time before his enemy attempted a similar alliance. He knew that Loarn was hungry for power, and wanted to expand his territory."

Mairwen nodded.

"He'd consulted *Eirianwen*, the wisest *Gwiddonod* in all the land, who'd informed him that such a request would be accepted. She also warned him of the steep price to pay for freedom from the ravages of war, one that might not be more favourable than the current situation."

The story came alive as the words spilled form her lips. A small army of men trudging through the heavy brush, the weight of their armor and weaponry burdening their progress. Their leader, the strong and handsome Llud LLaw Eraint, rode at the head if his men, flanked by several others on horseback. A gleaming sword dangled at his side, easily accessible for whatever challenge might present itself. His strength was irrefutable, as was the toll of the arduous journey to peace.

In the distance an assembly easily twice the size of Eraint's army waited, taking in the approach with respectful concern. This group stood tall, with lean, sinewy bodies and disproportionately long limbs. The snake-like digits of their pale hands gripped narrow staffs, and the occasional net. A soft wind tossed about the heads of unkempt dark hair, obscuring individual features.

Eraint pulled at the horse's reins, stopping about twenty yards from the Coraniaids. "Lonnog," he called out. "I come as friend. I ask for an audience before your leader, the good Ywain."

"For what purpose, Llud Llaw Eraint? Our peoples are known to keep to their own land."

"A common enemy."

"The Coraniaids have no enemy. We listen too well."

Eraint dropped from his horse with a controlled grace. He came closer to the collection of strange beings, with his shoulders squared and his expression serious. "We are well aware of your unique talent. As you must in turn be familiar with ours."

Lonnog stood silent. The change in perspective gave Sophie the first clear view of the being's face. Unlike Eraint who gave no outward reaction, Sophie tensed. Her breath sat in her chest as though afraid to emerge.

Reptilian was the first word that sprang to Sophie's mind upon seeing Lonnog's face without the obscuring veil of hair, though he was neither discoloured nor scaly. His skin tone was a soft mocha, pulled tight over an oval-shaped face that ended in a sharply pointed chin. Though his hair was thick and long, the face held not even a hint of mustache or beard, smooth like a pre-pubescent. Lips were but a slash, the nose long, but minimally raised from the height of the cheeks. Eyes like those of a giant fly searched Eraint's face, the orbs a gleaming ebony set high and wide from the other features.

"Magic." The single word hung between the two, taunting and desirable.

"Yes, magic. Of all sorts, depending on the beholder of individual talents. Access to such may prove useful to the Coraniaids, should they ever tire of only listening. One day you may desire action."

Lonnog stiffened as a ruffle of reaction wound through

both sides. At long last the large black eyes blinked. The tip of a narrow pink tongue ran along the lower lip. "Perhaps. A decision best left to Ywain himself."

"A sentiment I agree with completely."

Lonnog gave a quick flick of hand and the men behind him parted, allowing passage to the unknown lands. Eraint stepped into the enemy territory, with a handful of his best men following close behind. Lonnog stopped the men's' approach by pointing his long staff in their direction. "Just Eraint."

"Sir, you should not go alone," the closest man said.

"I'll be alright," Eraint answered before the Coraniaid army closed ranks, effectively swallowing him from view.

Sophie returned from the distant memory to find Mairwen and Nerys regarding her with concerned awe. She was seated, hands pressed against the map. Her heart was pounding, thumping about in her chest as though trying to escape.

"Are you quite alright, dear?"

Sophie shook her head, before taking a deep breath. "I think so. That was really intense."

"Indeed."

"What did you see?" Nerys asked.

"I saw Eraint meeting with the Coraniaids, and asking to meet with their leader…someone named Ywain. It was so real. I could hear and see and smell everything, just like I'd really been there."

"Hmm," was all Mairwen had to say.

Sophie waited, anxious for their take on what she'd just experienced. Even sitting there is Mairwen's room, far away in distance and time from the memory, she could still smell the damp earth and feel the cool breeze on her skin. The tenseness and excitement of the stolen moment refused to release its hold on her.

"I think this map is a conduit of some kind, like a familiar." Nerys choose her words carefully.

"Yes, I agree. Perhaps Eraint enchanted it, to help guide those after him. Certainly time has lost the truth of the matter. The map itself has only recently been found."

"What happens now?' Sophie asked.

"I think it best that I consult with Llyr, Nerys's father. I will send a messenger. In the meantime I think it's best for the two of you to return to Knob's End."

"Yes, mother."

"So that's it?"

"For now," Mairwen said, her answer firm.

Nerys stood, giving Sophie a pleading look. It took everything in her, but she managed to keep her mouth shut. Mairwen escorted the girls down to the main floor, where they found Brynmor overseeing a group of young women cleaning. She immediately came to them.

"Brynmor, take the girls to Gethen. Have him take them back to the portal. Their safety is his responsibility."

"Understood." She gave a quick bow of her head in Mairwen's direction, then stepped back and waited.

"Be safe, Nerys. You also, Sophie. Annwn has need of you yet." She gave her daughter a kiss to the cheek.

"I will see you soon," Nerys said.

"Ah, yeah. Nice to meet you, Mairwen."

She gave her daughter a long, pained look before retreating from the room. Brynmor hurried them back down the stone staircase, to the same door they'd entered. Gethen and his partner were still at their posts, alert and imposing.

"Mairwen has asked you to take the girls back to the portal, Gethen. They are not to be harmed." Brynmor addressed him in a prim, formal manner.

Gethen bristled at the order. "Of course, Brynmor. A task I am honoured to undertake."

Brynmor gave Nerys a quick hug. "Be safe." She disappeared inside, the door making a sharp clang behind her.

"Ladies," Gethen said, indicating they should walk before him.

Sophie went along with the maintaining the image of respectability as the three made their way through the village. She was bright enough to understand that certain protocols had to be followed, but she also knew that Nerys might not get another chance to speak with Gethen in private. As soon as they passed through the protective enchantment at the edge of the village's land, she gave her friend a sharp poke in the side with her elbow.

"Hey!" Nerys grumbled.

"Go and talk with him."

"I can't."

"Why not?"

"Because that's not how things are done here."

"The Nerys I know is brave and head-strong, and wouldn't let antiquated traditions keep her from the chance of being with her true love."

Nerys gave her a look. "Antiquated? Really?"

"Too much?"

"A tad, but you're right. Who knows when I might get another chance?"

Sophie hurried ahead, giving the two some relative privacy. A quick glance back showed Nerys falling in step with the object of her affection, as a nervous smile appeared on Gethen's face. As they continued over the narrow bridge Sophie couldn't help but look into the area of the forest where the *cyhyraeth* had appeared from. She shuddered as she remembered how its presence had made her feel, as though it had turned her blood to ice.

She did not want to see that thing again.

Stepping onto the dirt trail was an enormous relief, and also a disappointment.

Sophie would have loved the chance to explore the village more, and spend more time with Mairwen and Brynmor, and the members of the household she'd not had the chance to interact with. Perhaps when the trouble with the Coraniaids had been put behind them, there would be an opportunity for a visit of pleasure, not necessity.

Soon the vivid fields of Blodeuwedd appeared, touching them with its impossibly sweet aroma. Sophie searched, but did not locate the Mistress herself, yet the environment itself was enough to lift her spirits. Even Gethen broke into a brief smile as they began to walk the trail that cut through the endless rows of giant blooms. He and Nerys continued to chat as they made their way back to the portal, though Sophie could tell that his focus was still on their safety, as he continued to glance about. His hand rested on the hilt of his sword, to be drawn quickly should the need arise.

The flowers thinned, the landscape changing to open fields, and at last the small body of water from which they had emerged came into sight. The Morgens were gone. All was still and unspoiled, waiting to whisk them back to the unsuspecting inhabitants of Knob's End. Sophie waited politely as Nerys and Gethen said their good-byes. The body language of both spoke to their desire to cross the line from friendship. At last Nerys leaned in and pressed a kiss to his cheek. Sophie turned away, grinning and fighting the urge to cheer.

Gethen continued to watch as they entered the water. As the cool, swirling sensation began Sophie's last glimpse of Annwn consisted of his concerned expression and the sun glinting off the sword at his side.

CHAPTER 8

Mairwen had been right on the money with the time difference Sophie noted as the girls made their way home. The clock on the outside of the library showed it was only about twenty-five minutes later than when she'd passed it on her way to the cemetery. The rain continued as if they'd never been gone at all. Only her exhaustion from the miles of walking they'd done revealed the truth of the time spent in Annwn.

When they reached Sophie's house Nerys gave her a quick hug, before continuing on to her own home. She entered the front door, finding her grandmother was still away, running errands. The solitude was a relief, it gave her an opportunity to digest everything that had happened. She felt as though she'd been put through the proverbial wringer.

Her wet boots were left on the mat in the front hall before she made a beeline for the kitchen. Soon she had her hands wrapped around a mug of hot tea, with a plate of her grandmother's cookies before her. Her mind regurgitated a series of faces as she munched and sipped, forcing Sophie to consider each individual encounter she'd had, both real and borrowed, carefully. Removed from the circumstances it was hard to believe what she'd witnessed with her own eyes.

The map.

For some unknown reason Sophie was certain the map was the key to finding the dagger, but not in any traditional sense. While it might guide the way, helping to mimic the path taken so many centuries before, she thought there was more to it. A hidden message of some kind, whether in code or by magical manipulation she wasn't yet clear about. The answer seemed to be hovering just outside of her mental grasp, forcing her to dig deeper.

The sound of her grandmother pulling into the driveway interrupted her musings, in truth a welcomed distraction. Together they emptied the car of packages and grocery bags, settling into a comfortable routine of putting things away. It wasn't long before the mouth-watering aroma of home-made chili filled the small house.

By eight o'clock Sophie's eyes were drooping. There was no way she could finish the movie she and her grandmother had been watching. She used excessive studying as an excuse for how tired she was and slipped upstairs. The comfort and familiarity of her bed pulled her into an almost immediate sleep.

The hours till morning passed with unsettling dreams that often had her waking with a pounding heart and sweat dripping down her face. She witnessed bloody, violent battles of the past and glimpses of a murky future where the screams of Nerys and her family warned of terrible events yet to unfold. As was becoming her habit, she ended her slumber with the scene of she and Cadoc meeting by the water's edge.

Sunday vanished without even a whisper of threatening unknowns. Sophie kept expecting Nerys to call, but she never did. Maybe she needed a breather as well.

She was waiting for Sophie at the end of her driveway on Monday morning however. The sight of her safe and smiling lifted Sophie's spirits like nothing else would have. She fell into step with her friend and they walked down the block, neither commenting on events that had been unlike anything either one had ever experienced. When they met up with Marcy, she and Nerys shared a private look. So-called normal life was now a façade, hiding the girls in plain sight from a reality that most would not even be capable of believing in.

As they walked through the pleasant suburban surroundings Sophie half expected strange, mythological creatures to appear. There was only the rattle of engines, and the occasional barking from your run-of-the-mill dog. Instead of wide expanses of emerald fields and rolling hills, there were tidy lawns and privacy fences. Everything seemed so—ordinary.

The school was the same as it had been when she'd left it Friday afternoon, which in a strange way disappointed her. It seemed that life should be different, better, bigger, yet everything continued as though none of what she'd experience had ever occurred. Marcy had rattled on and on about her boyfriend, oblivious to the fact that her friends were thinking about something else entirely.

"I'll catch you guys at lunch," Marcy said before heading off to her homeroom. Sophie smiled and waved, feeling like a fraud. It wasn't that she didn't care about Marcy's life, her problems just seemed so mundane.

Sophie entered their homeroom just ahead of Nerys, immediately catching Mr. Sampson's eye. Something passed between them, causing the hair on Sophie's neck to dance. When she paused he smiled, making her realize she'd never seen him with anything but a serious or concerned expression on his face. The smile softened him and made her wonder about the suspicions she'd been harboring against him. As the trip to Annwn had proven, things were not always what they seem.

The rest of the week passed in quiet ordinariness, which sat in Sophie's stomach like an undigested meal. Waiting and wondering was far more difficult than anything she imagined could happen in Annwn.

At last Friday appeared, beginning as normally as each of the days before it. When the lunch bell sounded the usual group gathered together, all happy for the break away from classes. It had started to rain again, so they sat at a table near the back of the cafeteria, instead of at their spot under the large elm tree. Sophie noticed that Nerys's attention often drifted, eyes wandering over the crowd about them. In one corner Mr. Henry sat eating his lunch with a female English teacher, smiling and seemingly oblivious to their presence.

"So what do you have planned for the weekend?" Liza asked Sophie between bites of her turkey sandwich.

"Not much. Studying and helping my grandmother around the house." The lie rolled easily off Sophie's tongue.

In class Mr. Henry smiled as she and Nerys entered, as he had every day that week, but as soon as they passed him a shiver raced down Sophie's spine. If a person's gaze could bore into flesh, then that's what Mr. Henry was doing. She took her seat as quickly as she could, slumping down in her seat to try and avoid further scrutiny. Nerys also looked perturbed; a soft flush was creeping up her neck.

The minutes ticked by like hours. Sophie repeatedly glanced at the clock and to where Mr. Henry sat at his desk. Each time it was barely more than a few minutes from the last time she'd checked and the teacher meet her look every time, his neutral expression unwavering. Yet there was something about him that was different, frightening. When at last the bell rang, she all but leapt from her seat.

Just a few more steps, she thought.

"Sophie," Mr. Henry called.

Crap. She turned, feeling Nerys hesitate beside her. "Go on, Nerys. We'll just be a minute."

Nerys walked slowly to the door, seeming reluctant to leave.

Sophie came to stand before Mr. Henry, irrationally thankful for the large desk separating them. It wasn't as though he would attempt something in such a public location, but Sophie couldn't shake the feeling of unease. She looked anywhere but directly at him.

"Did you have a nice weekend, Sophie?"

The question surprised her. "Uh…yeah, I guess."

"Good. I just wondered after seeing you Friday evening. You looked a bit upset?"

"Nope. Everything's good."

The lack of response continued for so long she was compelled to lift her gaze from the desk's cluttered surface. As soon as their eyes locked he smiled. He had her. The tension in the room expanded, making her breathing tight. Her feet wouldn't move, she was trapped.

Without a movement that she could not perceive he was beside her. The blue of his eyes was so electric it terrified her. An intense shudder rocked through her body. All the moisture evaporated from her mouth, leaving her tongue the consistency of a shed snake skin. He closed the space between them, lips pulled wide in a smile more like a grimace.

Sophie whimpered.

"Mr. Henry?" A male voice called into the room from the doorway.

The sound wiped the smile from Mr. Henry's face. As soon as he turned his attention away from Sophie, the sensation evaporated. Her shoulders dropped and a breath expelled from her with such force it made her light-headed. While making herself not to look at Mr. Henry again she charged toward the door, almost colliding with the person standing there.

Mr. Sampson.

His fingers brushed Sophie's arm as she passed, surging through her flesh like an electric current. He gave her a nod so brief it could have been a figment of imagination, and then she was swallowed up in the dense collection of students getting ready to leave for the day.

Nerys appeared at her side. "What was that about?"

"I'm not sure, but he was doing something to me. Using magic I think." Before she could stop herself, Sophie cast a look behind herself. She was more than relieved to find that Mr. Sampson had not followed her.

"That's a serious no-no. What did he do?"

"He...looked at me, and then I couldn't move, I couldn't breathe. He didn't have a chance to do anything else because Mr. Sampson interrupted us."

"I saw him go in." She stopped, pulling Sophie alongside her. "I wonder what he's up to."

"Maybe your mom will know?"

"She would have said something to us if she knew there were others from Annwn here."

"Right."

"Let's go to my place and talk this over with Gruddyeu and Talar."

The girls walked home with Marcy, as they did most days, with Sophie doing her best to project an easiness that she did not feel. Marcy didn't seem to pick up on anything out of the ordinary, as she prattled on about a number of typical teenage girl topics during the fifteen minutes it took to get from the school to her house. After bidding good-bye she and Nerys continued on, at a decidedly quicker pace.

Passing by Sophie's home she was overcome with an urge to run inside and dive into her bed to hide under the covers. She swallowed back her reticence, soldiering on. There were no words as they walked on, the space about them a void.

At last they turned onto Nerys's street. They both broke into a trot, their destination beckoning them with the promise of safety and answers. This time the security measures about the property felt justified. The sound of Nerys's fingers on the alarm keyboard was music to her ears. The triumphant feeling didn't last.

As soon as they entered the curving hallway leading from the front foyer the indications of trouble were evident. Several of the portraits lining the walls had been knocked askew, one lay on the ground with a sprinkle of what appeared to be blood across its surface. Nerys pressed a finger to her lips, which Sophie acknowledged with a quick nod. Slowly they continued, listening intently for any sign of the person responsible for the damage.

The doors to the study were wide open, the soft sounds of scurrying feet wafting out to them. Nerys mumble something that Sophie could not understand, then she felt the warm tingle of magic on her skin. She put her faith in what she hoped was some type of protective spell, and followed closely at her Tylwyth Teg friend's heels.

The room lay in shambles. Books were strewn about, along with overturned shelves and tapestries pulled from the walls. At the centre of the chaos stood Gruddyeu, dangling some type of charm over a parchment spread across the table. His hair stood in untidy tuffs about his narrow head, and when he briefly turned in their direction there was a deep gash across one cheek.

As he turned back to his activity, Sophie asked, "What's he doing?"

"Scrying."

"Of course." Sophie had no idea what scrying was.

A glistening smear of blood could also be seen about the

bottom of the teardrop- shaped charm that was furiously swaying over what Sophie could now see was a map. Not dissimilar to the one she had seen in Mairwen's chambers, this one lacked the handwritten notes and markings.

"What happened, Uncle?"

"A group of *Tylwyth Teg* came here. They tore the place apart before taking off again. Whatever they were looking for they didn't find it."

Shock made Nerys's eyes widen. "I don't understand. Our kind came here? To fight against us?"

"The rumour of descent is true, dear one. Not all of Annwn fights on the same side."

"Where's Talar?"

"She's gone to warn your mother."

Nerys righted one of the chairs, and sunk down onto the seat. "We have a traitor in our ranks then. There is no way to have known where we were or the magic to get here otherwise."

"You're absolutely correct." For the fourth time in a row the charm came to a stop over a specific area on the map. "What the Dewi is going on here? This makes no sense at all." Gruddyeu's irritation made him tremble.

Sophie leaned on the table, studying the area of the map. It was a small island off the mainland of Annwn's territory. "What are you trying to find out?"

"Where these traitors came from, of course! But no citizens of Annwn lives on that wasted island. In fact no at all has lived there for centuries. Those bastards came from closer to home."

Nerys came closer. "Anffrwythlon. What is that place? I know the name, and it rings some bells about some superstition, or something bad that happened there."

"There are many stories, though the land has been abandoned for so long there's no clear access to the truth any longer. All I can say for sure is that it is a terrible, desolate place where no plant life will grow, and any who stay too long come to find themselves in the grips of a crippling despair. There have been whispers that this is the source of the *cyhyraeth*."

Sophie shuddered, remembering the sight of one approaching them on the bridge before Nerys's village. The idea of a collection of such beings was too awful to fathom.

"Yes, yes," Nerys agreed. "But there's something else. Something tied to what's going on now."

"It was the supposed resting place of the Dagger of Everlasting Truth, but that has long been dismissed as nothing more than fable. No one rightly knows where the dagger was laid, or where it's been taken to or by whom."

"But someone lived there once. I mean it wasn't always the way it is now."

"Yes, it was once the home of the *Coblynau*, the small people who mined the land for silver. But they were overtaken by a group of *Pwca*, shape-shifters who appeared as harmless hares, slowly killing the *Coblynau* in their sleep. When only a few remained they were forced to flee to the mainland of Annwn, where they remain to this day. One such *Pwca* fell for beautiful young woman named Tegwen, who he whisked off to the island in the dead of night. The young girl was so terrified it says she cried for an entire decade, her tears turning the once plentiful soil to rock. The conditions became so harsh that even the *Pwca* did not want to stay, so it was abandoned."

"What happened to the girl?"

"I'm not sure. Some say she died, others say she was reunited with her family."

"Sounds like the perfect place to hide something you'd never want to be found," Sophie said.

Gruddyeu looked at her as though he'd forgotten she was present. "I suppose you're right."

"Maybe that's why the thingy-ma-jig keeps coming back to this place. Maybe the people that came here were in whatchamacallit before coming here."

"Looking for the dagger you mean?"

"Yeah. And when they couldn't find it they came here."

"They must have thought we knew something they didn't."

The room began to spin. Sophie gripped the edge of the table with all her might to keep from tumbling to the floor. The vision gripped her brain as though it meant to rip it from her skull. Snap, the room was gone. Instead she found herself in a long boat, oars manned by an odd assembly of Tylwyth Teg and Coraniaid men. The wind screeched across the frigid, grey waters, touching exposed skin like the hand of death. In the distance a land mass could be seen, an indistinct shape but a few shades darker than the sea.

Powerful arms rowed on, pushing the boat to its destination. Within a hundred yards of landing, the jagged, rocky shore arose, resembling a mouthful of broken teeth. With care the men brought the ship in, narrowly missing being smashed against the rocks by a sudden, violent wave. The boat was lifted and carried onto the flattest area that could be found. From this landing only two men ventured further, one Tylwyth Teg and one Coraniaid.

Together they travelled a vast distance, never once speaking to one another. The Coraniaid carried a large sack over one shoulder, the strap of which he often adjusted throughout the walk, a seemingly nervous gesture. As the sky began to bleed violet from the approach of night, they came upon a large, pyramid-shaped pile of stones that could not be the making of nature. Ducking around one side the two men paused, giving each other a thoughtful look. They passed out of Sophie's unnatural view and disappeared.

"Are you alright, Sophie?" she heard Gruddyeu asking as her vision of the present place and time returned.

She attempted to answer, but her throat was too restricted to allow sound to escape.

Nerys rushed to her side, placing a warm hand on her arm. In that instant her feelings of fright and pain dissipated and within thirty seconds normal breathing returned. She looked to her friend and understood.

"You can affect how I feel?"

Nerys nodded, almost shyly. "I'm an empath. I can alter how people feel and I have an affinity with spirits of all types."

"You did this to me before, at school."

"Yes, I try not to unless someone really needs it. You were panicking."

"I couldn't breathe." She looked into Nerys's eyes, burning with nervousness. "It's alright. It totally helped me to calm down, and then everything was fine."

"Another reason the Coraniaids want the sisters. They possess unique gifts that could be exploited to their advantage," Gruddyeu said.

"What gifts?"

Nerys gave a bitter smile. "In addition to the magical knowledge that has been passed on to me from my ancestors, my sisters and I have abilities that few others do. As I said I am empathic, and often able to control or change a person's physical or emotional feelings. I can also communicate with most spirits or creatures that are not flesh. Aderyn can control animals and transform into a bird. Eira can make the elements work for her to both beneficial and detrimental consequences."

"Wow." Sophie had a hard time wrapping her brain around the new information.

The silence that had enveloped the room was disrupted when a bloody and shaken Mr. Sampson stumbled into the room. Sophie shrieked. Nerys and her uncle began to chant, different but equally strange recitations, the words tickling along her skin.

"No...wait. I'm here to warn you..." Mr. Sampson said before collapsing to the floor.

They heeded his words, approaching his prone form with caution. A serious cut ran across his right temple, weeping a sluggish stream of blood onto the highly-polished floor. His shirt was ripped, showing more wounds to his torso.

Nerys knelt. "Warn us about what?"

Before he could answer Mr. Henry burst through the door. He also appeared to have been in a recent scuffle, but was not as badly hurt as the other man. "Don't believe a word he says. He's trying to trick you."

"What in the name of Dewi is going on here?" Gruddyeu demanded.

"I have been sent here by Gwyn ap Nudd. I was to watch over Nerys without your knowledge. A second set of eyes as it were."

"There was doubt about my ability to protect Nerys?"

"There is no question of your skill or loyalty, Gruddyeu. The King had been told that the Coraniaids have infiltrated the noble ranks of Annwn, turning some of our own kind against him in secret. If one of the sisters were taken, it has been surmised that it could force him to honour the agreement."

"No... don't..." moaned Mr. Sampson.

"Don't listen to him," Mr. Henry snapped as he gave the man a kick to the ribs. "He attached me. I was just about to get away when he pulled an entrapment spell on me. It took several minutes before I could figure out which one and release myself. He got a head start on me."

So that's what had been off about the teachers; magic. "What should we do, Mr. Henry?" Sophie asked.

"Domnall, please."

"I don't recall having heard that name before," Gruddyeu said.

"I am one of the sons of Howell, in the north."

"Have proof, do you?"

Domnall fished about in his pocket before pulling out a ring with a large red stone and a line of script about the band. Gruddyeu took the piece, and examined it carefully, while Nerys passed her gaze between the unconscious man on the floor and the one standing with her uncle. At least, satisfied, he handed it back.

"Nerys, go with Domnall. Sophie, too. It's obviously not safe for you here any longer. Tell your mother what has happened. There could be others after your sisters."

Nerys did as she was told, grabbing Sophie's hand and following Domnall from the room. They headed to the cemetery, stopping to tell Sophie's grandmother that she planned to spend the weekend at Nerys's. Once at the enchanted pond they waded in and allowed the magic to whisk them off to Annwn.

When they emerged from the other end of the portal they discovered a small group of men waiting along the water's edge. They smiled at their approach.

"Your men?" Nerys asked.

"Most definitely," Domnall answered.

Sophie wasn't surprised to find herself in different clothing, along with Nerys and Domnall, outfits that reminded her of some strange fusion of fairy tale and Medieval England.

Strange how easy it had become to accept everything that was happening to her.

"Domnall," one of the men called. "So glad to have you back."

"As I am to be free of that ridiculous place."

He joined his men and the girls waited for his direction. In addition to his clothing his appearance had also altered. He appeared younger, and if possible, even more attractive than he had in his guise as Mr. Henry.

"You never fail to amaze, sir."

Domnall chuckled. "No praise is needed. She handed herself right over." He turned in Nerys's direction. "Didn't you?"

When he turned to look at the girls the façade of goodness had completely drained away. Though still handsome, the face before them was a monster's. The ring that had convinced Gruddyeu of his authenticity was tossed into the pond. His haunting blue eyes were hard and angry.

Two of the men seized Nerys's arms at the same time she called out, "Run, Sophie!"

So she did. She ran faster than she ever had in her life. The only problem was she had no idea where she was running to.

CHAPTER 9

Belatedly Sophie realized she'd run off in the opposite direction of Nerys's village. With her heart pounding and blood hissing in her ears, she plunged into the dense forest. The sounds of Nerys's screams and the angry calls of the men kept her from looking back. She needed to lose her would-be captures and find her way back to the land of Rhiannon.

The trees in the forest were so tightly packed it was difficult to maneuver, the soaring canopies blocking out all but the infrequent stream of sunlight. Sophie moved through the heavy, damp air, her fear giving her a stamina she'd never before possessed. Her frequent changes of course shook the pursuers from her trail, but also completely disoriented her from which direction she was headed in. At last she saw a break in the line of trees and bolted for it.

Stepping out from the dark into the powerful afternoon light left her temporary blind. She blinked several times. Slowly the flashing groups of multi-coloured dots became solid objects; a green field with a narrow dirt road curving along its expanse. Her gaze travelled from right to left to settle on a sight both startling and expected.

The young man from her dreams known as Cadoc, stood with his horse at the pond's edge. He held the reins loosely, letting the animal drink. Sophie took a step in his direction and the movement caught his attention. He turned, meeting her face on. A brief expression of shock, though not surprise, crossed his face. Then he smiled.

"Hello there, miss. Lost, are you?" He asked as she walked toward him.

"I guess I am," Sophie agreed.

She stopped a few feet from where he stood. They continued to smile at one another while the horse gave an exasperated snort, then returned to her drink. Cadoc laughed.

"Seems to me we've done this before," he said.

"You've dreamed of this moment?"

"A few times. I believe your name is Sophie?"

"That's right. And you're Cadoc."

"And now that we have been properly introduced, would it be presumptuous of me to ask how in the world it's possible to have dreamt of this moment?"

"Annwn is a magical place."

"In truth, Sophie. But I am not possessed of such abilities. Are you?"

"Not at all. I think this is of something bigger than the both of us, yet it seems we will both have a part to play."

"Make your meaning clear."

"Nerys of Rhiannon has been kidnapped."

His hesitation turned to alarm, tightening his eyes and mouth. "Then we must let her parents know at once."

"Of course."

Cadoc mounted the horse in one fluid movement. Sophie let the young man help her onto the animal, to ride behind him. She clasped her arms about his waist, faced pressed to the rough texture of his shirt.

The horse raced along the dirt trail, past the flora of Blodeuwedd, where she felt unseen eyes watching their progress. Just as she had seen in her dreams, a flock of *Adar Llwch Gwin* flew overhead, casting a wide berth of shadow on the land for several seconds.

At the road before the gates to Rhiannon they dropped to the ground, walking the horse with them. Sophie had warned Cadoc of the *cyhyraeth* guarding the entrance. He seemed to take the comment in stride, and after the strangeness surrounding their meeting, there was no reason not to take her at her word.

When the hideous creature appeared Sophie stood her ground. She did not remember the hand gestures and recitation that Nerys had used to stop the creature's approach so she raced toward the gate, pulling Cadoc along with her, who in turn led his horse by the reins. She did best to pronounce the difficult words clearly. "*Bendith y Mamau.*"

The door opened and they raced inside. As they closed behind them the specter was stopped mid-shriek, much to Sophie's relief. They skidded to a stop once safe, resuming their voyage to the castle at a more dignified pace. A few villagers cast concerned or curious glances their way, but no one attempted to block their progress.

They were stopped once again at the enormous doors to the castle's private land.

Sophie knocked, waiting for a response. After several minutes an older man appeared along the wall, pulling thoughtfully at his beard as he scrutinized the callers.

"What business have you?" he called.

"Get Gethen. It's very important," Sophie called in response.

The man gave her a strange look before disappearing from view. When the gates swung open, revealing Gethen, Sophie was so happy she could have burst. Once in her sight she raced ahead, diving into the arms of the surprised guard. Cadoc had no choice but to follow. Despite Sophie's actions, Gethen kept his poise.

"Gethen, I need to speak with Mairwen. Something terrible has happened."

"Slow down. Tell me."

"Nerys has been taken."

Gethen looked from Sophie to Cadoc, then to the other guard who had trailed along behind him, and was listening in on the conversation. "I need to take them inside."

He took Sophie's arm, heading to the castle.

"Wait. My horse," Cadoc called.

"Go ahead," the other guard said and took the reins from his hand. When Cadoc didn't move he added. "She'll be here when you get back."

Gethen ushered them inside, personally taking them to Mairwen's private quarters.

He knocked. A full minute passed before the door opened, revealing a troubled Talar. "Gethen, Sophie. And is that Cadoc? What in the world is going on?"

"We must speak with Mairwen."

Talar stepped back to allow them to pass. The seriousness in Gethen's voice was all the prompting she needed. Mairwen rose to her feet upon seeing the odd assembly filing into her room.

"What's happened? Is it Nerys?"

Gethen nodded, a sharp, angry movement. "She's been taken. I don't have the details."

"Speak to me, Sophie."

"A man named Domnall has been pretending to be a teacher in Knob's End. He staged an incident to make us think that he was helping us, but it was a trick. He had men waiting for us when we came through the portal. I managed to get away, and Cadoc helped me find my way here."

"Domnall? You're sure?"

"Yes, that's what he said."

Mairwen looked to her sister. "This is not good. The only chance is to find the dagger."

"I volunteer to help in any way I can," Gethen said.

"Bless you, boy. I need everyone I can trust at the moment. Please everyone sit down. There are things to discuss."

Sophie followed her to the table, feeling a deep apprehension at the sight of the Llud LLaw Eraint's map open on the surface of it. She feared another vision, yet she knew them to be a potentially helpful phenomena. She was certain the answers were somehow tied to that piece of paper. Figuring out what they held and how to access them would be the challenge.

"Are you alright. Sophie?"

She realized she had stopped, staring at the map. "Yeah, sorry."

Once seated Sophie passed along all the information she had. The sisters exchanged thoughtful looks, while Gethen appeared angrier with every passing second. His hand kept touching the sword at his side, and if his eyebrows had drawn any closer together they would have been one solid line. When she reached the part about the scrying and the location of *Anffrwythlon*, where the charm kept stopping, Mairwen's eyes grew large as saucers.

She grabbed Sophie's hands. "You're certain?"

"Yes, Mairwen. Gruddyeu told us a story of how the island became so desolate. I remember it very clearly."

"This is most troubling," Talar said.

"Yes, but the truth is often not one of our choosing."

"Ladies, please, I mean no disrespect, but can you just tell us what you think is going on?" Cadoc blurted. He'd been so quiet that his venture into the conversation was startling.

"Domnall is the son of Loarn, the current ruler of Gaidheal. They must be helping the Coraniaids with this mission to force the agreement through. They'd know we will do anything to have Nerys returned safely. All they have to do is hold her until the allotted time passes and they win."

"What of *Anffrwythlon*?" Gethen asked.

"It was rumored to be the resting place of the dagger, but the passing time has made this a guess at best."

"The dagger?" Cadoc asked.

As Mairwen explained to the men the agreement made between the long ago King Llud LLaw Eraint and the Coraniaids, Sophie's hand began to slide across the map, movement not of her control. As her fingertips touched the area depicting *Anffrwythlon* the vision of the men in the boats came to her. She was suddenly certain the voyage had been to place the dagger there, and that the two who had laid it in its resting place had given their lives to keep the location secret.

"It's here," Sophie said. "Or at least it was." Her words drew everyone's attention. "You're certain?" Mairwen asked.

"Yes."

Talar looked to her sister, eyes wide. "I told you. She is to help us. We must trust her word as absolute truth."

"I'm inclined to this conclusion also, Talar." Mairwen let her gaze settle on the map. A single tear escaped, trailing down her cheek to dampen the old parchment. "Nor do I think it coincidence that Sophie would run into one of Annwn's most travelled inhabitants. Sophie, Cadoc, the two of you must go to *Anffrwythlon* together. Take the map, as there is certain to be secrets and help to be found within in it yet."

"And if the dagger is not to be found there?" Cadoc asked

"Then keep searching. You know these lands better than

anyone. With your knowledge, the map, and Sophie's visions, the answer must be available. The time line is not far off." Her meaning was plain.

"Mairwen," Gethen said before being cut off.

"I have need of you as well, Gethen," Mairwen continued. "I have lost contact with Llyr. I fear he has been injured…or worse. You must organize the guards. Enlist the help of any who will join us. My husband and daughter must be found."

"What of Eira and Aderyn?" Talar asked.

"Safe for now."

A few seconds of heavy silence passed. Gethen rose suddenly, his sword clanging against the table. The sound jarred the others from their reticence, setting events into motion.

"Talar, make sure the staff provides food and water for Sophie and Cadoc's journey, and have a horse brought up from the stables. Cadoc, take a copy of the official seal of Rhiannon, it may help your passage through difficult lands." She rolled the map, tying it with a thin band of leather, then handed it to Sophie. "I need to contact Geraint of Dyfed. He has always been our closest friend and ally. Gethen, I will instruct him to treat you as my ambassador in this matter."

"Understood." His hesitation met Mairwen's pain. She came and pressed a chaste kiss to his cheek, which sent him on his mission faster than any order could have. The well-being of his land's ruling family was now on his shoulders.

Talar followed Gethen from the room, with Sophie and Cadoc trailing behind in quiet bewilderment.

"Sophie, wait. A word in private," Mairwen called.

The request stopped her in her tracks. When she turned her gaze back to Mairwen, she found her opening the tall bureau with the key worn about her neck. From inside she withdrew a small red velvet pouch. Her hand trembled as she handed it over to Sophie.

"Take this. It can offer some protection from the things you might encounter."

As the bag changed hands there came a soft tinkling sound. Something solid, and with some heft, was concealed within the soft cloth. Mairwen nodded, prompting Sophie to pour the contents onto her palm. A silver charm on a long, intricate chain emerged, baring the strange symbol she had once doodled in her science text book.

"Truth," Sophie said.

Surprise made Mairwen's eyes shine and her lips moved as though attempting to smile. "Yes, truth. Wear this for protection. Only those of the purest intentions can tap into its power."

"I don't understand," Sophie answered, slipping the chain about her neck.

"For brief moments of time the charm can cloak its wearer, basically making them undetectable. It may come in handy on a journey such as yours."

"It can make me invisible?"

"More a trick of the eye, but you will be visually undetectable."

She let the explanation settle in.

"Do you think I can do this, Mairwen?"

"I have hope."

Sophie took the words to heart, knowing how Gethen must have felt upon receiving his instructions. Not knowing what else could be said, Sophie left the room. As the door closed she thought Mairwen had started to cry.

I can't screw this up, she thought, while at the same time imagining about a thousand ways should could just that.

Talar and Brynmor met her on the lower level with water and neatly packed bundles of dried meat, bread, and fruit. The three carried these outside, where Cadoc was packing other items onto his horse. A sturdy, chocolate-brown horse stood beside his, equally laden with blankets and other essentials for their journey. When their food provisions had been added, he helped Sophie onto her mount.

"Her name is Jili," he said, adjusting the reins to a comfortable length for Sophie. With a stroke across the creature's fur, she leaned forward. "Well, Jili, I hope you and I will be good friends. I need you."

In response the horse gave a soft whiny and trotted on the spot, bringing a grin to Sophie's face. She'd never been a big animal lover. Maybe this experience would change her mind.

Turning her attention back to the humans about her, she found Cadoc looking at her as though she'd suddenly grown a second head. She straightened up, pretending indifference to his scrutiny.

"Be safe, Sophie," Talar said. "We need you."

There was nothing more to say. Cadoc led the way back to the main gate and out across the stone bridge. Instead of heading back the way they'd come he moved along the southern edge of Rhiannon, following a well-worn dirt trail. Though he'd barely glanced at the map, which Sophie had tucked in the soft leather bag, he led the way with unassuming confidence. She liked that about him.

Many hours later they were still following the same trail, with little change in the surrounding geography. The sunlight was softening, letting shadows elongate and the air chilled. At last they entered a small valley, where the forest receded from the trail, and a small pond sat undisturbed. Cadoc stopped his horse, dismounting with a graceful strength that Sophie had no hope of mimicking. Not getting caught in the stirrups was about the best she could hope for.

He took a quick scan of the area before giving her his attention. "This is a good place to stop for the night."

"Okay," Sophie agreed. He would know better than she.

She lowered to the ground with a small stumble, but didn't fall. Under his watchful eye they gathered some wood for a fire and unpacked the blankets and rations. She organized the food as he got the fire started. His arms were well-defined, and Sophie felt heat creeping up her throat as she watched him. He didn't seem to notice, or at least he didn't comment if he did. The circumstances of being alone with an attractive young man in the middle of nowhere struck her full force.

After they had eaten, and night was closing in Sophie lay wrapped in a blanket, with her head on the leather bag. Cadoc assumed a similar position on the opposite side of the fire, his knife with an inch of his hand.

"Tell me something about yourself, Cadoc," Sophie said when she could no longer stand the silence.

"Not much to tell I'm afraid."

"Why do they call you the wanderer?"

With the question he rose on his elbow, not quite smiling. "I've been riding since I was a small boy, my father taught me. I have always loved the feeling, being able to go anywhere I fancied." His gaze clouded as his mind visited some private memory. "Anyway, my parents were both killed in an accident the year I turned twelve. After that riding was my salvation. I literally wandered from one end of this land mass to the other. I've seen every square inch of Annwn, Gaidheal, and even Tir nan Og. I even snuck into Coranis once, though I didn't much fancy it. The land is very dark and flat, and I could never escape the feeling of being watched."

"How did you get in other lands? Don't they have magic like they do here?"

"I have my ways, Sophie. My father was an apprentice to the highest order of *Y Dyn Hysbys*. He taught me more than just riding."

She was too tired to ask what a *Y Dyn Hysbys* was. "I'm sorry about your parents. I lost my mother last year, so I can understand how you must have felt."

"Yes, so now there's just Roshyn and I."

"Oh, is that your horse's name? That's pretty."

He chuckled. "Thank you."

"Good-night, Cadoc," Sophie said after another long pause.

"Rest well. We have a long journey tomorrow."

The sound of his voice was the last thing she remembered before the sun rose on a new day.

CHAPTER 10

A barely audible rustling sound began to seep into the thin veil of sleep. Sophie tried to ignore it, but once she'd been pulled to the realm of wakefulness there was no going back. She rolled onto her side, expelling a deep yawn. Her eyes were reluctant to open, and once they did the image brought to her brain did not make the least bit of sense. From her prone position the view ahead of her was turned on its side, and furthermore was completely unfamiliar to her.

Sophie snapped upright so quickly the motion came with a wave of dizziness. Her sudden movement startled Cadoc, causing him to drop the map he'd been holding.

"You alright there?" he asked.

"Yeah, sorry. Didn't know where I was for a sec."

"There's some tea, still warm, and some fruit. We must head out soon. We should make the shore by afternoon."

As Sophie puttered about, eating and cleaning herself up as best she could, Cadoc continued to stare at the parchment. Sophie finally realized he wasn't actually studying the map, as in to follow its direction, so much as examining it.

"What's up?" she asked.

He lowered the parchment to meet her gaze. "There is something about this map. I can't quite put my finger on it, but it gives me the feeling that it's something more than a directional guide."

"I think so, too."

"Do you?"

"Yes, when I touch it I experience visions, like I'm seeing the things that happened back when this pact was made with the Coraniaids." She shuddered.

"You think that Llud LLaw Eraint put a spell of some kind on it? For what reason?"

"Maybe to help prevent this marriage form happening. At the time it may have been the only way, but he must have suspected that it would have been bad for Annwn if the deal actually succeeded."

Cadoc leaned back, letting the map rest on his lap. The early morning light touched his eyes in such a way they glimmered, highlighting their unusual shade of green. Sophie did her best to keep her expression serious, which was not an easy feat when he looked so adorable. Even the smudge of dirt on his cheek could not detract from his appeal.

"You think he would have left some type of clue."

"Maybe he did and it's been lost or overlooked. This is a very long time we're talking about."

"And yet, it seems connected to you somehow. A human girl."

"Yes," she agreed, sitting down next to him. She was very conscious of how close he was to her, yet he seemed completely indifferent. "I wish I had the answers, but I don't."

He smiled at her then, making her heart give an anxious jump. "Maybe we'll find the truth of your past as well."

She looked down at the map, trying to hide her flustered reaction. "Maybe."

Cadoc soon retrieved the horses, taking them to drink at the pond before they set off on the next leg of their journey. He'd explained to Sophie about the lands they would cross that day; *Matholwch* the land of giants and *Cobblywn*, where the *Coblynau* had been expelled to after the *Pwca* overtook their original homeland. Though both members of Annwn, they were also factions that kept to themselves. They didn't interfere with other groups, and seldom ventured from their own areas.

With the noon sun bright and furious in the sky the two entered Matholwch. For the better part of the morning the path they'd followed had traversed a forested area heavy with ancient trees, and the sounds of multiple animal species. This woodland at last begin to thin, exposing rolling fields under a carpet of blooming heather, and the odd farmhouse.

The closer they came to *Matholwch* the larger the dwellings became. When they passed a fenced-off pasture containing three of the largest horses Sophie had ever laid eyes on, Cadoc informed her they had arrived.

Not surprisingly the road widened considerably. Sophie gripped her reins with all her might, scanning near and far for any sign of movement. Cadoc did not seem as alarmed as Sophie felt, but his movements had become tighter, and more cautious. After several miles, and a handful of villages they had yet to see any of the area's inhabitants, save for cattle and the occasional bird.

Coming around a bend in the road, which followed the outcropping a large rock formation raising high above the otherwise flat landscape, Sophie was consumed with a pressing urge to flee. On the far side of the curve they all but ran into an enormous and extremely hairy man standing with menacing determination in the middle of the road. He didn't flinch, but both Cadoc and Sophie expelled grunts of surprise, in turn eliciting nervous whines from the horses.

Even on horseback neither of them was as tall as the man's chest. The width of his massive shoulder extended almost to each side of the road. Both fists were clenched, drawing attention to hands ten times the side of human man's. His shirt and pants strained at the seams, fighting to contain his massive form. Dark eyes stared out from under heavy brows. The rest of his face from the cheekbones down was cover in scraggly, course hair, culminating in a beard that hung almost to his waist.

"What business have you here?" the giant asked at last.

"Just riding through, sir." Cadoc meet the man's eyes with his own, steadier than Sophie could have managed.

"Not the first," he answered.

"I beg your pardon?" Cadoc asked.

"You're not the first stranger to pass through here in recent days."

"Is that so? Have you had conversations with any of these parties?"

"Every one." The giant seemed fond of blunt, yet not entirely informative statements.

"Have there been many such groups?"

"Three."

Cadoc looked sideways at Sophie, but she wasn't certain what he was trying to convey to her. She looked back at the giant who continued to stare at them. Unless he chose to move they had no way to continue. The swamp to the far side of Cadoc, and the rock protrusion to Sophie's left had them essentially blocked in.

"May I ask your name, sir?" Sophie asked. She was quite pleased that her voice had quavered only on the first word.

To her surprise the giant grinned, revealing teeth like a shark. "No one's ever asked me that. They call me Ysbaddaden."

Sophie groaned inwardly. Another name she couldn't pronounce. "I must confess that I have difficulty with your language. Would it be alright to call you Badda?"

This time he laughed. "Of course, child."

"And may I ask Ysbaddaden, if the previous groups were allowed to pass?" Cadoc asked.

"They were not."

Sophie cut in, "Will we be allowed to pass?"

"State your business."

"We are on order of Mairwen, Ruler of Rhiannon. Her daughter has been taken, and she has entrusted us to help find her."

"You have proof?"

Cadoc handed over the seal for Ysbaddaden's inspection. The paper looked tiny within his large hands, and he did not hand it back until he had reviewed every square inch of it.

"Where are you off to?"

"*Anffrwythlon.*"

The giant took a sharp inhalation of breath at the mention of their intended destination. "What in the name of Dewi could there be in a cursed place like *Anffrwythlon* that could help you with such a matter?"

"We cannot say, lest we break a royal secret that has been shared with us."

Sophie nodded her agreement to Cadoc's statement, while Ysbaddaden seemed to consider several options before finally speaking again. "You realize that the closest port is in *Cobblywn*?"

"I do, sir. Do you have advice? It's been many years since I travelled through those lands."

"All I can say is be on alert. The Coblynau are mean, suspicious little creatures, with a hatred for any but their own kind. If they can stop you or disrupt you in any way, they will. Their magic is strong...and dark."

He gave them each a long, hard look before standing aside. The horses took some prompting before they would move past the massive form.

"Wait!" Ysbaddaden called out.

They felt as much as heard his rapid approach. Each step made the earth below them quiver.

"Yes?"

The giant pulled a small drawstring pouch from the pocket of his shirt. He handed it over to Cadoc. "It's *Hieracium cambricum*. The Coblynau hate the stuff. It may buy you some time if you need to incapacitate one of them, or make a quick getaway."

"Thank you."

"Be safe you two."

They didn't speak again until Ysbaddaden was long from sight, and the smell of the sea burdened the air. The pastoral setting had given way to rocky soil and stunted trees. An oppressive, heavy feeling saturated the atmosphere like fog.

"We're close to the sea now, and the border between this land and *Cobblywn*. Keep your eyes open."

A prickly feeling scuttled across the damp skin at the nape of her neck. Though the flat, open landscape spread out for many miles in all directions, Sophie wasn't entirely sure they would be aware of the Coblynau's approach. Sophie was fast learning that magic could do many strange things, including changing one's perception of time, surrounding, and feeling. She would not expect that creatures known for hostile and selfish behaviour would send out the welcome wagon for them.

A long desolate stretch of rocky shore line came into focus as they continued on. The air became heavier, pungent with salt and sea life. Sophie could just make out the lines of a small harbour, where several odd vessels were tethered to wooden launches worn grey by long exposure to water and air.

The road took a sharp turn, running parallel to the shore. The hard-packed dirt turned to tiny stones, which crunched beneath the horses' hooves. The once even topography started a gentle rise on the oceanless side of the path, turning to prickly grass several hundred yards from where they travelled. Except for the occasional boulder or stunted tree, there was little vegetation, and no sign of wildlife. A fine mist touched her skin, bringing a chill.

Sophie was not aware of any movement on Cadoc's part, but found his dagger suddenly gripped in one hand. His posture became tense, his upper body pushing closer to the length of Roshyn's neck.

"What?" Sophie asked, startled at how loud her voice sounded against the soft shush of the water lapping against the land.

"We're being watched. I've spotted two near the harbour, and another small group on the knoll to our left. Don't let on that we're aware."

Sophie swallowed hard, but managed to not dart a look in either direction. Her heart took up sudden residence in her throat, making it a struggle to breathe normally.

"What's the plan?" she asked.

"Keep heading to the harbour. We need to get on a boat."

A loud, rumbling commotion stole away any answer she might have put together.

Jili reared in response to the noise, almost dumping Sophie to the ground. When the horse's front legs connected with the ground again, Sophie's jaws snapped together with such force she tasted blood. From her peripheral vision she had the awareness of something large and fast-moving headed in their direction.

"Hurry!" Cadoc screamed, using a sharp gouge with his heels to spur the animal into action.

Sophie followed suit. Jili burst into a run, narrowly missing an avalanche of stone and debris. Looking behind she found the spot where they had stopped moments before buried in rubble, an amount that would have caused serious injury to horse or person. They raced to the harbour, away from a possible further attack, and straight at two of the most hideous creatures Sophie could ever imagine.

Two leathery faces were caught in a snarl, their sparse hair little more than peach fuzz across the tops of their pointy heads. Beady, black eyes watched Cadoc and Sophie approach with stern disapproval. Both were dressed in a similar fashion, ill-fitting overalls and shirts so filthy the sight of them made Sophie's skin crawl. The crossed arms and tight posture gave them an angry, menacing pretense. Even with the two frightened horses charging toward them, the Coblynau didn't flinch. They stood their ground, openly challenging them.

At the last second, Cadoc gave a sharp tug at the reins, bringing Roshyn to a skidding stop. The difficult movement kicked up a cloud of dust, the touch of which also failed to elicit a reaction from the loathsome creatures.

"What business have you here, strangers?" the closest Coblynau demanded. When his thin lips parted, a mouthful of jagged, blackened teeth was revealed.

"We need access to this port to travel to *Anffrwythlon*."

Both creatures stiffened and gave each other pointed looks.

"For what purpose?" the second, and slightly smaller Coblynau asked.

"We go by order of the *Tywysoges* Mairwen. That is all I am at liberty to discuss."

"You lie," the first creature said.

Cadoc dismounted, pulling the royal seal from his pocket. As he held it out before him, the two creatures took a hasty step backward as though the piece of paper might do them harm. Realizing the move betrayed weakness the larger Coblynau returned to his previous position, shaking his head with vehemence. "Easily faked."

Sophie had an idea. She also dropped to the ground, coming to stand slightly behind Cadoc. Without a word she slipped her hand inside the outer pocket of his jacket, fingers brushing the small sack that Ysbaddaden had bestowed on them. As quickly and discreetly as she could she worked her fingers inside, forcing herself not to react when her skin came in contact with the cold, slimy contents within.

"You think I would dare pretend to be on official orders? Only an idiot would conduct himself in such a manner," Cadoc answered.

"I know you not. Perhaps you are an idiot."

At the insult Cadoc lunged forward. Sophie jumped between the two. Without warning she reached out, touching the creature on his bare forearm. For a few moments there was no visible reaction, then his eye began to twitch and his knees trembled as though suddenly unable to bare his weight.

"What magic is this?" he croaked, mouth clenched so tightly he could barely utter the words.

"This is but a small demonstration of what we are capable of. We came to you in good faith, only to be met with tricks and challenges. We wish to borrow one of your boats, one large enough for my friend and I, and the two horses. If you cooperate I will forget this insult."

The smaller Cobblynau's eyes bulged from his now reddened face. He seemed torn between assisting his companion and running for the hills.

"Agreed," the afflicted creature said.

Sophie pulled back her hand, and slowly he regained control of his faculties. His face screwed up like he'd sucked a lemon, and with fists tightly clenched at his sides he escorted them down to the harbour. They walked behind him, taking in the fact that the smaller Coblynau had joined the small group watching from up the hill. He did not utter a sound as he made his way to the end of the main dock.

"Lead the way then," Cadoc instructed.

The creature looked at Sophie, a twitch pulling at one eye. "Death and misery are the only things to be found in the place to which you venture."

"Is that a threat?" she asked.

"A warning." He pointed toward a mid-sized ship with a black and red sail. "There," he said, and turned abruptly on his heel.

Cadoc led the horses aboard, making sure they were secured

for the voyage. He and Sophie settle on the deck, looking over the map once more before setting sail.

"Shouldn't be more than a couple of hours, unless the wind dies out on us." Cadoc had a habit of running a finger along his lower lip when lost in thought, which he began doing then. Sophie found the habit charming, but would never have told him so.

"You know how to sail, I hope."

"I do. What kind of adventurer would I be if every body of water I encountered had to be travelled around?"

She smiled. "Not much of one?"

"Exactly. You take a seat over there. Don't worry I'll get us there safely."

Sophie didn't doubt him for a second. Despite the fact that she had known him for less than two days, or only for a few hours if she tracked their relationship on her real time, she felt secure in his abilities and his dedication to the mission and her safety. Her confidence in him was a great thing she realized, making it easier to concentrate on getting to the truth. Time was surely working against them, and worrying about every little thing was only going to slow her down more.

"Do you think we'll see some Morgens," she asked after the boat was out in the open sea. She looked about expectantly.

"Not in this water, Sophie. They stick to streams and ponds. You might catch a kelpie, or a Cirein-cròin though."

"What's that?" she asked, almost against her instincts.

"A sea creature, like a giant eel with razor sharp teeth."

"Fantastic. Just what we need at a time like this."

She'd lost Cadoc's attention, his gaze was fixed on the sea. She waited until he seemed satisfied that they were on the right course, and came to her side. She had pulled the map from her bag, and set to studying the area they would soon come upon. The depiction showed the island to be small in area, yet contained a few strange symbols. Cadoc plopped down beside her.

"Find anything helpful?"

"Not at all."

He moved his hand toward *Anffrwythlon*, brushing the side

of Sophie's arm. The touch sent warm tingles through her flesh, but she willed herself not to have any visible reaction.

"Not much there," he commented.

Sophie nodded, scanning the area for what felt like the thousandth time. The island was an almost perfect circle, save for a small appendage on its northwest side. The crude drawing indicated a space of moderate elevation, a near complete rocky landmass, devoid of life. There were no settlements indicted within its borders, though Sophie already knew that it was uninhabited from the discussion she and Cadoc had shared on the way to Cobblywn. What symbols were on the map had been obscured by time and wear, but the longer she stared the more they came to resemble the *cyhyraeth* she was so wary of.

"Do you know the legend of this place?" she asked.

"Only the silly folk tales about the *Pwca* and a woman whose tears turned the island to rock."

"Don't most tales come from an origin of truth?"

"I suppose. What are you getting at?"

"I'm not sure. But those Coblynau sure didn't seem to want us going to the island."

"You think they know something?"

"Could be."

"Could also be that they're a bunch of nasty, selfish creatures who don't like to help anyone."

"Maybe."

Sophie ran her finger along a deep grove in the parchment, which crossed off-centre of the island's interior. At her movement a strange expression crossed Cadoc's face. She had a question on the tip off her tongue when he abruptly stood up and returned to the area from which to steer the ship. The remainder of the voyage passed without conversation. The soft, chilly cry of the wind over the sea and the crashing waves were the only sounds about them.

Soon the desolate, jagged shore appeared. The sky darkened around its shores, the air turning to fog. Dread washed through her, making her stomach feel as though it had turned to stone. Setting foot in such a place was the last thing she wanted to do, but she knew there was no choice in the matter. Nerys's father was preparing for the battle, should one come, but the best thing for all involved would be to prevent such an event from happening at all. Finding the dagger had to be her only concern, fear and discomfort taking a far distant second.

Cadoc maneuvered the ship close to the island and dropped anchor. He lowered a long plank to bridge the gap from the deck to the shore, and Sophie followed behind as he led the horses to land. Even the animals seemed nervous, as both whined and bared their teeth. Sophie felt like doing the same, but she kept up a brave front.

Cadoc looked up from the map. "We should set up camp nearby. The map says it's near six miles to the interior and it'll be dark before we reach it."

"Alright."

Sophie started to pull her pack from Jili's back. Cadoc hadn't moved, and was watching her with a strange expression on his face.

"What?" she asked.

"You're incredible."

Sophie shrugged. "So everyone here seems to think. You guys really need to set some higher standards."

Cadoc laughed, a deep hearty sound that made Sophie's insides flutter. "I mean it. You take everything you see and all the burdens put upon you in stride. Are you incapable of fear, girl?"

It was Sophie's turn to be amused. "Are you kidding? I'm terrified. I am so not prepared to be doing something so important or dangerous. I'm just Sophie."

"Perhaps that's all you need to be."

He looked at her for a long time before turning away. When he did he strode with confidence toward the island's interior. Sophie was glad to let him take the lead, also happy for the break in conversation. She had never been one to take compliments well, and considering how unsure of herself she felt, she didn't feel at all deserving of Cadoc's praise.

He found a small clearing, with a shallow, but passable body of water to let the horses drink from. Once they had been fed and settled, he gathered a few pieces of wood from the stunted and reluctant trees that grew in sparse clumps about the area. Enough was collected to start a small fire, which the two used to heat their supper. Afterwards they sat side-by-side, studying the map.

"See these lines, here and here," he said after some time, pointing out areas of wear in the parchment. "I think this was folded at some point. I noticed it last night. Do you think it was done purposely?"

Once the words were out Sophie saw what he meant.

"You're right."

She handed over the map and let him play around with it until he managed to have the lines mesh in such a way that they made they made a new version of the island appear. What before had been the odd line or squiggle about the periphery of the land mass came together over top of the original, highlighting an area to the northwest of the island's interior. There was a symbol, which appeared to Sophie to resemble a mountain and a word in an unfamiliar language.

"Can you read it?"

"I think so." He squinted as though the words caused him pain, before uttering a series of strange sounds.

"What does that mean?"

"The Stone of Providence...I think. It's an old dialect."

"Well, that's promising isn't it?"

"Depends on whose providence you're talking about." There was only one way to find out.

CHAPTER 11

Six miles seemed a very long distance as they travel the bleak, scarred land, moving toward what at best would be a dead end. Sophie didn't even want to let her mind wander to the grimmer possibilities of what might be waiting for them. The rocky terrain made it difficult for the horses to progress with any speed, prolonging the worry and anticipation.

The mountainous area indicated on the hidden map of the island appeared suddenly. At the sight of it Sophie's heart gave an odd off-tempo beat. Jili slowed even more, making an alarming sound deep in her throat. To one side of the path a strange rock protrusion caught her eye, and as she realized what she was seeing she gave the horse's reins a sharp tug, halting her movement altogether.

She dropped to the ground, approaching the pile of rocks with trepidation. She didn't imagine that the pile would spring to life and begin chasing her, but in such a place you could never be too cautious. As she neared she became certain it was the same formation she had seen the men in her vision pass as they had gone to hide the dagger.

"Cadoc, come see this," she called out.

He came to stand at her side. Sophie had carefully folded the map, showing a small symbol in the area in which they now stood. The same symbol was barely visible on the surface of one of the largest base rocks.

"What does it mean?" she asked him.

"I'm not sure, but I think we're headed in the right direction." He took a quick scan of the area about them. "Let's leave the horses here."

Sophie agreed. They tied them up, off the main path and hopefully out of harm's way. As they continued along the path toward the base of the incline, a damp, suffocating coldness crept in. She felt the effect down to her bones, causing her lips to tremble. Beside her Cadoc tensed, as though experiencing something similar. His movement became slow and deliberate, and he progressed with a protective arm held out in front of her.

She heard the creature's approach long before she saw it. The terrible, grating wail assaulted her ears, digging into her brain. Her impulse was to flee, causing her to expel a soft whimper as she forced herself to keep going. Soon a *cyhyraeth* materialized, stopping about ten feet before them. It regarded the two with its soulless eyes, set deep into the withered, graying skin draped over the contours of its skull. Its lips pulled back and it emitted another deafening wail. Sophie though she might throw up. As before its presence evoked a heart-clenching, gut-twisting desperation.

Cadoc pulled his dagger out, waving it before him. The movement was enough to snap Sophie back to relative coherence, forcing her to deal with the situation head on.

"You can't kill it. It's already dead, I think."

"Then what is your suggestion?"

Her mind was completely blank. All the saliva in her mouth evaporated as she stood there staring at the creature, while trying to force some semblance of a plan from her brain. As the seconds ticked by more and more *cyhyraeth* came to fill the path, turning into a small but terrifying army. Her hand drifted to her chest, as she found it suddenly difficult to breathe.

While clutching at the thin fabric of her dress her fingers brushed over the charm about her neck, the one Mairwen had given to her before leaving. She grasped it with all her might with one hand, grabbing Cadoc's arm with her other. He turned to her in concerned surprise, eyes wide. She forced her mind to calm, thinking only one thing; truth, truth, truth.

It took a painful, anxious thirty seconds, but the charm's power sprang to life. The metal began to warm, the heat seeping into her flesh. A small cluster of *cyhyraeths* began to twitch and sway, some filtering away from the main group. Within minutes all had dispersed in various directions as though they had lost sight of their intended victims, even though Sophie and Cadoc remained in the spot at which they had been stopped. When the last creature had dispersed in search of its prey, the two broke into a run, not stopping until they were in the camouflaging shade at the mountain's base.

Sophie realized then that she still had hold of his arm and that they were pressed so tightly together she could feel his warm breathe against her neck. With reluctance she dropped her hand.

"What just happened?" he asked, still staring in the direction they'd come from. "Mairwen gave me a protective charm. I took my chances that it would work."

He turned as she held out the charm in his direction, touching it briefly before smiling. "Well, that was lucky."

Before she could answer another strange sound came at them from some distance away. Cadoc made eye contact, giving a quick shrug before moving ahead to investigate. About a hundred yards in the distance a section of the mountain appeared to be opening, revealing a gaping maw of darkness. A cloud of dust sprang into the air, stinging Sophie's eyes and pelting her bare arms with tiny bits of debris. Her pounding heart was too loud in the sudden silence.

"What do you think?"

Sophie was seized with a compulsion to move forward, a sensation so overwhelming she didn't think she could have resisted if she tried. As it was, she didn't. It seemed obvious that the uncertain destination had presented itself. Whether the outcome would be good or bad was yet to be determined.

Cadoc called out behind her as she stepped into the velvet blackness. As her eyes adjusted to the change in light Cadoc caught up with her. He took her hand, squeezing it firmly as though to impart that she was not to rush away from him again. There was barely time to react to his touch when a light became visible in the distance. Her heart hammered, and her blood took an icy course throughout her body. She moved forward, legs trembling.

"Who comes?" an as-yet unseen woman asked. Her voice

filled the dark space, a soft and breathy sensation as disorienting as it was lovely.

"S-Sophie," she stammered. "And Cadoc."

A shadowy figure stopped before the distant source of light, casting a shaky halo about its form. "You managed to pass the *cyhyraeths* unscathed?" The woman asked with undisguised surprise.

"We did," Cadoc answered.

"Come forward then. Such people I must observe more closely."

They did as instructed. What they were headed toward came to be clear. From the narrow passage way emerged a large, cavernous space rising at least thirty feet above their heads. A slithery, fluttering sound came filtered down overhead, the source lost in the shadowy crevices of the stone ceiling. Sophie didn't want to know what was causing such a noise.

Once into the space it became apparent that the light had no identifiable source, it simply filled the area with a ghostly luminance. There was movement in the light, swirls of shadow that slipped from focus to quickly to ascertain what it was. When something cold and slimy brushed her side Sophie cried out.

"Enough," said the figure, and the separate moving entities came to a standstill at her side. When no longer moving, it became clear that a handful of *cyhyraeths* were in attendance.

"Cadoc," Sophie whispered.

"Do not be afraid. Here on *Anffrwythlon* these creatures do as I say. It's only when they wander from these shores that my control sometimes falters."

Sophie took a several steps toward the figure, who in turn mimicked her action. In seconds they were standing less than an arm's length from one another. With great amazement, Sophie found herself standing before a delicate young woman, whose beauty could not be hidden even by the gloom of their current environment.

Sophie raised her hand, reaching out to the figure. She had expected a spectral being of some kind, so when her hand touched flesh she took a stumbling step backward. Cadoc caught her elbow, keeping her upright.

The woman smiled. "I am real. I offer no tricks here."

"Who are you?"

"My name is Tegwen."

It took Sophie a few moments, but the connection was made. "You're kidding."

"I can assure you I am not." Her words were accompanied by a sad smile.

"You know her?" Cadoc asked.

"No, but I know of her. Nerys's uncle told us the story of how this place came to be. Tegwen was supposedly abducted by a Pwca, and brought here. She was so terrified that she cried for years, her tears turning the island to stone."

"And birthed the hideous *cyhyraeths*. You must not forget that."

"That was only a story," Cadoc said, shaking his head.

"Yet I am here, before you now."

The *cyhyraeths* continued to hover just behind Tegwen. Sophie couldn't help but look at them, as though that would somehow make the story sensible.

"Why do you stay here if the Pwca have gone?"

"I cannot leave this place."

"I don't understand."

"I am cursed."

"There must be something that can free you," Sophie said, horrified at the thought of such an existence.

"Only true love, from whom I was stolen. Unfortunately he passed many centuries ago, thus there is no chance to break my imprisonment. Believe me I have tried." With these words she gave the two before her a tight look. Then with a quick flick of her hand the *cyhyraeths* disappeared, an event that Sophie welcomed.

Tegwen turned and walked away from the spot where they had been standing. After a look at Cadoc she followed, coming to an area where several stones had been grouped into what resembled a table and chairs. Close by were two larger stone pieces that presented a curiously humanoid shape. Tegwen sat, so Sophie and Cadoc did likewise.

"Do you know why we have come?" Sophie asked.

"For the dagger I suspect. That is the only reason anyone comes to this awful place."

"Yes."

"A handful have attempted to come to this place over the years, fewer still have made it past my companions."

A shimmer of light cascaded over the two large stones near where the group sat, catching Sophie's eye. In a flash she realized that the rock didn't simply resemble human forms, that they were in fact depictions of two adult males. She jumped to her feet, moving in for a closer look. Tegwen watched her with solemn eyes.

Recognition grabbed her brain. If nothing else, the strange, flattened features of the shorter figure would have given the men's identities away. It was clearly a Coraniaid.

"These are the two who brought the dagger to this place?" Sophie asked, already sure of the answer.

"Yes. And here they have remained ever since."

Sophie came to stand before Tegwen. "You did this?"

"I did."

"Why?"

"Because they asked it of me. They didn't want there to be any way for their destination to be shared with anyone. The others simply dropped them off and left."

"Your tears did this?"

"Yes, it was the early days of my imprisonment then, and the *cyhyraeths* had yet to appear. They were a strange after-effect of the residual magic of this place and the desolation that the land eventually succumbed to. Then it was simply me and my sadness that they stumbled upon. The men explained their mission and I agreed to help them."

Sophie looked back to the stone figures, feeling Cadoc come to stand beside her. "So the dagger is here?"

Tegwen sighed. "I'm afraid not, Sophie."

"What do you mean?" Cadoc demanded.

"Please, sit." When it appeared that she would not speak until they had re-joined her at the table, they both sat. "It has been gone for more than a century now. As I already told you

I have tried many things to escape this place. This was simply an act of desperation."

"Explain," Cadoc said.

Tegwen met his gaze, eyes steady, yet sad. "A pair of Coblynau came to me. They had heard of the dagger's magical capabilities, and promised me that if I gave it to them that they would return with the spell I needed to be released. I had nothing to lose, I'd tried to harness the dagger's magic many times to no avail. So I handed it over."

"Let me guess, you've never heard from them again?"

One tear slipped from Tegwen's eye. "Correct."

Sophie tried to put the pieces together, but they just didn't seem to fit. "Wait, how did they even know about the dagger in the first place, if it was such a secret. And what did they think it could do for them? Isn't it about deciding truth?"

"I do not have your answers, Sophie. The Coblynau are powerful creatures, and have access to many secrets. I confess I cared not what their purpose was, if there had been any chance to help myself."

"I guess that explains why they didn't want us coming to *Anffrwythlon* in the first place," Cadoc said.

"Now that we know the truth I don't suppose they're just going to hand it over either."

"Probably not," he agreed. "Tegwen, why are you telling us this?"

Tegwen's sigh rattled her thin frame. "I've had many dreams in my long existence, but none as frequently as the one in which I have engaged in a similar experience to the one we are having now. This meeting, between us here and now, is part of all of our destinies. If there is a chance for any of us, total honestly is the only option."

The three fell into an anxious silence. Sophie felt the two rock figures peering at her, certainly a figment of her imagination, but an unsettling feeling all the same.

"The one you want an audience with is Daegnar, the current leader. Like many here in Annwn the Coblynau are long-lived, and it was his men who came to make a bargain for the dagger."

"Thank you, Tegwen. We will make good use of this information," Cadoc said.

"Unlike the Coblynau, our word is good. Thank you for giving us this information and I promise to do my best to find a way to help you in return," Sophie said.

"I know you will, Sophie. Though I would love to spend more time in conversation with you, I know that time is of the essence. You must go to Cobblywn and find the dagger." She touched Sophie's hand lightly.

Cadoc nodded, and made his way to the door. Sophie followed, invigorated by the information they'd secured and also disheartened at the thought of leaving Tegwen alone again.

"If nothing else, I will come back to see you," Sophie assured the other woman.

Tegwen smiled. "Your kindness will be remembered. Now there is one last thing I must tell you. The *cyhyraeths* have been whispering about an event that is about to happen. A great battle, where many lives will be lost. My creatures revel in death, and are drawn to it. Their understanding is not clear, but from what I can ascertain this will happen soon, and when it occurs Llyr will be in grave danger."

"Nerys's father?"

"Yes. He is leading a great army at the moment, preparing to defend Annwn with force if the dagger is not found."

"Will he...be killed?" Sophie felt sick at the thought.

"It is not certain. If you would permit me to touch you, perhaps I can share the vision with you. If I am not mistaken, you possess such a gift?"

Sophie hesitated. The weight of all the expectations upon her and the broad assumptions of abilities she was not convinced she possessed came crashing down on her. She took a deep, hitching breath before she could speak. "I sometimes see things, yes, but I don't know that I'd call it a gift. I mean, I can't really control it..."

"Gifts come in many forms, often in presentations that one overlooks or misunderstands. Do not fall prey to doubt, Sophie. There are many that believe in you."

Without waiting for her reply, or consent, Tegwen stepped

forward to clasp Sophie's hands. The touch of her skin was warm, but unsettling, like the delicate husk of something left to dry out for a long period of time. Despite the lack of heft her grip was strong, almost painfully so, but Sophie did not try to pull away. For the first time she gave herself over fully, freeing her mind of doubt and fear. Whatever information came her way, she wanted to be able to access every bit of it. Many lives might rest on the smallest of details, some seemingly unimportant action or word.

For the first time Sophie saw Llyr's face, a strong, handsome man on horseback. His hair was damp and gritty from the number of weeks spent on the move and his clothing and armor had become slightly worse for wear, yet there was no mistaking his noble presence. The other men and women in his party followed with loyal reverence, allowing him his leadership position while still maintaining a protective stance. As the vision closed in Sophie noted the striking colour of his eyes, a trait passed on to his daughter.

In the larger group flanking Llyr's inner ranks was comprised of not only Tylwyth Teg, but other creatures that Sophie did not have names for. Like those of *Cobblywn* and *Matholwch*, the beings were vaguely humanoid in composition, but also very different in other respects. Sophie's gaze settled on a group of *cyhyraeths* off in the distance, just visible on a rock crest at the edge of the field in which the assembly had gathered.

Sophie tried to force the details of the area deep into her brain, lest she might need to figure out where the meeting had taken place at some crucial time in the future. She noted the rock crest, the stream, and the odd, misshapen building barely visible to the naked eye. It reminded her of pile of crumpled clothing.

"Sophie." Her name being called broke the moment. Cadoc was regarding her with curiosity and concern. "What did you see?"

"I saw Llyr and his army gathered in a large field. Not much to go on, but I think I'd recognize the place again."

"No battles, or glimpses of the enemy?"

"Sorry, nothing like that."

If Cadoc was disappointed he didn't let on. Tegwen didn't comment or offer any further information either, leaving the two no choice but to head back to the boat. Her last glimpse back caught Tegwen turned away from their departure, shrouded with shadow and *cyhyraeths*. At the sight a bone-rattling chill rushed through her body.

The walk back to the horses was uneventful. Sophie suspected that Tegwen had recalled all her creatures, no longer needing them as a deterrent to strangers on her island. A strange, desperate bond had been formed, one which Sophie had every intention of honoring.

The trip back to the beach was made in short order. Since they'd started their day at the break of dawn, there was enough time to make it safely back to the mainland before nightfall, there to begin the next leg of their unpredictable journey.

Sophie stood on the deck, letting her eyes travel over the endless expanse of grey- blue water. She let her mind wander, wrestling between plans for the future and the still-unsolved riddles of the past. For every answer found, several new questions seemed to appear.

A loud crash to the right of where she stood, along with the accompanying splash of cold salt water turned her attention from what might lay ahead. Cadoc yelled, his words obscured by an even louder and closer bang then the previous one. The noise startled her so much she jumped, coming back into contact with the deck by slamming her shins against the cubby she'd been leaning against. Cadoc yelled again, what she realized much too late to be, "Get down!"

The next crash hit the side of the ship, not ten feet from where she was standing. In response the ship tilted, knocking Sophie off balance, and sending her tumbling down the slick deck. She crashed into the center cabin, smashing her head so hard she saw stars.

When she pulled her hand back from the throbbing wound she'd acquired it was coated in blood.

Cadoc was suddenly before her, his mouth moving yet no words reached Sophie's ears. He gave her a hard shake and the sounds from all about them came rushing at her. "Are you alright?' he demanded.

"I hit my head," she answered, holding out her bloody hand.

"My word, Sophie. Let me see."

The ship tilted again in response to another loud crash. Cadoc's weight pressed down on her and for one crazy moment she wanted nothing more than to just hang on to him.

"Are we under attack?" she asked.

"Yes, a ship from the direction of Cobblywn. They're firing at us." He pulled off his jacket and pressed it to Sophie's wound, before placing her hand a top of it. "Keep the pressure on." Then he returned to the helm.

Sophie rose on shaky legs, the unsteady ship and her emerging nausea both threatening to send her back down. She managed to make it to the rail, gripping on to it with the hand not at her wound. She scanned the sea until she found the source of the attack.

A ship of equal size to the one on which they travelled was coming straight at them.

The dark red sails strained with the force of the wind, reminding Sophie of freshly spilt blood. As she stood staring another item came hurtling toward the ship, a cannon ball that struck the main mast before landing in the sea. The giant piece of wood split, bringing the sails and the suddenly fast-moving lines of rope crashing to the deck. One of the damaged lines caught Cadoc about his leg, dumping him in an unceremonious heap on the deck.

As Sophie started in Cadoc's direction another crash sounded behind her, with enough force to make the ship tremble. She dropped to her knees and crawled toward her friend, who she realized with despair was not moving. Water sloshed over the sides of the careening ship, impeding her movement.

At last she reached him. "Cadoc, Cadoc please," she sobbed.

The rope was still wrapped about his leg, which she removed with care so as not to cause further injury. A stain of red spread out within the puddle of sea water beneath Cadoc's still form. The shallow rise and fall of his chest was the only indication that he was still alive. Sophie felt panic clawing at her brain.

Her wound throbbed, and she was soaked to the bone, more terrified than she had ever been before.

Another crash sounded, this one louder and more powerful than any of the previous assaults. She rose to see what was happening, praying that there were not more ships coming to aid in their demise. To her despair she found that another ship had indeed joined the first.

"Somebody help us!" she cried.

To her complete astonishment the second ship opened fire, but not on them. The red-sailed ship was struck in a series, tossing it back and forth like a child's plaything. The last movement kept it toppled over to one side, dangerously close to sea level. From this strange angle the attacking ship was revealed, a giant black vessel. It moved alongside the damaged ship, firing once more with obvious results. It was sinking.

The black ship continued past, moving toward her as Sophie watched with astonishment. It came alongside her ship, sails lowering to slow its movement. Once in proximity it became clear that the strange vessel was more than three times the size of hers, and she knew that there was nothing she could do if its occupants decided to attack.

"Sophie," a deep baritone called out, and when she saw the owner of the voice appeared she broke out in a grin so wide it made her cheeks ache.

"Badda!"

The giant came to stand at the rail closest to her ship, and she was glad to see that he was also smiling. Several others of equal size and stature scuttled about behind him, tending to various tasks.

"Hello, Sophie. I told you those Coblynau were nasty creatures."

She laughed. "Obviously you were right. And you came to check on us?"

"Yes. There's more to this, but perhaps we can talk about when we get back to shore. Throw me a line so we can tow you in."

She did, and then sat with Cadoc's head cradled in her lap as their surprising new ally brought them to safety.

CHAPTER 12

Ysbaddaden steered them to a small port in Matholwch, a farther journey than returning to the one they'd left from, but a decidedly better option. Cadoc had opened his eyes briefly, and looking up into Sophie's face had managed a small smile. She found that he'd also suffered a head injury but unlike hers it wasn't bleeding, instead swelling up into an alarming lump at the back of his skull. His leg wound had been the source of red, mixing with the sea water on the deck.

Once docked, Ysbaddaden and two of his men had boarded their ship, and after ripping the door of the Captain's room off its hinges, had used it as a makeshift stretcher to bring Cadoc to shore. There they were met by a small group of giants, both men and women, who took the appearance of the two strangers in stride. One young woman immediately came to Sophie's aid, leading her to a nearby dwelling where her wound was treated with a foul-smelling concoction that stopped the bleeding and ebbed the pulsing ache. She also gave her a mug of steaming tea, promising that it would help with her healing.

With her stomach warmed by the brew she asked the young girl, who had identified herself with the unlikely name of Leolina, to take her to Cadoc. He was being tended to in the dwelling next to hers, where Ysbaddaden stood waiting outside. He nodded to Leolina, who then left. Sophie came to the giant, the furious pace of the day's events making it impossible to even consider that she might still be in danger. After all she knew nothing of the giant, or the intentions of his companions, but felt secure that he meant them no harm.

"How's Cadoc?"

"He's given his head a fair knock, but he'll be alright. Not a good idea to move him until at least morning."

"We need to go to Cobblywn."

The giant didn't seem at all surprised at her comment. "They'll be on alert after what's happened today. It won't be an easy task."

"I know that, but we have no choice."

"Why is it that you must go to this place?"

Sophie didn't even bother with the idea of secrets, she took a leap of faith that Ysbaddaden was on her side. "We must locate and destroy the Dagger of Everlasting Truth to prevent the Coraniaids from being able to force a marriage between Llyr and Mairwen's daughters and the sons of the current Coraniaid King. This union will change things for everyone in Annwn."

"And not for the better," he wisely surmised.

"That's right. They will have access to your lands, people, and worst of all, magic."

"How is it that the Coblynau have possession of this dagger?"

"Through lies."

He was quiet for a few minutes. "Perhaps this acquisition was not entirely of their own instigation."

"What do you mean?"

"They are a mean, petty bunch, smart in their own way, but I don't think wise enough to have planned this on their own. From what you are saying, having this dagger is a major bargaining chip."

"I hadn't thought of it that way. Who could be pulling their strings?'

"I suspect those who have the most to gain, or lose."

"The Coraniaids."

"That would be my guess."

"You have any ideas?"

"A few, my best advice would be to bring some backup," he answered, while making a gesture toward himself.

Just then another male stuck his head out of the door, motioning that they should come inside. They entered a dimly-lit space with ceilings that soared above Sophie's head, yet actually caused Ysbaddaden to duck at intervals. Cadoc was laid out on an enormous, if crudely-built bed, an oily, lumpy sack applied to the swollen area of his head. One of his pant legs had been opened along the seam, displaying a nasty furrow in his flesh where the rope had snagged him. The wound itself appeared to have stopped bleeding as dark hardened scab had formed along the ridge, and the surrounding skin flared an angry pink. To Sophie's happiness his eyes were open, and he appeared to have control of his faculties.

"Can we clear the room for a bit?" Ysbaddaden asked, to which the others immediately responded by exiting the dwelling.

Sophie took a seat on the chair vacated by the giant who had been tending to Cadoc. "How are you?"

He chuckled. "I've been better, but treatment here has been topnotch."

With some effort he turned over and pulled himself to a seated position. One hand kept the sack pressed to his head. Once facing her Sophie saw that one side of his face had blossomed into a rainbow of bruises. Before she could stop herself she'd reached out and brushed a finger along his cheek, prompting him to lock gazes with her. Something powerful passed between them, to which they both awkwardly withdrew.

"Miss Sophie tells of your need to get into Cobblywn," the giant said.

Sophie turned to him, grateful for the interruption. "Badda has offered to help us."

"We can't ask this of you."

"No asking, I offered."

"Why?" Cadoc asked.

"A simple truth. I want to protect Annwn. This is my home."

Cadoc's reaction fell in line with Sophie's, taking the man at his word. He nodded. "What do you propose?"

"We have been neighbours for far too long not to have gained some knowledge that will be helpful. I can get us in unnoticed, I am sure of that. What is your exact destination?"

"The area where the land's current ruler lives."

Ysbaddaden made a deep whistling sound. "That will be tricky. Not impossible, but we need be prepared."

"We need to speak with him. Make him hand the dagger over."

"Not something he'll be inclined to do willingly. You've seen what these creatures are capable of. Are you prepared to act in kind?"

"I will do what I must." Cadoc's meaning was clear.

"Then let us attend to you until morning. We will feed you well and give you a safe place to sleep. In the morning I will join you, and I give my word to help you in any way that I can."

Cadoc and Sophie agreed, prompting Ysbaddaden to retrieve the man who had been attending to Cadoc's injuries. With swiftness and surety he had Cadoc's leg wrapped and a steaming mug of tea in his hands. Sophie watched as he sipped at it, noting his drooping lids and relaxing posture. He was all but asleep when she took the cup from his hands a few minutes later.

Leaving her friend to rest, Sophie followed Ysbaddaden from the room. The warmth of the sun was welcomed after the events at sea, helping to take the last of the dampness from her clothing. The giant indicated to an outside sitting area, centered within a cluster of similar dwellings. Others milled about, giving them a wide berth, making Sophie think their behaviour was more than simple politeness. Ysbaddaden commanded a deep respect among his people, obviously a leader of some kind.

"This will be dangerous," he said after lowering his large frame onto one of the chairs. Upon closer inspection the piece of furniture turned out to be a modified tree stump.

"I know. But what choice is there? Annwn needs us."

An odd expression crossed his face, and his eyes squinted as though a sudden pain had taken him. "Yet you are not of Annwn yourself. Why are you putting yourself in harm's way?"

Sophie didn't see any reason to keep the truth from him. "One of my relatives was a Tylwyth Teg, which connects me to this place." She dug the toe of her shoe into the soft soil, conflicted as the true motivation for her assistance. "I think that I need something to believe in right now, something bigger than me, if that makes any sense."

Ysbaddaden looked at her for so long her skin started to itch.

"I do, Miss Sophie. It takes a wise person to see beyond one's immediate needs."

Again with the praise. "Thanks. Now I'm starving. Any chance I can get some of that food you were talking about?"

In a surprise gesture of compassion, he patted her hand with his much larger one. "Of course. Let me get Leolina to put a plate together for you."

As he left, two children who'd been hovering in the periphery became emboldened enough to come over to where she sat. With huge grins on their faces they approached, a boy and a slightly younger girl. They both past six feet tall, towering over the much smaller Sophie. They regarded her for a few moments before running away in a gale of laughter.

Ysbaddaden returned with a large plate, steam rising from the biggest meal she had ever laid eyes on. A chunk of dark meat in gravy, potatoes, and mashed carrots filled the dish, the heady moisture of aromas making her mouth water. She began shoveling the food into her mouth with enthusiasm, making small moans of pleasure as she ate up every last bite. The giant had watched with a mixture of amusement and awe, while eating his own meal. The food was washed down with a cider-like drink that had a decidedly sour aftertaste. When she burped Ysbaddaden chuckled.

"That was delicious," she said.

"Glad you liked it. I'll make sure to tell my daughter."

"Oh, is Leolina your daughter? I didn't realize."

"I didn't tell you as much, but yes she is."

"Her mother?" Sophie asked.

"Passed away many years ago," he answered, unsuccessful in keeping the sound of regret from his voice.

"We have that in common. My mother is also gone."

"But never forgotten."

Sophie lowered her gaze. "That's right."

An awkward silence followed that neither attempted to fill. At last he led her back to Leolina's house and handed her over to his daughter. In turn Leolina provided a comfortable bed and warm blankets, and with her belly full, and mind and body exhausted Sophie fell into a deep sleep.

A warm hand to her shoulder gave her a gentle shake. She'd been awake for some time, but had yet to open her eyes. While lying in the quiet and warmth she'd been replaying the scenes of an odd dream, where she had been reunited with her mother. It was an image she would have liked to hang on to, but knew would fade with each minute of wakefulness.

She rolled over, surprised at the figure to whom she opened her eyes. Leolina had been expected, but she found a chipper-looking Cadoc instead.

"C'mon then. Can't sleep all day." He smiled broadly as he teased her.

"Give me a sec."

"I'll wait outside. There's some breakfast for you, then we need to get moving."

Sophie was dressed and fed in short order. The horses, whose existence she had all but forgotten about in the commotion of the previous day, were waiting to depart with their riders. She gave Jili a stroke along her nose and whispered how happy she was that she'd come through the incident in one piece. As though she understood Sophie's words, she bobbed her head and pranced in place. Then they were off.

Ysbaddaden had organized a small group to assist in their effort to infiltrate the land of Cobblywn. Like the beings who rode them the horses of *Matholwch* were oversized, standing at least double the height of Sophie's animal. The footprints left behind were the size of serving platters, gouging the earth to a considerable depth. The giants moved in what Sophie thought of as a migrating bird formation, with she and Cadoc safely in the middle.

About a mile from the border the assembly stopped, where Ysbaddaden ordered smaller group to move out in various directions, in effect coming at the Coblynau from multiple directions. Some would advance directly, others under concealment, but all with their eye on the same prize: Daegnar, the leader of the Coblynau. She and Cadoc, with Ysbaddaden as their protector, carried on alone after that.

Sophie had been schooled in the ways of the Coblynau

on the way to their destination. She knew that in addition to being naturally gifted in magic and spell-casting, that the small people were excellent miners also. Silver was their specialty, but they would work to unearth anything that would bring them a profit.

So when a ragtag group of the little creatures, clutching pickaxes and shovels, stopped them less than a minute after passing over the border to their lands, it did not come as a surprise. The one that Sophie had tricked the day before led the group, and immediately gave her a serious dose of the stink eye. She touched the small pouch containing the *hieracium cambricum* in her pocket, which gave her a sense of protection.

"Back again?" the familiar Coblynau asked.

"Yes. We wish to speak with Daegnar."

"Not likely," he snorted. The group of Coblynau chuckled at his retort, which quickly died out when Ysbaddaden took a step in their direction.

"I do think it's likely," Ysbaddaden said.

"You think you can scare us with the big ones, do ya? 'Tis not size that matters here, just talent." With those words a billowing cloud of black smoke appeared, which when dissipated showed that the creature had disappeared.

"Here I am."

The three whirled about, shocked to find him standing behind their group. His grin widened, displaying the terrible state of his teeth.

"I warned you they were tricky little things," Ysbaddaden said, not seeming at all surprised at the display.

"Might we have a name for the one we speak with? I am Cadoc."

The creature sneered. "The wanderer?"

"Yes."

"Hmmm. I thought you'd be older."

"Sorry to disappoint." Cadoc kept his gaze steady, though the presence of the Coblynau appeared to be unnerving the horses.

"I am called Iffyd."

"The King's man?" Ysbaddaden asked.

Iffyd narrowed his eyes in obvious displeasure. "I am."

"Then take us to him."

"As it is, he is waiting for you. You will be moved only after being properly restrained."

Several things then all happened at once, creating a chaotic, overwhelming environment where it was impossible to track a single person's actions. The small group of Coblynau suddenly became four times its original size, whether by magic or clever concealment of additional parties Sophie could not discern. The horses panicked, dropping both Cadoc and Sophie to the ground. A flurry of small arrows descended upon the three, several of which pierced Ysbaddaden's wide back, the easiest target to hit. He swatted at them, but they did not seem to impede his movement in any way. The large net that seemed to appear out of thin air was another matter entirely.

The heavy leather came down on them like a ton of bricks, causing Ysbaddaden to join them on the ground. Before they could shake it off or scramble out from under it, hands had grasped them by the arms, yanking them out with painful force. Lickity-split their wrists were bound together, and the three attached to a length of rope. Several others of the foul creatures captured the horses, also binding them together for easier transport.

Sophie was hauled to her feet by two grimy sets of hands. She found herself between Cadoc and Ysbaddaden, all three physically prevented from accessing the substance in their pockets which could have facilitated their hasty retreat.

"I don't remember this being part of the plan," Sophie muttered.

Cadoc cast a pained look over his shoulder, garnering a sharp tug at the rope that caused all three to stumble. They trudged on for several miles. Sophie tried to be aware of their surroundings, but the gaggle of Coblynau obscured her view. There was no way to tell if any other members of their party, whom they had separated from earlier, were aware of their predicament. She wanted to believe that the reason they had yet to appear was because they were devising a brilliant and fool-proof plan for their rescue.

The group came upon a small settlement nestled against the

first in a series of rolling hills, adorned with intermittent clumps of short-statured trees. The largest of the unsophisticated dwellings looked as though it actually extended into the hillside, the front a bulbous protrusion with a lopsided roof. A wide chimney belched out a suspicious black smoke. Their captors marched them straight toward this building, and the group assembled on its rickety veranda.

The procession was watched with undisguised contempt. More Coblynau appeared, emerging from the other dwellings to line the path to the main house. Once at the base of the steps Sophie easily picked out the group's leader, a male standing slightly apart from the rest gathered with him. Though by no means taller or cleaner than the others, he did have an extremely large belly hanging over his leather belt.

"Daegnar," Ysbaddaden said, confirming Sophie's assumption.

"I should not be surprised to find you messed up in this, Ysbaddaden," Daegnar answered.

"I am surprised that a man of your stature would sanction the involvement of his people in something that could be detrimental to all in Annwn."

Those gathered about Daegnar bristled at Ysbaddaden's statement.

"My loyalty is to my own, and to that end I must do what will be most beneficial."

"Most rewarding, you mean," Cadoc said.

"Where is the dagger?" Ysbaddaden asked.

Daegnar made a dismissive gesture. "No longer here, though I do not understand why this piece of metal is so important. We held it for many years, and even with magic as strong as ours we could not get it to produce anything of worth."

"What did you do with it?"

Before Daegnar could answer a new group of beings came about the side of the large house. Front and centre of the new group was someone whose presence should not have been the least bit surprising; Domnall.

Sophie felt like she'd just been punched in the gut. "That's the man who took Nerys," she whispered to Cadoc.

"Why he gave it to me, of course," Domnall said. His smug grin assured his captives of how pleased he was with himself.

Cadoc and Ysbaddaden were both regarding the man is if they knew him, or of him. As he passed her, he gave Sophie an exaggerated wink. Daegnar had descended the steps, and the two came to stand together.

"Why are you doing this, Domnall? This is not an issue for Gaidheal," the giant inquired.

"Not an issue for Gaidheal? You must be forgetting the origin of this whole matter. Long ago, far from any of the lives here today was a dispute between my land and that of Annwn. This whole arrangement with the Coraniaids was nothing more than a stall tactic, one that's lasted many hundreds of years, but the matter still remains."

"Of this dispute, do you even know the origin?"

"Of course. This all started by one of the oldest reasons for war. A family divided."

If this was news to Ysbaddaden he made no indication. "A family long dead, Domnall."

"Is it not time to lay this to rest?"

"A slight is still a slight, no matter the years that have past."

"I'm going to have to disagree with you there," a confident male voice called out, startling all in attendance.

The crowd about them began to move, and the expression on Domnall's face indicated he'd been caught off guard. Sophie heard the distinctive sound of horses approaching, and the ground beneath her feet started to tremble. Ysbaddaden had managed to break free of the rope about his wrists, and he grabbed Sophie's arm to pull her out of the way of those advancing. She and Cadoc, still tied to one another, stumbled along behind him.

Leading the group of giants was a man who Sophie had to look at for several moments before recognition set in. He'd lost his conservative dress and close cropped hair, now appearing in his true Annwn guise and laden with weaponry. As he rode by he made a careful swing of his sword, taking the binding from Sophie's wrists.

She smiled as he continued past. Mr. Sampson had come to save the day.

CHAPTER 13

"Geraint. How lovely of you to join us." The tight set of Domnall's lips contradicted his words. Geraint, it turned out, was Mr. Sampson's real name.

Daegnar gave Domnall a hateful look. "What is he doing here? I thought you said he'd been eliminated."

"Domnall has always been overconfident in his abilities," Geraint answered.

Once close to the dwelling Geraint dropped from his horse, while those flanking him remained mounted and tensed for action. Sophie counted fifteen men, not much of an army when compared to the hundreds of Coblynau they were surrounded by. She reached over and unfastened Cadoc's binding as quickly as she could. His hand went immediately to his side, where his dagger would have been had their captors not removed it earlier.

Quicker than the blink of any eye the fight began. Domnall launched himself from the veranda, hitting Geraint hard enough to take both men to the ground. Geraint's men drew their swords, engaging those closest to them. Many of the Coblynau retreated, though some returned with bows and arrows in hand to join in the confrontation. The strongest drew on their magical abilities, sending out streams of flame and transporting from one place to another to avoid contact from enemy swords.

Ysbaddaden scooped Sophie up into his arms and took off at a surprisingly quick pace, with Cadoc close on his heels. The giant managed to force his way through the scurrying Coblynau, knocking aside many with the heft of his free hand. Sophie spotted their horses several yards ahead, tied to a wooden rail. The lone creature guarding the animals held Cadoc's sword in his hand, jousting with a make believe opponent. Too late for any movement that might have helped him, he became aware of their approach. By then Ysbaddaden had gotten a hold of him, and Cadoc was removing the dagger from his grip.

With one powerful knock from Ysbaddaden's meaty fist the Coblynau crumpled to the ground.

"You stay here, Sophie," he ordered.

"If anyone approaches you, use the charm," Cadoc advised. "Or get on Jili and ride far away from here."

A commotion behind them cut off the conversation. A number of their original party came riding into town, a group of strangers fighting to keep up with them. A glance at their clothing in passing made Sophie reasonably certain they were allies of Geraint. She might have even seen the emblem of Rhiannon.

Cadoc and Ysbaddaden joined the ranks, charging ahead to join the cries and chaos of a battle fully underway. Once alone Sophie pressed alongside Jili, casting her gaze about. A sudden movement in her periphery caused her to turn, only to find a handful of armed Coblynau heading in her direction. A spasm of adrenaline shot through her. There was nothing in close enough proximity that she could use to defend herself, and no sooner had the though passed through her mind a terrible, sharp pain exploded in her brain.

Though it could not be so, Tegwen appeared. "I send some of my children your way, Sophie. Be strong, and let them feed on the fears of others."

The vision cleared, taking the pain with it. In its place were several *cyhyraeths*, hovering just above the earth. They regarded her intently, as though awaiting her command. She raised her trembling arm and pointed to the group of Coblynau, who upon the sight of the *cyhyraeths* had stopped in their tracks. The swarm rushed forward, their wail crawling along Sophie's skin. At their advance the Coblynau turned and ran. Within minutes the creatures lay on the ground, withered and still. The *cyhyraeths* lingered, returning their attention to a cowering Sophie. Understanding they were somehow under her control she mounted Jili and indicated that they were to follow with a flick of her hand.

She rode into the swarm of bodies, her small congregation of *cyhyraeths* dropping many in their tracks. Others simply fled on sight of the horrid creatures, knowing full well what their appearance could mean to those who crossed their tracks. As she neared the main dwelling her supernatural followers began to wane. In succession they slowed, fading until nothing remained but a wisp of smoke. By then she had delivered herself to the densest area of battle, not the wisest move for an unarmed, untrained human girl.

Geraint had Domnall backed up to the dwelling. Several of his men, plus Ysbaddaden were fighting against the much larger enemy ranks. At last Geraint struck a blow that knocked Domnall's sword from his grasp, and he raced in to wrestle the man to the ground. Once down he pressed the tip of his weapon to the other man's throat, bringing the swell of violence to a standstill.

"Give me the dagger," Geraint ordered.

"It's not here," Domnall spat back, while still struggling to free himself.

"Then you're going to take me to it." Geraint stood, pulling the other man from the ground. One strong arm wrapped around Domnall's throat and the sword was pressed to his side.

"This one comes, too," Ysbaddaden said, pulling Daegnar over the back of his horse. The smaller creature yelped, but he was no match for the giant's strength. Not to mention the fact that Ysbaddaden had wisely coated his hands with *hieracium cambricum* before setting out.

Geraint led his men, including the giants, Sophie, and Cadoc out of the village. Once clear he tied Domnall's hands and had one of the giants place him on the back of a horse, before mounting his own. Natural leader that he was he moved to the front of the procession. When the group had safely crossed over into Matholwch, Ysbaddaden ordered two of his men to take Daegnar to a specific location, and to make sure he did not get away.

Ysbaddaden led the group back to his village to attend to those who had been hurt. He and Geraint immediately went off together, leaving Sophie to suspect it was not the first time they'd worked together. Domnall was under the watch by several men, with no chance to escape. He did not look pleased.

Cadoc came to her after tending to a minor cut along his cheek. "How was that?"

"Pardon?" she asked.

"You alright? How did you get right into the thick of things like that without a scratch on you?"

Taking a broad look about, she understood what he was getting at. Not one who'd been in their attendance had walked away without a minor bump or bruise. "Tegwen helped me."

"Speak sense, please."

"Somehow she sent a band of *cyhyraeths* to help me. They cleared a path for me."

"How can that be?"

"Don't know, but it happened. Some kind of magic. They didn't last, they kinda faded away after a few minutes."

"One strange thing after another with you, Sophie."

"Yep," was the only answer she had.

After about an hour the group reassembled. Geraint came forward to address those who'd gathered, with Ysbaddaden a silent ally.

"First, let me thank you, people of Matholwch, for welcoming my men into your land. We are honoured by your allegiance, and know by your actions that you are true to Annwn. The only way to ensure that we keep the Coraniaids out is to be as one. They have strong backing with Gaidheal, and defeat will not come easily.

"For those who do not know, I am Geraint, son to the current Gaidheal King and brother to the foe we have now in our midst."

A murmur of surprise and dismay circulated through the crowd, and many turned to stare openly at the bound Domnall, who scowled in return to the scrutiny. Sophie looked to Cadoc, who appeared as shocked as she was at the news.

"Listen!" Ysbaddaden roared, capturing everyone's attention. "Geraint is true, having turned his back on his own family to help us. He has put his life on the line many times to defend us."

"Why?" a male shouted from the mass.

"I do this because it is the honourable thing. We have no need or right to your lands, and the Coraniaids are merely pawns in this battle. Even so, they are not a kind that should be allowed to enter, they are dangerous in their own way. This disagreement needs to be laid to rest once and for all." Geraint spoke his words with conviction, letting his gaze settle on Sophie.

She smiled, and as though in reaction to the silent exchange Cadoc moved close enough to her side that she could feel his warmth.

"Bring the prisoner here!" Ysbaddaden commanded.

Domnall was hauled to his feet by a choking tug to the back of his jacket, and forced to come before his brother. The hatred emanating from Domnall soured the air.

"Where is the dagger, brother?" Geraint asked.

"Far from here."

"Tell us where it is so we can retrieve it."

"I will not."

Geraint and Ysbaddaden exchanged glances, and the giant stepped into the inquisitor's shoes.

"Where is Nerys?" Ysbaddaden asked.

"Also far from here." Though Domnall kept an angry, defiant stance Sophie could feel the cracks beginning in his resolve.

"Then arrangements need to be made to return her to Annwn. An exchange—her life for yours," Geraint said.

"What about the dagger?" Ysbaddaden asked.

"I think Sophie can assist us with that," he answered.

When the attention of the anxious crowd shifted in her direction, her blood ran cold. Cadoc gave her a nudge with his arm. In response the crown parted, allowing enough space for her to travel to the front of the gathering where the men waited for her. Every serious expression she passed made her legs heavier and her heart pound faster.

At last she was within arms' reach of Geraint, Ysbaddaden, and Domnall. The captive began to struggle, requiring two men's strength to keep him in place. Sophie knew what the expectation was, and didn't want to disappoint. She thought of how she'd opened her mind, freeing herself to the connection

Tegwen, which had produced the most vivid and lasting vision yet. Domnall jerked violently as she reached out to him, his tongue working at the saliva crusted in the corners of his mouth.

Her fingers brushed his shirt sleeve, tentatively moving down until they met his warm flesh. They both had a visible reaction to the union, and a collective bristle circulated through the crowd. Sophie's arm began to shake, making it difficult to maintain her grip on Domnall's arm. Reality slipped away, the pressure of her impending escape into Domnall's thoughts squeezing along her body, a sensation she would have gladly fled from if able.

When the pressure closed in about her chest, restricting the depth of her breathing she gave into it, letting her mind go onto its supernatural journey.

An impressive collection of horses and riders moved across a far-reaching section of flat landscape, kicking up dust and determination in its wake. Domnall sat front and centre of this group, the men who'd been waiting for them at the pond's edge flanking him. Nerys was behind one of these men, hanging onto him for all she was worth lest she slip and be trampled under the hooves of the racing animals.

Till the sun began to slip form the sky they rode, passing through the flat, dark lands of the Coraniaids and beyond. That they passed without issue or challenge prove the depth of allegiance between the two people, joined enemies of Annwn. Once in what Sophie presumed to be Gaidheal the land opened, where the men passed a series of small villages and various bodies of water. Full dark had arrived by the time they came upon a large fort, where a large door opened in greeting for the malicious party.

Inside Nerys was pulled from the horse and escorted by Domnall into a large structure within the thick stone walls. With unnecessary force Nerys was taken to a chamber under heavy guard. Several times she stumbled, only to be yanked back onto her feet, yet in no instance did she cry out. Only the pallor of her skin and a slight tremble in her hands betrayed her fear.

The last set of guards greeted Domnall as a returning hero,

all but falling over themselves in their enthusiasm to open the door they stood before. He paid them no mind and rushed inside, the massive door shutting behind them with an ominous thump. The space was dimly lit, but what could be seen was expansive and held little furniture. A large man with a long fall of white hair sat at a table, watching. At the sight of Domnall he rose, and came to greet the man.

The older man embraced Domnall, then placed a kiss to each gritty cheek. As Domnall stepped back the man turned his attention to the other person in the room. Nerys meet his gaze with steadfastness. He neither smiled nor frowned as he appraised her, seeming to have no reaction to her presence whatsoever. Sophie knew that taking her was meant to give them some advantage, or else such effort to find her would not have been made.

"Nerys, sit please." The man pulled out a chair form the table for her. She sat, going along with the misplaced graciousness.

"Do you know who I am?" the man asked.

Nerys shook her head. "Not by appearance, but I am going to assume you are Domnall's father. From what I've overheard I understand he is of Gaidheal's royal family, and your greeting indicates closeness."

"Bright girl. You're quite right in your assumptions. I am Albanach of Gaidheal."

"I hope you'll excuse me being able to say it's a pleasure to make your acquaintance, but considering the circumstances…"

He gave her a chilling smile. "Of course. Now I will make an assumption that you understand the reason for such brutish actions on our part."

"You wish the pact to go forward. You want my sisters and I married to the Coraniaid sons." The words triggered a shudder, and Nerys pressed her lips together as though she might be sick.

"Yes."

"May I be so bold as to ask why?"

Albanach smiled again, this time with genuine amusement. "Of course, the truth will not impede our plans in anyway, certainly not at this junction in our plans." He and Domnall shared a look, a private understanding passing between them.

"It is a means to an end, a way to reclaim what is rightfully ours."

"I don't understand."

"Once your people and mine where the same," he said, taking a pause to allow his words to make to make an impact. "You see the people of Annwn, the Tylwyth Teg at any rate, come from the bloodline of Gaidheal. Not unlike the current division in my family, a son of the ruling family of olden days defied his father to marry a girl beneath his standing. If that weren't enough, he left his family completely, even his homeland to settle in what is now called Annwn. A few loyal followers left with him, and to his father's great surprise the settlement flourished."

"This makes you believe that Annwn in rightfully yours?" Nerys did nothing to hide her disgust and incredulousness.

Albanach chose to ignore her question, instead turning to his son who remained silent during the exchange. "A decision has been made about the dagger. It must be taken to *Eirianwen.* She is perhaps the only one who can tell us how to use it."

"*Eirianwen*, the *Gwiddonod?* She's still alive?" Nerys interjected.

"You know of *Eirianwen?*" Albanach asked.

"Yes, she was the one who told of the prophecy."

"Why take it to that witch, father? If we can't destroy it, then we should take it and drop it to the bottom of the sea."

"Your vision is too narrow, son. An instrument like the dagger could be used to uncover the most profitable truths."

The truth of his father's words gleamed in his eyes. "Of course, father."

"She still resides in the Passage of Glyndwr. I want you to organize a small army of your best men, and get it there before the time is upon us."

"Without the dagger there should be no worry of Gwyn ap Nudd being able to stop the union. And with the Coraniaids our firm allies, their access to Annwn becomes our own."

"Then what?" Nerys asked, eyes wide.

"Then we take over and impose our rule. Should be very simple with your father and many of the other house's rulers out of the way."

The colour drained from Nerys's face, leaving her looking young and frail. Her green eyes welled with tears.

"Plans are underway, father?" Domnall asked.

"Yes, I planted a false story of the dagger's whereabouts through our men on the inside, and as I suspected the various leaders of Annwn are on route. They have no idea they are walking into a trap."

The two men leaned over a map spread across the table's surface, where Albanach's skeletal finger pointed out the spot for the would-be battle. Sophie tried to read the name, fought to hang onto the letters that appeared before she was forced from the vision.

With the fall of Nerys's tears and the caustic bellow of Domnall's laughter Sophie was thrust from the past, slamming back to present reality with bone-rattling intensity. She stumble backward, her grip ripped from Domnall's arm. He cast her a look of pure loathing. His chest rose and fell in rapid succession, and he was sweating so profusely that his hair had turned to clumps of damp curls and a ring of wetness could be seen on the tall collar of his jacket.

"Llyr," Sophie barked out, her tongue dry and difficult to move.

Geraint stepped closet to her, disregarding the effect her connection with his brother had taken. "What about Llyr? What did you see, Sophie?"

"They tricked him. He's leading his men into a battle he's not prepared for."

"And Nerys?"

"Albanach has her, but she is safe."

Sophie tumbled forward, overtaken by a sudden wave of dizziness. Bile burned at the back of her throat, the sensation dimming only in respect to the tears scalding their way down her cheeks.

Geraint fell to his knees to take her in his arms. "Sophie, what's happening?"

She let herself sag against him. When the feeling began to dim she opened her eyes, finding a face tight with concern peering down on her. He was so close it would have taken little effort to kiss him, a thought that made her cheeks burn. With as much grace as she could muster in such a situation she moved away from him. Cadoc offered his hand, which she took with silent gratitude until she realized she had in effect sandwiched herself between the two men. Both stared, waiting for her explanation.

"Sorry. I get dizzy after the visions. That was a doozy."

"But you're alright? No lasting effects I mean," Geraint said.

"Yeah, I'm fine now. Thanks."

He paused, seeming as though he were trying to think of the best way to proceed. "Do you know where they're headed?"

Sophie tried to force the name to come to her, difficult from the all too brief glimpse she'd been privy to. A jumble of letters swirled in her brain, incoherent at first, but slowing until they hovered along an invisible line. Like most places in Annwn the word did not resonate as something she could pronounce. Her tongue bunched inside her mouth, ready to take a stab at the utterance. "Cigfa."

"I know of it," Cadoc said, making no comment on Sophie's painful attempt to speak the name correctly.

"Yes, near the border with Gaidheal. An ideal place for an ambush," Geraint said. "They must have more on the inside, those knowledgeable enough to use the rightmagic to allow them inside Annwn land." Ysbaddaden said, not realizing he was echoing words that Albanach had spoken in the vision.

The giant moved to join the small group of Sophie, Cadoc, and Geraint. Behind them Domnall smiled, a reaction that didn't pass any of the men unnoticed. Geraint turned his full attention on his brother.

"This has been nothing more than a distraction, hasn't it, brother?" Domnall continued to grin.

"Without Sophie we may not have known the truth in time," he continued as he moved closer. "At least your inside knowledge didn't extend to her talents."

"No matter. Llyr is as good as dead."

Geraint struck his brother hard enough to take him to his knees. Domnall raised his face, blood dripping from his lip and laughed. "Hit me all you like. It won't save your men."

Geraint's fist clenched at his side, but he didn't take the bait. Instead he turned back to Cadoc, giving the younger man a hard, direct look. "I'm counting on you, Cadoc. You are the best man here to get the rest to Cigfa quickly. You must stop what is about to happen.

Many lives depend on this."

"I understand, Geraint. I won't let you down. Sophie, get your things." He started to walk toward the area where the horses were kept.

"Sophie cannot go with you. It's much too dangerous. Moreover I need her help in tracking down the dagger. Saving lives may be of little importance if control over them is lost. The Coraniaids and my father must be stopped."

Cadoc stopped dead in his tracks. The expression he turned in Sophie's direction made her heart feel as though it dropped from her chest. Their gazes locked, and she could feel his conflict, as though it filled the space between them like fog. He grabbed her arm, pulling her along behind him. The others moved to allow them to pass, and not a word was spoken until they were far from sight of the crowd.

Once alone Cadoc leaned forward and met her lips with his own, drawing her into the most wonderfully, butterfly-inducing kiss she'd ever experienced. Once broken, they both drew back. Cadoc flushed and had difficulty meeting her eye. He seemed unsure what to do with his hands. Sophie was equal parts embarrassed and thrilled. She threw her arms around him, hugging him as tightly as she could. Less than thirty seconds later he relented, embracing her in return.

"Be careful," she whispered against his chest. "After that you need to come back to me in one piece."

"After that I have something to come back for."

She looked up to find him with a gentle smile on his face and his eyes impossibly bright. This time she took the initiative and kissed him, letting herself linger. She felt his hands move up her back into the long fall of her hair. It seemed impossible that he couldn't hear the furious pounding of her heart.

The sound of someone clearing their throat intruded on their intimate moment. In surprise they pulled away from one another and turned toward the sound. Geraint stood at the corner of the building, staring at the ground. "I'm sorry, but time is of the essence."

"Understood," Cadoc said in a rough voice. He placed a quick peck to her cheek and strode off to meet the men he would be leading.

Sophie fell into step with Geraint, feeling very self-conscious, but unable to keep herself from grinning. To his credit he didn't comment on what he'd witnessed or her subsequent demeanor. Sophie all but tripped over herself as she followed along behind Geraint, as her gaze kept wandering to where Cadoc stood organizing his men to leave. Then with a smile and a wave he mounted Roshyn, and the group departed in a haze of pounding hooves and dancing sand.

Domnall had been placed on the back of one of the horses, his bound hands attached to the leather harness to prevent his escape. Two determined guards flanked his horse with their own. The bright sun gleamed off the unsheathed sword dangling at the side of one of the men, touching Sophie's eyes with blinding force. The effect triggered something deep within her brain, transporting her far from her current place and time.

A dark, cramped space, slowly revealing itself to be a one room dwelling with nothing more than a single table and chair, and a blanket-covered pile of hay for a bed. Before a low hearth a young woman knelt, grinding the contents of a crude bowl with a smoothed bit of stone. The fire flickered, dancing a myriad of colours over her long strands of hair. A sound catches her attention.

An unnoticeable door opens and a woman with a pronounced hump in her back enters, a large basket clasped in one hand. The young woman comes to meet her visitor, her attention drawn to the basket as the unmistakable sound of a baby's cry fills the small space.

"The child lives?" the young woman asks.

"Yes," the older woman answers.

A cover is pulled back from the basket to reveal a plump, and decidedly unhappy newborn. As the young woman leans down to kiss the child a blast of light consumes them, inexplicably radiating out to Sophie. Within the light the young woman turns, peering out from the vision to meet Sophie's gaze. Her smile is almost as blinding as the light.

Unseen hands seem to push her from the scene she is supernaturally spying on, knocking her backward with enough force that she stumbled. Her heel catches on an even piece of earth. The light is drawn back to its source, pulling away until there remains only a tiny pinprick of radiance. From this fading apparition, drawing away from her like liquid through a straw, a voice could clearly be heard to say, "The blood of this child will one day save Annwn from the most wretched of fates. She must live, so that her descendent may someday return."

The words died in a howling blast of hot wind. Sophie fell, landing hard on her backside. Her teeth clacked together, bringing tears to her eyes. Hands were on her shoulders, shaking her until she could focus once again. Geraint, whose eyes she discovered while in such close proximity were the colour of milk chocolate, stared down on her. His mouth had become a narrow slash across his face, and his apprehension pulled the tanned skin of his forehead into a series of furrows.

"Are you alright, Sophie," he asked in a gentle voice.

She was, but felt like a total idiot sitting there in an unceremonious heap on the ground. "Fine. Surprised, but fine."

With true gallantry, he offered his hand to help her back onto her feet. After a brief hesitation she took it, meeting warmth and strength. Back on her feet she found herself face-to-face with the man, neither one rushing to release their hold on one another. Then with heat in her cheeks she turned away, taking long, determined strides to where Jili was tied, waiting for her rider. She stroked the horses mane, bidding her time until the effects of her embarrassment had passed.

By that time Geraint and his men had assembled. As a collective force moving with mesmerizing precision they began the two day journey to Llediaith. Time was against them. A little less than seventy-two hours remained until the pact would pass and they would be forced to live with the fall-out of such an action.

Geraint gave her a smile, which she sure was meant to be

reassuring, but failed to make her feel anything but unworthy of the faith the people of Annwn had in her. She felt like a fraud, nothing more than a frightened child whose inadequacies were about to come to light in a phenomenal way.

How had the fate of so many people fallen on the shoulders of such an ordinary girl?

CHAPTER 14

Sophie and the twenty-odd men and women in her attendance backtracked to the midway point between Arawn and Rhiannon before taking a sharp turn to the north. From there the group would pass through the lands of Tywi, Arianrhod, and finally Llediaith. Their destination of Gofannonlay resided deep in the heart of Llediaith, a wild and mostly undomesticated land, where *Eirianwen's* home lay hidden in the Forest of Ysbrydion. The woods were rumored to be haunted, full of all manner of spirits, shape-shifters, and other supernatural creatures.

One of Geraint's men parted from the group to continue to Rhiannon, where he would pass on information of recent events to Mairwen. There was still time for further back-up to be sent to join Cadoc, should the battle that was suspected materialize. The intended battle site was closer than the area Sophie and company needed to travel to, with a much easier terrain to pass through. Llediaith lay on the fringes of Annwn, for the most part secretive and suspicious, and as Geraint had explained not clearly committed to any one cause. When intruded upon or put under threat, it remained uncertain how the different groups that called the land home might react. Or whose side they may choose to align with.

By nightfall the group had passed through most of Tywi, accompanied at times by a small, nimble-footed people, the first to resemble the fairies Sophie had learned about as a child. Though wingless they were lithe and graceful, every movement a dance, and when so inclined could travel at impressive speeds. A handful had appeared near the beginning of the journey through their lands, curious and cheerful at the sight of the group on horseback. A larger group appeared toward supper time, offering food and water. At Geraint's approval they stopped for a brief respite.

The map of Llud LLaw Eraint had remained in Sophie's pack, and after filling her belly she pulled it free for yet another perusal. Her actions garnered the attentions of one of the younger creatures, who came to sit at her side. His large, oval-shaped eyes scanned the parchment, sudden comprehension eliciting an enthusiastic response. One elongated finger touched the spot on map that approximated the place they had stopped at.

"Yes, this is where we are," Sophie agreed.

The creature bobbed up and down frantically, making Sophie chuckle. "Do you know of Llediaith?" she asked.

At the question he all but leapt from his seat in his eagerness to answer. He tapped the area on the map, looking to Sophie for confirmation.

She nodded. "Yes, yes. Do you know how to get to the Forest of Ysbrydion?"

His eyes grew round as saucers at her question, and for the first time his body went completely still. Then, like the flick of a switch, he began to chatter away at her, a delightful, chirping gibberish she could not understand at all. His excitement spread to Sophie, bringing a grin to her face. He kept drawing an imaginary line along the map with his finger, marking a trail that seemed to veer from the one they were currently following.

One of the men she travelled with picked up on their interaction, and seeing her confusion came to her side. He listened intently to what the creature was chattering about for a few minutes, his focus indicating an understanding of the strange language. At last the creature stopped his long recitation, clapping his hands in sheer delight.

The man smiled as he turned his attention to Sophie. "Well, talkative little guy isn't he? Well, most of the *Ellyllon* are, truth be told."

"He seems quite jazzed about the map," Sophie said.

"Yes, he says he know of a quicker way to get to *Ysbrydion*. He's offered to show us."

"Oh, and his name is Fial."

"Fial?" She asked, making the creature squeal with delight. "I'm Sophie."

"So-phie," Fial said, then started giggling.

"I'll let Geraint know about his offer, and see what he'd like to do," the man said, standing. He looked to Fial, who continued to fidget and chatter. "Looks like you have a friend for life."

At his parting words Fial emitted a sound that made Sophie's teeth clench. Her ear drums puckered up, making their best effort to block out the offensive noise. She pressed her fingers to her ears and shook her head, trying to impart to her excitable, little friend that he should not do that again. He responded with a sheepish look, and toned the volume down on his incessant nattering.

After some debate, and a small spell to detect deceit on the part of Fial that he passed with flying colours, Geraint agreed to take him up on his offer. Full dark had come to rest, prompting the group to do likewise. Watches were organized and blankets passed about. Domnall had been tied to a large tree and had his own personal guard, a fact that gave Sophie great comfort. Fial plopped down at her side, pulling part of her blanket over himself. He must have fallen asleep immediately for his chatter ceased, and Sophie didn't have the heart to wake him again. She lay down, exhaustion pushing aside any thoughts of impropriety.

A sound intruded into the comforting numbness of sleep, burrowing deeper until recognition snapped her from her slumber. She sat upright, so quickly she was sure she'd felt her brain slosh about in her skull. Her sudden movement caused her to bump Fial, who mumbled incoherently in response, but didn't wake. Her heart hammered, feeling as though it had somehow managed to become lodged in her throat. The darkness was so intense she could make out nothing more than vague shapes, except for the lone man on watch, who kept a small oil lantern at his side. The small bit of light it emitted seemed very far away.

The sound came again—footsteps.

"Who's there?" she asked. She'd drawn her share of the blanket up to her chest, as though it might offer her some type of protection.

"It's me, Nerys," a female said, the sound alarmingly close to where Sophie lay.

"It can't be."

Then from the darkness a figure emerged. Sophie blinked several times, unable to believe what she was seeing. Before her a small figure was kneeling, so close she could have reached out and touched it. "It's me," she said again.

The voice sounded just as she remembered, pulling her insides into a painful series of knots. All about her the others continued to sleep, as though nothing out of the ordinary were happening. The figure of Nerys watched her intently. When she'd managed to pull her wits about her, Sophie leaned toward the figure, trembling fingers moving to touch the long fall of red-gold hair. At the moment when her flesh should have connected with the silky strands a shallow buzzing sound was heard, and the image of Nerys flickered, for a moment replaced by the unending blackness of night. Sophie leapt back as though she'd been burnt.

"Holy crap!" she squawked, garnering another series of incoherent mumbles from Fial.

The image of Nerys snapped back into focus, bringing with it a wisp of cinnamon scent. "Don't be afraid, Sophie. This contact is made with only good intention. Please listen closely, as I will only be able to maintain this affect for a short period of time."

"What is this?' she asked, again attempting to touch the image of her friend.

"A projection," she answered, then looked behind her at some unseen action. "I've managed to influence a couple of the guards here with my empathic abilities, gaining a small amount of trust and compassion. By collecting the correct items from them I have put together a contact spell, but it is not one I have mastered with any strength. Be warned I may make an abrupt departure."

Sophie didn't even begin to understand, but she went along with her friend's words nonetheless. "Gotcha."

"Albanach is in league with the Coraniaids, and even more alarming has pulled some of Annwn's own inhabitants into his alliance. In particular he has infiltrated the northern lands, most deeply in Llediaith, where the dagger is being taken. He is certain that he will be able to make it to one known as *Eirianwen*. He knows that time is against us, and by keeping it from us until the pass of two days the pact will be complete. Even more sinister is his belief that *Eirianwen* will be able to show him how to use the dagger for his own selfish and twisted desires. He longs for nothing less than total dominance over all the lands of the people of magic."

"That doesn't sound good."

"I assure you it is not, Sophie. He must be stopped. Now warn your party that Ceridwen has been turned, and as such all the ones with shifter powers cannot be trusted. Do you understand?" Her desperation was plain to see, even as her form began to fade.

"I do, Nerys. Please be careful. Next time we see each other I expect to be able to give you a big hug." She couldn't help herself. A flood of tears slid down her cheeks.

"Soon, my friend. I trust you...." The vision of Nerys vanished, leaving a smothering, angry silence in its place.

Sophie allowed herself a few moments of quiet crying. The brief moment of weakness actually refreshed her, made her feel as though at least part of the burden had been lifted from her shoulders. After drying her face of the sleeve of her dirty shirt, she stood up and walked over to where Geraint lay sleeping. Within five feet of his prone figure his eyes opened and he snapped into a seated position with a small knife pointed in Sophie's direction. The sudden movement and appearance of the weapon stopped her in her tracks.

"On my mother's name, Sophie! What are you doing sneaking up on me like that?" The knife lowered as he spoke.

"I'm not sneaking up. I have something that I need to tell you."

"Right now?"

"Yes, right now. It's important."

"Alright then, lassy. Let me hear it."

She took a deep breath before launching in. "Nerys says that Albanach has infiltrated the area we're going to and that you can't trust someone named Ceridwen, or any of the shape-shifters."

"Nerys told you this?" His tone suggested disbelief.

"Yes."

He took a quick scan of the area. "She's here then?"

"Not exactly. She came to me in a vision, said she was projecting herself or something. You know, some kind of magical thingy."

"You sure you weren't dreaming? I can imagine how worried you must be for her."

"I was not dreaming. She told me she'd cast some kind of spell to reach me, and that
I needed to pass the information along. Now I have. If you don't want to believe me, then that's your problem."

Geraint stood, placing a hand to her shoulder. "Now, now. No need to get in a huff. It's just a strange bit of knowledge to be passing along. Give me a minute."

Without waiting for her reply he wandered a few feet away to rouse one of his men. Once the man was fully awake he brought him back to where Sophie was standing, feeling sheepish and uncertain. The other man, who Sophie recognized as one who always rode with Geraint's inner circle, did not look pleased to have had his sleep interrupted.

"Please tell Rhys what you just told me."

Sophie felt her cheeks flame, something she hoped the darkness would hide. "I was contacted by Nerys through some spell she'd worked, and she warned me about not trusting Ceridwen or any of the shape-shifters we might encounter."

"She said Ceridwen? You're certain?"

Agh! This place and all its crazy names. "Yes, I'm sure that's what she said."

"A most telling bit of news, Geraint, but something hard to translate to action. No one has seen Ceridwen in her true form in countless years. If she lives still she could come in any form." His attention had turned from Sophie to his leader.

"I came to you because of your knowledge of such creatures. What would be your suggestion be on how to proceed?"

"The only thing to kill a true shifter is silver. Even then the stronger ones may be able to heal. They are fast, cunning, and at times vicious. We should see if our friends the *Ellyllon* could provide some silver to tip our arrows with. Other than that we need to step up our protection and detection spells, and keep on the lookout for any movement. All living creatures should be approached with caution and suspicion."

"In the morn I expect you to make arrangements to acquire the silver, and prepare instruct the archers of the new threat. I leave this in your capable hands."

Rhys paused for a moment, then nodded agreement to the command and unspoken dismissal. The situation was getting more dangerous by the minute. In addition to Albanach's men and the Coraniaids, now there were shape-shifters to be on the lookout for.

Geraint looked to Sophie, concern drawing his face into a series of tight lines. "You must stay close, Sophie. Mairwen spoke to me of the prophecy. If true, then you may be the only one to end this."

"Why me? We have the map, we know where Albanach's men are taking the dagger. How can I be of any more help?" Her voice sounded the tinniest bit desperate, a sound she did not enjoy.

"I think you know this is more than your gift of foresight. You have a natural affinity with many of Annwn's inhabitants. Something from your past connects you to this place. It's in your blood."

"I don't understand," she said, finally breaking down. "I don't know what to do." Geraint pulled her into a tight embrace. "You will," he whispered against her ear.

They stood for a few moments in the darkness, letting the enormity and imperativeness of their mission settle in. There was no turning back and no alternative to meeting their fate head-on. She had to be brave, at least outwardly.

When Geraint cleared his throat, she realized they were still pressed together in an intimate, though not unpleasant way. As soon as the thought passed through her brain an image of Cadoc flashed before her, and she took an abrupt step backwards. Geraint also seemed uncertain, as he looked away and moved his hands about as though he wasn't sure what to do with them.

"I guess we should both try and get a bit more sleep. We need to be rested and alert tomorrow. We still have a ways to travel, and it seems the elements are against us, as is time."

"Yes, you're right. Good-night, Geraint."

"Good-night, Sophie." He gave her one last look before striding back to where he'd been sleeping.

Likewise, she returned to her place beside Fial, gently sliding under the covers so as not to disturb him. He gave a loud snore and turned so he faced away from her. As she lay still her mind raced, chewing on her concern for Nerys, worry for the safety of Cadoc, Ysbaddaden, and the others marching into battle, and her doubts about her ability to do anything helpful in the coming hours. She began to tremble, but not from the cold. Sleep remained elusive for some time, despite the total physical and emotional exhaustion she felt.

The dream came on with startling vividness, an occurrence she should have been used after all the crazy, inexplicable events that had happened during her time in Annwn. Yet, unlike the dream of her meeting with Cadoc, which had come to her as a strange, yet-to-be memory, this came to her more akin to one of her visions. What she was to witness was from the distant past, long before the time the pact had been made.

The vision moved across the low-ceilinged, shadowy space to focus on a young woman. She lay in a damp, disheveled mess, the pain from the impending birth of her child causing her to rock about and grip the tangled sheets beneath her. The pain seemed too great to allow her to do more than groan. Her paleness shocked Sophie, something was definitely not right.

Another figure came to the bedside, with a cloth clutched in one gnarled hand. The second woman mopped at the brow of the one on the bed, and brushed the long locks of hair back from her face. A flash of lightning filled the small space, highlighting the misshapen form of the woman attending the birth and the dankness of their surroundings. After placing the cloth aside, her claw-like fingers moved across the swollen belly of the soon-to-be mother. Her reaction to what she deduced from her examination made Sophie certain that the labour was progressing normally.

After the child had been born the mother lay still; her life had been sacrificed for that of her child. The hearty cry of the baby brought a smile to the old woman's lips, despite her tears. A quick succession of practiced moves and recitation over the still form of the mother it appeared ended with a small bouquet of what looked like dried wild flowers being placed in the corpse's hands. The old woman left soon after that, the baby safely wrapped and stowed on a large basket that she carried out into the night with her.

A hasty voyage through a dark and dense forest brought the old woman to a small cottage. Inside she met another woman whose beauty had no comparison. She checked the child, their connection of flesh filling the cottage with a blinding flash of light. Sophie broke from her dream with the woman's final words ringing in her ears, "The blood of this child will one day save Annwn from the most wretched of fates. She must live, so that her descendent may someday return."

The sound of the woman's voice came to her with such force she couldn't stop herself from looking about, as though she'd managed to transport her from the dream into reality. Her heart beat out a painful tempo in her chest. Above the sky was turning from ebony to violet, the first hints of the sun on the horizon. She drew her knees up to her body, wrapping her arms about her legs and tried to rock the lingering presence of fear away.

The movement roused a sleepy Fial, who turned in her direction. For a moment he looked confused, then a huge grin spread across his face. With the smile came the endless barrage of chatter that Sophie could not make heads or tail of, yet found so amusing. He accompanied her to the small gathering who were putting together breakfast for the group before they departed. Many long minutes passed as the group ate, the tension saturating the air like fog. Fial was the only one present who seemed indifferent to the anxiety stemming from the impending last leg of their journey. Sophie wondered briefly if the creature was ever bothered by anything.

If we could all be so carefree...

The meal passed too quickly, and Sophie soon found herself again on the back of her horse Jili. Fear anchored itself in the pit of her stomach, a state she found she could no longer shrug off. Even Geraint looked grim, not quite able to smile when she met his gaze.

Absentmindedly she touched the amulet about her neck, finding its presence gave a small, but welcomed, sense of comfort.

Rhys had done his part, gathering enough silver to tip the majority of arrows in the archers' packs. The early morning sun struck the metal, casting about brief flashes of prismatic light. Sophie found the affect delightful and ominous.

A small group of *Ellyllon* had joined their ranks, running alongside the sure-footed horses. Fial had chosen to ride on Jili with her, his never-ending babbling intruding into her heavy thoughts. Each step the horses took counted down the seconds until the moment they had all been working toward. The forest began to change about her, subtle at first, but then impossible to ignore.

The foliage encroached on their procession, the larger tree taking on a hostile appearance, ever ready to block, scratch, and impede their progress. Sophie felt the sting of a thorny branch on more than one occasion, even having her hair yanked with such force at one point that she almost toppled to the ground. The sky darkened, clouds doing their best to block out the weakened sunlight. A cold, ominous feeling touched the group, worming its way into their flesh, impossible to shake. All about her were similar reactions to the change in atmosphere. Even Fial had slowed the chatter, his voice barely a whisper.

Several of Geraint's men unsheathed their swords, prepared to offer protection should something or someone overtly threaten them. Sophie had gravitated to the centre of the group, where she felt less exposed and vulnerable. Geraint had given her a short sword at camp, but she was no warrior. Unless absolutely necessary, she'd be leaving the fighting to the more experienced members of her party.

The twisted trail become more difficult to travel with each mile, as the ground grew rockier and inclined to steep, sudden rises and drops. The horses strained to keep steady. The deeper into the strange territory the more intense and foreboding the atmosphere became. As Sophie strained her faculties, drawing on every reserve of energy she had, a sudden and absolute silence could not be ignored. The wind ceased to blow and no sounds of life could be heard, which the grim looks of her companions told her they had noticed also.

Their *Ellyllon* companions, who had till that point been running ahead and all about the procession of horses, closed ranks. Deliberate, controlled movements belied their discomfort, as did the wide-sweeping perusals taken of the eerily still forest. The horses' hooves over the rocky soil beat an ominous song against the tense silence, making anxiety jump and tingle along Sophie's bare skin. Her shirt clung to her back, drenched with nervous perspiration. Her jaw ached from how hard she was clenching her teeth. Fial suddenly whispered something that caused the hair on the back of her neck to stand at attention.

Geraint made a sharp gesture with his arm, which the group collectively took as an order to halt. Jili let out a soft, but nervous whinny and pranced in place. Fial pressed even more tightly against Sophie's back, a move that unnerved her more than anything else. The *Ellyllon* seemed a sensitive folk, in touch with the environment in a way that most would be oblivious to. His reaction was telling.

The stillness erupted into a flurry of movement, cries, and startled horses. Jili bolted, an abrupt movement that had Sophie all but smashing her face off the top of the saddle. She felt Fial slip behind her, but with her focus on keeping herself upright she didn't have the chance to reach out for him. He hit the ground with a soft thud, followed by a shrill cry. She didn't have to time to look back to see if he'd been hurt as Jili had taken a sharp turn off of the path the group had been following, a move that cut her off visually from much of the action underway.

In the distance her name was being called out, she thought by Geraint, but couldn't be certain. After several minutes of panicked racing, which neither verbal nor physical commands could temper, Jili finally began to slow. At last she acquiesced to Sophie's sharp tugging at the reins, coming to a stop in the shade of a small cluster of misshapen trees. A breath she hadn't been aware she'd been holding escaped with a painful, gulping sound. It took several minutes before her heart stopped beating so hard that it felt as though it were slamming against the inside of her ribcage. She felt wetness dripping down the side of her face, and with a quick swipe of her hand discovered she was bleeding. No doubt from being unable to protect her upper body from the assault of overhanging tree limbs, as she'd had to hold on tightly to the horses reins to prevent being dumped to the ground.

The sound of blood hissing in her ears was replaced by the thunder of multiple hooves. Without thinking she drew the sword from her belt, holding it tightly with both hands. Jili seemed to understand her fear and became completely still. Sophie had the vantage point, for a few brief seconds she would be able to see her pursuers before they saw her. The canopy of trees obscured the faces of group until they were almost upon Sophie, who by that point was brandishing her weapon before her.

A beam of sunlight pierced the gloom, striking the profile of the man closest to her.

When she recognized him as one of Geraint's men she let the weapon drop. "Sophie," the man cried out.

Another horse came to stand alongside the first, this one carrying Geraint and a seemingly unhurt Fial. When the creature saw her he let out a happy squeal, leaping from Geraint's horse to hers. He reclaimed his former spot with much excitement, a reaction that garnered chuckles from those in attendance.

"Are you unhurt?" Geraint asked.

"I'm fine. Where's everyone else?"

"Scattered. There were attacks from several different locations, which frightened the horses and caused the group to split. The *Ellyllon* are trying to round everyone up."

"Who were they?"

"Just some Binn." When her look indicated she didn't know what he was talking about he added, "Lesser fairies. Not capable of much more than being annoying."

"Powerful enough to startle a group of experienced soldiers," she answered.

A sheepish look crossed Geraint's face.

"True."

"Perhaps that was the point, Geraint," the other man offered.

Geraint answered with a sharp whistle, drawing all those within range into a tight cluster. A quick flick of his fingers told Sophie she was to come to his side, a position she kept as he led them back to where they'd been before the attack. Several others were already waiting, and within a few minutes the remaining men, giants, and *Ellyllon* had returned. None were harmed beyond a few bumps and scratches, and none could sense the presence of any remaining Binn. Whatever their intention, they had fled.

The group proceeded on, almost as though the interruption had never occurred. Sophie couldn't quite shake the feeling that there had been more to the appearance of the Binn than a simple stall tactic. The whole episode had put them back less than a half hour.

Onward they trudged along the overgrown, serpentine trail until at last emerging into a small valley with a crescent-shaped lake and a view of a small mountain range.

Geraint halted his horse and dropped to the ground. Coming to Sophie's side he made a gesture to her pack. "May I see the map, Sophie?"

Fial snatched it from the outside pocket and as he dismounted handed it to Geraint.

As he spread it out on the ground before him Fial broke into an excited series of chirps, drawing in the other *Ellyllon*. He tapped the parchment with one bony finger, drawing nods and undecipherable feedback from the others of his kind. Geraint allowed the exchange to transpire without interruption, waiting until they all began to nod, as though finally having reached some kind of agreement. The man who'd come to her aid in translating Fial's words while at camp joined the small group. His name, she'd come to learn in the time since their initial encounter, was Owain.

He'd crouched alongside Geraint, listening with intent to the chatter amongst the *Ellyllon*. When they stopped speaking, a collective first, he turned to his leader. "They say that about a five miles north, along the lake edge is the access for the trail Fial spoke about. Otherwise we have to continue to the far end of the lake, and essentially double back over many more miles of terrain, along a more established path."

"He's sure he can lead us. We have no time to get lost."

Owain shared the inquiry, to which Fial gave an enthusiastic nod.

"He's certain."

Geraint gave a wide-sweeping perusal of the still water and surrounding forest.

Unlike the rest of the land there the sun was bright, but the tranquility of the place was unsettling. Though there was nothing but peaceful stillness, Sophie felt a dark presence lurking, waiting for the right moment.

"Alright then," Geraint said. He stood to address his troop. "This is it. We have about one and one-half days to find the dagger and break the pact. All our training and planning have come to this moment. We cannot let the people of Annwn down."

These words led the odd assembly into the most dangerous situation they would ever know.

CHAPTER 15

In Rhiannon....

A t about the same time the group in Llediaith had stumbled onto the quiet lake, a young man, tired and dirty from the hard ride, was being led to Mairwen's private chambers. Once ushered inside he was greeted not only by the lady herself, but two young women. Though he didn't know it, as he had never met any in the house of Rhiannon personally, the women shared a startling resemblance to the sister being held in Albanach's castle.

He bowed as Mairwen rose from her seat. "*Tywysoges* Mairwen, I beg your pardon for this intrusion. I bring word from Geraint."

"Yes, speak plain."

The two younger women joined their mother in standing, a dazzling display of beauty the man found difficult to ignore. "Cadoc is leading a group of men to Cigfa to join your husband who is unknowingly walking into battle. In turn, Geraint and the Mistress Sophie are on their way to Llediaith to intercept Albanach's men who have possession of the dagger."

Mairwen quickly absorbed the implications of danger to both factions of her people. "Daughters, I think we know what must be done."

Two solemn faces met their mother's gaze and nodded.

The group pushed on. The trail alternated between following along the shore and abruptly veering back into the treacherous, old-growth forest without rhyme or reason. One such excursion away from the hazy, morning warmth took them quite a ways into the damp interior of the woods, a place where an intense silence swallowed their group as though they had been completely cut off from the rest of the world.

Their progress slowed to allow cautious observation of their surroundings, with Geraint's soldiers and the two remaining giants taking arms in an offensive move. Sophie and the Ellyllon, save for the pairs traveling at the head and back of the pack, had grouped in the middle of the assembly for protection. The Ellyllon who were not with the rest had gone scouting, moving in and about the surrounding forest with their superior speed to be able to give a warning should they meet anything or anyone who may wish to do the group harm. So far they had come across nothing, which in and of itself was alarming. A forested area so rich with plant life and shelter should be teaming with life, but nary an insect or animal crossed their path.

The sound of someone moving with rapid progress sounded to the rear of the group, startling several of the horses with its suddenness. Sophie turned in the direction of the sound, detecting the tell-tale sign of flapping tree branches. The Ellyllon who had been placed to the back of the procession burst into view, eyes wide and chattering as though they'd been put on fast forward. Owain dropped to the ground to meet the closer of the two, unable to understand what he was trying to convey until he slowed his recitation down.

"He says there's a small group of men on horseback about a half-mile down the path," Owain translated.

"Did he recognize them?" Geraint asked.

Owain conveyed with the Ellyllon who gave a short response and a vigorous head shaking. "He says he didn't see them clearly enough. He raced back to give us notice about their approach."

"Alright then." Geraint took a brief look about, seeing as they all did, nothing but endless woodland, and no path a horse could travel except the one they were on. He pointed to two archers close to him. "You, and you. Take a man with you and go into the forest. Find a vantage point and be ready."

Four men dismounted and vanished into the forest. Sophie

felt Geraint look her way, letting his gaze dropped to her side where the small dagger was tucked into the waistband of her dress. She nodded her understanding and pulled the weapon free, its heft feeling wrong in her hand. Fial mumbled, a sound that Jili echoed with a soft whine. After a few tense minutes the distinctive sound of hoof-prints could be heard. Sophie drew in a sharp breath, unable to let it out. Her heart thumped, and the dagger slipped in her hand that had become damp with perspiration.

Soon the source of the sound came into view, four riders of indeterminate gender. When they were all within a few feet Sophie recognized the brown leather cape draped over the torso of the closest rider. His gaze locked with Sophie's, bringing a huge smile to what had been a grim expression.

"Cadoc!" she cried.

Several of the group moved to allow enough room for his horse to pass, wherein he came to Sophie's side. The three men with him were from the party that had departed from Matholwch. All appeared tired, with dirt coating their clothing and person.

"Explain your presence, Cadoc," Geraint instructed, his voice carrying across the small space between the two men.

"We were ambushed, sir,' he answered.

"The rest of your men?"

"Killed."

The sound of his voice was so welcome that the harsh implications of his words took a moment to settle in. "Badda?" Sophie asked.

Cadoc nodded and her heart dropped like a stone. A cold wave of shock washed through her. True she'd known the man only a few days, yet she'd come to have a great respect for him.

Fial broke out into a fervent speech, which when not immediately responded to he took to Owain's attention. He sailed from Jili to the back of the horse on which the soldier sat, directing his gibberish to his attention. The other Ellyllon also began to chatter, but the sound took on an urgent, frightened quality that had not been heard before. Their stance turned defensive, with many backing away from Cadoc and his men.

Owain clearly did not understand what Fial was trying to tell him, which made the creature pound his hand against the soldier's protective breast plate in frustration.

"He's not making any sense," he said.

Geraint didn't respond, but Sophie noticed his hand creeping toward his sword.

Fial abandoned his conversation by leaping back to Jili. There he grabbed the dagger from Sophie's hand and in a blur of movement had it at Cadoc's throat.

Sophie tried to grab him, but the creature was too quick. A look of understanding passed over Owain's face and whatever message hadn't been delivered in words was made apparent with the bold collective action. The Ellyllon supported Fial's aggressive move with an unnerving hiss, a sound that crawled over Sophie's skin.

Geraint maneuvered himself next to Owain, who by then also had his sword pointed in Cadoc's direction. Strangely, Cadoc had not cried out or attempted to defend himself. In fact he did not seem the slightest bit surprised by Fial's behaviour at all.

"What's going on?" Sophie demanded.

"This is not Cadoc, nor your men, Geraint," Owain said.

"What do you mean?" Geraint asked.

"They're shape-shifters."

Shock took Geraint like a slap to the face. "You're sure."

"I am, sir. Look at how the Ellyllon are reacting. They are very sensitive creatures."

As a feline would when fearful, their bodies had tensed and their elongated ears lay flat against the side of their heads. The hissing continued as they pressed together, becoming a coiled, provoked mass, ready to strike. Sophie looked from Cadoc's face to Owain to Geraint, seeing nothing that reassured her. Her focus returned to Cadoc, less than five feet away.

He met her eyes and his expression pleaded with her, an action that triggered a palpable guilt. Her stomach clenched and her trembling hands made it difficult to maintain her grip on the reins. The images racing through her brain made it impossible to know what to do. Cadoc turned away from her to look at his accuser, an action that sparked alarm in her brain, bringing the cyclone in her mind to a standstill. She tried to focus on whatever her subconscious self had picked up on, but it stayed just below the level of true understanding.

"Geraint, please. I don't know what this man is talking about. It's me, Cadoc."

When Cadoc turned his troubled gaze from Geraint to Sophie again, it hit her. A slim stream of sunlight touched his face, highlighting exactly what was bothering her. His eyes, normally so bright and engaging, were entirely the wrong shade of green. His eyes had been the first thing Sophie noticed when she first met him, as they were like none she had ever seen before, a hue falling somewhere between spring grass and the flesh of a ripe lime. The eyes in the face staring at her were dull, devoid of the warmth and vivacity the real Cadoc had been unable to disguise.

"Sophie. Help me," he said, reaching out to her.

"That's not Cadoc!" Sophie cried out, at the same time attempting to back Jili out of such close proximity to the unknown creature.

Her outburst caused several of the Ellyllon to latch onto the legs of the horse the Cadoc imposter rode. Fial swung the blade, slicing the metal across the front of his shirt. A bright line of red appeared on the exposed chest, letting forth a thick liquid that started to froth and hiss as it ran down the front of the creature's clothing. A wild, guttural shriek came from the creature in response to the injury, causing Fial to stumble backward and ultimately fall to the ground. The creature's horse reared as its rider thrashed about, a potential liability to the Ellyllon clustered about. Fial hit the ground hard. The horse's hoof came down mere inches from his head and still he didn't move. Sophie surmised the intensity of the impact had knocked him unconscious. With no though to her own safety Sophie dropped from Jili's back and reached out for her vulnerable friend, while dodging the erratic milling of a fear-frenzied crowd. She heard Geraint barking orders and the soft whisper of arrows flying through the air.

Just before she became the recipient of a painful stomping

from the horse herself she pulled Fial out of harm's way and managed to awkwardly carry him to the edge of forest. He had started to moan, and as she lay him against the trunk of a gargantuan tree she spotted a thin trickle of blood leaking from one pointy ear. In the heat of the battle there was nothing she could do to help him, a truth she swallowed with a painful lump in her throat. From her low vantage point she spied the blade where it had fallen from Fial's grasp. The metal, still coated with the Cadoc imposter's blood, had started to flake and pit from the corrosive nature of the liquid.

In addition to the four who had brazenly ridden into their midst, many more of the creatures descended on the group. They came from all directions, charging into the mass of bodies with fangs and claws bared. Most appeared in semi-humanoid guise, betraying only a small glimpse of their true nature. Yet any substantial wound they incurred revealed more and more of their real form, as though draining the energy needed to keep up the false appearance.

A snapping, pain-filled growl near her right side drew her attention to one such creature who'd lost one arm and lay writhing on the blood-soaked ground. Coal black eyes stared out from a porcine face, covered in course quill-like stubble and the elongated limbs ended in claws as large and sharp as any grizzly bear. A thick, grey tongue protruded, hanging over the jagged, crowded teeth and leathery lips.

From his chest protruded one of the silver-tipped arrows, the wound weeping a sluggish, fizzy substance.

She turned her back on the dying creature, snatched the dagger and crawled back to Fial. When within arm's reach of her injured friend something large and moving with impressive speed passed by her side. Turning to identify friend or foe, a hand swooped down and caught the back of her shirt and began to drag her alongside the horse that her attacker rode. She struggled, twisting from side to side with no avail. The dagger slipped from her hands.

The grip on her was firm, forcing her to concede her most prudent action would be to protect herself as best she could until the movement stopped. As such, she crossed her arms over her chest with hands to her face, and drew her knees in close to her body. Still the jarring pain from being bounced along the ground at such a speed was almost more than she could bear. Tears streamed from the corner of her eyes and a particularly hard collision with an upturned chunk of rock sliced a gash along one shoulder. The sudden drop to the lower ground level made her vision blur. Her mouth filled with blood, enough to make it difficult to breath.

Then as abruptly as she'd been snatched, she was released. The objectionable voyage came to a sudden, brain-sloshing stop. She leaned to one side to spit out the mouthful of blood, unable to control the waves of swirling dizziness. All she could see were bright points of light, flashing and dimming in rapid succession. The world had lost sound, except an annoying, burning whine, like a nest of mosquitoes taking up residence in her ear. Her heart attempted to explode out of her chest, pounding harder than she had ever experienced before. Rolling to one side she was overcome with a violent coughing episode, and when she attempted to come up on her hands and knees she collapsed as though her bones had liquefied.

Slowly her senses returned to normal. When she could focus the first thing she saw was the tips of two very muddy leather boots close enough to her face to do damage. She took a sharp intake of air, bracing for the pain. A few more seconds passed and the boots did not move. At last the owner dropped into view. The green eyes were now black, glaring at her with unrestrained anger.

"Sophie James. You've caused a lot of trouble, do you know that?" The creature was no longer mimicking Cadoc's voice, and his own was much deeper.

"So it seems," she agreed, wracking her brain for some way to defend herself.

While he seemed to decide on his next course of action the guise of her beloved Cadoc started to melt away, leaving in its place one of the most hideous beasts she could imagine. A foul smell wafted to her, triggering her gag reflect and causing a tremor to ride her body for head to toe. Fear overcame her physical pain, and she scrambled back from the thing advancing on her.

"Lucky for you my orders are to bring you alive."

"Yeah, fantastic." She'd back up against a thicket of trees, barring any further retreat as surely as a brick wall.

Her shoulder throbbed from the cut she'd sustained earlier, the pain blatant after the initial shock had dissipated. She grabbed at it, the top of her hand grazing the charm as she did so. The beast licked his lips as he moved forward. In desperation she grabbed the charm, clutching it so tightly the metal bit into her skin.

Truth, truth, truth, she thought, triggering a slideshow of strange images in her mind; Mairwen, Tegwen, a great battle.

"Where did you go?" the beast demanded. "I don't like tricks."

Sophie held her breath and forced her terrified and injured body to remain still. He was so close that he could have touched her, but thankfully mistook her invisibility for having been transported to another location. He turned away, scanning the area about them and then started to double back along the path he'd dragged her along. His horse whined and chomped at the air, all the while staring directly at where she sat. The beast paid the animal no mind and disappeared back into the woods.

She could hear others close by, the air heaving with screams and clanging swords. She rose on shaky legs, still gripping the charm. Like a channel not quite in focus her image filtered back and forth from nothing to a hazy, ghost-like version of herself. Each step made her presence more solid until whatever magic she'd summoned died.

"Damn, I wish I understood how this worked!"

The horse responded to her outburst with a loud snort. Footsteps could be heard coming in her direction. There was nowhere to go but toward whoever or whatever was coming. Quicker than the blink of an eye a figure appeared before her, startling her so badly that she fell. At first the form didn't make any sense to her brain, filling the narrow path with a humanoid shadow so translucent that the foliage behind could still be seen. It floated forward, causing the horse to flee in terror. Sophie wanted to do the same, but her feet had turned to concrete, rooting her in spot.

"Trust me, Sophie," the thing said before resuming the form Sophie knew. "Tegwen," she cried, so happy to see the woman she burst into tears.

"Remember the *cyhyraeths* are now under your control. Do not be afraid. Use themto do your bidding."

"How are you doing this?"

"I'm not. You are." She smiled, though the statement terrified Sophie.

"I don't understand. I don't know how to use this power, whatever it is."

"Just believe Sophie. *Bendith y Mamau.*"

She choked back her tears. "*Bendith y Mamau.*"

"I cannot stay, Sophie. This is not my place. But know that I am thinking of you, and my strength is your strength."

With a wave and a sad smile she faded away, leaving a small army of *cyhyraeths* in her place. They bobbed up and downing, staring at her with their soulless eyes as they awaited her command.

She took a minute to gather her wits about her, forcing her fears and doubts into a deep recess in her mind. One foot forward, then the next. With her heart hammering she moved toward the sounds of violence, leading her spectral soldiers into the battle they could not afford to lose. A smear of her blood glistened on the rock that had torn her shoulder open, a reminder of how serious the situation was, and how easy it would be to lose control of again.

She burst onto a flurry of movement so overwhelming it took several second to take stock of exactly what was happening. Men were on horseback and running along the ground fighting with fists, swords, and arrows. The Ellyllon flittered about, helping where they could with their limited magical abilities and small statures.

Several men and Ellyllon were down, obviously hurt and some so still she feared the worst.

Fial was still against the tree where she'd left him Sophie noticed, not appearing to have been hurt any further. As though aware of her presence he struggled to look in her direction, smiling. The small gesture lit a fire in her belly, bringing forth a determined, aggressive side of herself, unlike any sensation she'd ever known. She could not let her friends die, and she wouldn't let the people of Annwn down. Not without a fight anyway.

A brief count of those still in the area that she'd been snatched from told her that some of her group must have been chased off, or were themselves in pursuit of some of the individuals responsible for the current chaos. Geraint had maintained his place on horseback, effectively slashing his way through a dense collection of the foul shifters, all having been reduced to their offensive, but natural, appearance. A small group of archers had taken position several feet into the forest, their actual presence obscured by the density of foliage, but the consistent showers of silver-tipped arrows were evidence of their close proximity. The ground was littered with bubbling, leaking remains of many fallen enemies, thankfully many more than the noted casualties of her comrades.

Geraint had noticed her, and by the look of shock on his face the presence of the *cyhyraeths* hadn't escaped him either. Several of his men and many of the shifters floundered at the site of the reviled creatures, uncertain whose side they'd come to the aid of. Owain lay about ten feet from her, bleeding badly and struggling to drag himself from the path of further harm. A nearby shifter also caught sight of the vulnerable soldier and lunged at him.

"Now. There!" Sophie commanded, sending a handful of *cyhyraeths* onto the shifter.

The creature's fear immobilized him, making him easy prey for the hungry spirits who proceeded to drain his body until there was nothing left but an empty shell. The remains were left on the ground, nothing but a husk that was all but unrecognizable as something once alive. Only the eyes stayed life-like, shiny and wide with terror. Though she'd saved Owain's life, the destruction she'd ordered caused a stem of bile to rise at the back of her throat. She bit the inside of her cheek to keep from being sick.

"The rest," she said, releasing the full force of the *cyhyraeths* on the remaining attackers.

Too fast to track the spirits spread out, hunting down and draining all the shifters whose path they crossed. Their silent, methodical elimination was unnerving to say the least, chilling Sophie to the core. The Ellyllon must have felt the same way as they responded to the presence of the spirits by drawing together. The collective whimper they expelled rattled Sophie even further, making her question the barbarity of her direction.

"It was them or us," Geraint said, having joined her.

She nodded, her tears warm on her cheeks. When he reached out, as if the wipe the tears away she turned and strode over to where Owain lay, breathing heavily. She knelt at his side, surveying the numerous wounds, the one on his chest needing immediate attention. After tearing a strip from her skirt she pulled back the blood-soaked cloth clinging to the wound. It was deep, about four inches long and gaping like the mouth of water deprived fish. An alarming amount of blood continued to drain from the wound, which Sophie pressed the torn cloth against.

Another one of Geraint's men joined her, taking over tending to Owain's injuries. He gave Owain what look like a dried root to chew on, then proceeded to spread a sticky, yellowish residue along the seam of the wound. Within seconds the blood flow turned sluggish. Owain had closed his eyes and his ragged breathing resumed a more normal rhythm. When the other man pulled out a sharp needle and a bit of sinew Sophie turned away. She could stomach a lot of things, but watching a man be stitched back together was not one of them.

She stood, immediately colliding with someone behind her.

"C'mon, we need to find the rest," Geraint commanded.

She followed without argument, too shaken by recent events to trust her voice. He led her down a narrow offshoot of the main trail, where they were forced to step over the bodies of several fallen creatures, including one of the Ellyllon who was still clutched in the claws of a shifter. Geraint had continued on, indifferent to the loss that made Sophie feel like her inside were being twisted into unnatural configurations.

The trail curved sharply to the right, then opened up on a small clearing. One of women in Geraint's fold was tending to a man who appeared to have broken his arm. She looked up as they entered and motioned for them to continue on. Sophie spotted the second trail about the same time as Geraint, and as they made their way to it a lone *cyhyraeth* floated out. It hesitated, soulless eyes scanning the area for more prey. At the recognition of its master it came to her side. Sophie's chest filled with an icy ache, but she refused to give in to her frustration and fear. Even the loathsome creature at her side could not break her down any further. She forced herself to be mindful that it was under her control and not the other way around.

An anguished shriek from off in the distance brought the reality of the situation back to the forefront, sending the two hurtling through the resistant trail to the source of the sound. The *cyhyraeth* followed so closely at her back that the filmy edges of the shift draped over the skeletal form kept brushing against the back of her arms as she ran, instilling a feeling of being trapped between the horror she knew and the one still to be seen. A spot of light appeared a few feet ahead, penetrating the shadowy greyness of the trail. Geraint burst out into what lay ahead seconds before she did, taking the brunt of a lash of psychic power that met them.

The force knocked Geraint to the ground, where he sat stunned for several seconds. On instinct Sophie dived in the opposite direction, missing the second wave of energy that lashed out at them. She rolled to the ground, frantically casting her gaze about the space and trying to remember to keep breathing. Her adrenaline level was so high it threatened to overwhelm her, travelling through her body like an urgent, painful second pulse. If her heart could have beat even harder than it was, there would have been nothing left of her ribcage.

Think, dammit.

Geraint regained his composure, and after a swift glance to make sure she was still in one piece, he leapt to his feet and charged the source of power. One of the giants and two of Geraint's men were writhing on the ground before a woman with beguiling serpentine features and the Cadoc imposter, the latter of which appeared as though his guise had been abruptly stopped from melting off of him. A sloughed second skin hung from various areas of his exposed true form, clinging in places by a thick, translucent substance. The effect was disturbing.

The woman halted Geraint's approach with a simple pointing of her finger. He dropped to his knees, clutching at his throat as though invisible hands seized him. Sophie wanted nothing more than to turn on her heel and flee, but she didn't. With her hand clutched about the charm, she focused on one thing: calling the *cyhyraeths* to her side. The woman turned her attention to Sophie, and as she did so the pressure about Geraint's throat seemed to dissipate. He took in a deep, whooping breath and struggled back to his feet. The small clearing filled with a sudden chill, as cold as any arctic wind. The sharp temperature drop puckered the skin on Sophie's arm, announcing the arrival of the spirits before she could see them. The woman smiled, and soon the space crawled with an army of her own, a whole new wave of shifters unharmed and eager for battle.

"Get help!" Sophie shouted to Geraint, only vaguely aware of his departing form as she concentrated on directing the spirits who continued to wait for her instruction.

The new collection of shifters filed in, encircling the woman and the others with her in such a way that Sophie felt certain some type of magical barrier had been called about them. The otherworldly power surged to life within her, and she drew on this to call out to the *cyhyraeths* to meet the attackers full force, which they did with gusto. The two different, but equally vile supernatural beings engaged in a vicious and unrelenting battle with only one purpose: elimination.

A flurry of frantic movement erupted about her, hurtling both shifters and spirits throughout the small space. When either form came in contact with the protective ring the air snapped with static electricity and sent out a blinding flash of light that transformed into perpetual multi-coloured rings rising from ground level to the tops of the tallest trees. Sophie walked the outer most edge of the clearing, watching the shifters being drained of their life force one after another, all the while looking for some weakness in the seemingly impenetrable energy field. The woman tracked her movement with her cold, dead eyes.

Pounding hooves against the rocky soil announced the

arrival of her backup. The remainder of her group, including a weary-looking Owain, burst onto the battle, joining forces with the dreaded *cyhyraeths*. A second wave of shifters replaced the ones already destroyed, adding to the confusion and desperation of the situation.

The conflict raged, magic and brute force being used by both factions. Sophie did her best to stay out of harm's way, clutching tightly to the charm and calling out warnings to her allies when she could. After an indeterminable amount of time passed the last shifter fell, though the consequences to their own ranks were no less devastating. Of the twenty-six they'd started with, only eleven remained standing, including the three hostages. Geraint, bloody and with fury burning in his eyes, surveyed what was left of his army.

Though the shifters had been defeated, there still remained the issue of retrieving the three within the energy field. After several attempts to weaken or eliminate the protective ring with various spells, Geraint conceded that there were none among them knowledgeable enough to break such powerful magic.

"We can't just leave them," Owain said.

Geraint paled, obviously stricken at the thought. "The lives of three cannot be weighed against the rest of Annwn, my friend. We must stay true to our mission."

"That's right, Geraint. Fate has already chosen your path." The woman's voice surprised them all. She peered at them from the safety of her magical shield, her lips pulled back in a terrible grimace.

"What do you know of this fate?" Geraint asked, taking a confident step toward the one addressing him.

"I know many things. Many things that others lost sight of long ago."

As they watched the woman underwent a series of rapid changes, appearing in many guises, including those of Tegwen. The others were any number of Annwn beings, some that Sophie had already seen with her own eyes, others she could not have even imagined.

"We must leave this place," Sophie said, the prickly touch of dread crawling the length of her spine.

A tug at the side of her skirt caught Sophie's attention, and looking down she found a shaky Fial at her side. She dropped to her knees and threw her arms around the small creature, unable to contain her happiness. He squeaked when she drew him into a bone-crushing embrace, but laughed when the intensity eased. He pointed behind him, where the remaining Ellyllon had gathered. All regarded her with expressions mixed of wonder and apprehension.

"So-phie," Fial said in his awkward, childish tone.

"Yes, Fial," she answered.

He did not speak to her again, instead moving with the others to form a circle about the one they could not break. Each tiny body tensed, arms outstretched as though reaching for the one to either side. From the tips of their fingers a smoky thread of residue emerged, moving until it met the identical residue of their neighbour, then entwined. Once the last section had been closed a rush of energy escaped, scorching Sophie like the time she'd bent too close to her father's barbeque. Her face flushed, and her skin tightened in response to the heat, an action so quick and pressing it knocked her to the ground.

When she looked up she saw that the remaining soldiers, and the satiated *cyhyraeths* had also been pushed back from the circle of Ellyllon. They closed in on the energy field, fighting against the power lashing back at them despite the obvious negative effects. The Ellyllon closest to her twitched and bucked, struggling not to break the magical connection. Several were bleeding from their ears and noses. A painful, high-pitched keening accompanied their actions, so intense Sophie had no choice but to clamp her hands over her ears to block out the sound. Pressure built to painful levels.

A mushroom-cloud of energy and light exploded upward and outward, knocking aside the Ellyllon and scattering them like leaves in the wind. The sonic boom produced by the upsurge left Sophie's ears ringing, the carousel-ride-on-steroids dizziness furthering her disorientation. Despite not being able to clearly focus on any one thing she managed to pull herself into a seated position. When the swirling, shifting mass of colours and shapes slowly became actual objects again she realized she was all but sitting on top of an unconscious Geraint. The back of his head was bloodied, resting against a sharp protrusion of stone.

Fial scrambled over to her, favouring one arm and bleeding from a gash along the left side of his face. His injuries didn't keep him from grinning ear-to-ear at the sight of her, though. There'd been barely time to process her immediate surroundings when movement in her peripheral vision caught her attention.

Something hurtled toward her at an impressive speed, colliding into her before she could even bring her arms up to protect herself. She and the thing she'd been struck by spun away from the group, twisting faster than a cyclone. She heard Fial screaming, sounding muffled and far away.

When they stopped rolling she found herself pinned under the weight of the Cadoc-shifter, an experience she would have gladly passed up if given the choice. In addition to his hideous half-changed appearance, the creature produced a stench like a mixture of manure, rotten eggs, and skunk. It had its hands about her throat before she could blink.

The charm, so instrumental in the help she'd provided along the way, was ripped from her neck. She felt rather than saw it being tossed far from where she lay, its landing blocked from view by the awkward position she'd been forced into. The creature pressed its hideous face in front of hers, so close its rank breath wafted across her unprotected skin. She did the only thing she could think of to free herself; she leaned in and bit the creature's bottom lip as hard as she could. It cried out, using hands that had been immobilizing her to clutch at the surprise injury.

The distraction was enough to allow her to wiggle out from under the creature's weight, and once free she broke into a desperate run. Fear wrapped about her chest like a vice, making each breath laboured and painful. The hot tears pouring from her eyes blurred her vision, furthering her disorientation. She could not make any sense of direction or distance, every inch of space about her was an unending blur of green. The land seemed determined to impede her getaway, assaulting her with thorny vines and outcroppings of rock, and producing foliage so tightly packed there was no hope of passing through it.

A beam of light could be seen ahead and Sophie rushed toward it with hopes it would offer a means of escape. The trees thinned, offering flashes of blue sky.

Despite the protest of her aching legs and the burning in her lungs she pressed on, refusing even once glace behind her though she could hear the tell-tale sounds of pursuit. The end of the trail loomed, and she gave it all she had. As she burst from the forest into the light, she felt the ground beneath her feet give way and before she could stop her forward momentum she had pitched herself over the edge of an unseen hillside.

The hard connection her back made with the surface of the rocky hillside forced the air from her lungs. The suddenness of the pain seemed to freeze her brain, making it impossible to think, and as such her skidding descent turned into a violent roll. Above her she heard the creature shriek, followed by a meaty thump. A shower of tiny rocks and grit rained down on her.

The topography took a sudden ninety-degree turn, flattening and bringing her uncomfortable journey to an end. She lay on her back, the sun boring down on her and tried to catch her breath. When at last her lungs agreed to function, air filled them like fire. She coughed and sputtered, aching over every inch of her body. A numbing sensation raced along all her limbs, and for a few short, terrifying moments she thought she'd been paralyzed.

The sound of someone moving close to her left side propelled her into action. She leapt to her feet, stumbled and then righted herself. A quick glance back proved what she'd surmised; the creature was still after her. It had also risen, but seemed to be having some difficulty in coming after her. It staggered, dragging one leg along the ground at an unnatural angle.

A wild, terrified glance about showed there was nowhere to go but back the way they'd fallen. They'd landed on a short outcropping of rock, which overlooked the cool, blue water some ten stories below. To either side lay sheer rock face and the straggling attempts of wildlife to grow in the difficult terrain. She was trapped.

The creature grinned, having come to the same conclusion. Once within five feet of her it lunged, taking her to the ground. It wrapped its claws about her throat, taking malicious glee from her inability to protect herself. She struggled though she was no match for the creature's strength, and just as she was about to pass out a soft whisper of air disturbance touched her ear and the hands determined to choke the life out of her slackened. She blinked several times, trying to hang on to consciousness. The evil grin slipped, the jaw dropping open.

The thing atop of her slumped to the side, then crumpled to the ground. She scrambled away from the unmoving form despite the immense pain her movements caused. She kept backing away until she collided with something solid. She whirled about with fists raised to find the one thing she'd have lest expected.

Fial stood very still, regarding her with his wide, innocent eyes. A bloody sword was clutched in his hand, as much of a surprise as his presence. She followed his gaze when it moved from her face, watching as the head of the creature he'd just killed rolled away from its body. Sophie finally gave in, and began to retch.

Her friend waited with infinite patience until she had stopped being sick, then came to pat her hand, trying to reassure her. His touch was light and warm, skin as soft as silk. His eyes captured her, showing the depth of bravery and strength he truly possessed, which she had missed in her assumption of inadequacy. She had underestimated Fial.

And she'd forgotten all about the woman.

CHAPTER 16

Together they scrambled up the hillside, where the dust had yet to settle from their sudden and rapid encounter. Fial chirped and flitted about her, but she was too focused on getting back to chastise his annoying behaviour. Men's voices could be heard ahead, the tone imploring her to fun even faster.

She stumbled into the clearing, where a new figure had taken a place at the woman's side. Domnall glared in her direction, and as he clenched his hands into fists, Sophie noted the remnants of rope still about his wrists. The Ellyllon had retreated, now huddling in the shade of a large tree. The *cyhyraeths* swirled around the two enemy figures, swooping down at them in intervals, only to be thrown back by the woman's magical interception. One large energy blast sent them back from wherever they'd materialized from. Though the larger force-field seemed to have been dissipated, the woman still possessed the ability to protect herself.

"You cannot win, Geraint. The Annwn you know will soon no longer exist." Her words rang with confidence.

"I will see you die, brother," Domnall said.

The clearing erupted in a blinding flash of light, then dropped into total blackness. Voices cried out and someone bumped into her. Sophie moved her hands about until she found Fial. With a loud snapping sound, emitted with enough force to make her teeth rattle, the veil of darkness lifted.

Domnall and the woman had vanished. Luckily the three who'd been held hostage remained, a touch worse for wear, but still alive.

Geraint and Owain came to her, the former asking, "Are you alright?"

She couldn't help but laugh. "I think I have hurt every part of my body, but I'm still standing."

"Good, there is no time. We have to get to the dagger."

"What if I don't know what to when we get our hands on it?" Sophie asked.

"Then all will be lost."

Sophie turned away, choking back the cry threatening to escape. Fial kept his small hand entwined with hers, a comfort she clung to. She forced a deep breath in, counting to ten to let her pulse slow. A flash in her peripheral vision caught her attention, bringing the fear back in an instant. Yet instead of another attack she found one of the Ellyllon walking toward her, small hand outstretched. In it was clasped the charm, the small bit of sunlight that penetrated the clearing catching against the shiny surface.

Sophie raced to the creature, and after grabbing the charm from its hands, spun them around and around. The desperation of the situation faded at the recovery of necklace, and she allowed herself to laugh like she hadn't in months.

She would find a way to save Annwn. She had to.

True to his word Fial continued in his position as the group's navigator, leading them to a section of the forest surrounding the lake, which seemed unremarkable when compared to the rest of the visible topography. In fact, the specific area didn't appear to hold any type of travelable path at all, it was merely one small section in a wall of foliage so dense and deep that none in the procession could view anything past a length of five short feet. The ominous quality of the wooded area lay in stark contrast to the serene, unspoiled perfection of the crystal blue lake, but even its beauty could not lighten the heavy hearts of those remaining. Leaving their fallen comrades behind had been a grim decision.

Fial began to gesture wildly, his rapid cadence on par with the speed at which he flicked his limbs about. The other Ellyllon drew close to him, alternating between nodding their agreement and looking about the too quiet area with suspicion. Sophie could see nothing to indicate the cause for his assertion.

Owain stepped forward, listening closely to the excited chatter. "He says this is the spot." One hand hovered above the wound to his chest, an unconscious action.

Geraint referred to the map, which he'd keep in his hands while walking the miles along the lake's sandy coast. From there his gaze wandered over the expanse of land, and back to the map. As if to emphasize his point Fial began to tap at a spot on the map that showed nothing but a series of trees, indicting a section of woodland. Geraint frowned, and Sophie felt herself mimicking his response.

"There's nothing here, you silly creature," he said.

Fial emitted another burst of chatter and made a strange slicing motion with one hand.

Owain asked something of the creature, clarifying before addressing his leader. "He says it's magically hidden. He's not sure how to open it."

"Wonderful."

A sensation seized Sophie with such suddenness her knees knocked together, and without Owain snaking out an arm to catch her should would have fallen to the ground. From her feet emerged a curious tingling, which then ran up the length of her legs and made her belly squirm. She could not think at all, but acted only on instinct. She reached out for the map, and after all that had happened so far in their journey Geraint knew better than to argue.

As soon as the map touched her hand a cone-shaped energy force emerged from the parchment, with the image of a ramshackle cottage and surrounding meadow dancing at the top. Sophie immediately recognized it from her one of her visions. From the marvel emerged a voice, not so much heard as felt inside one's head.

"*Three drops of noble blood it will take to pass into the realm of Eirianwen.*" Geraint groaned. "That would be me, I take it."

"I would suppose, sir."

Geraint stepped forward, pulling a short knife from the inside of one dusty and cracked boot. With the barest grimace he drew the blade across his palm, then pulled the hand into a first, allowing three drops to fall to the rocky soil. Several seconds passed and the woods remained the same. Fial passed a worried look to one of the other Ellyllon, who shook his head in response.

A cool wind passed by Sophie's face, lifting her sweat-dampened hair. As the sensation waned a small sound intruded. A voice.

"It must be you, Sophie."

A startled murmur circulated through the group, with each set of eyes searching for the source. Nothing but forest, blue sky, and unspoiled waters were visible. Several of Geraint's men drew their swords, but no living thing made any advance on the group.

Without realizing he'd moved, Sophie found Fial at her side, where he tugged gently at her arm. With the most serious expression she'd yet seen on the creature's face he regarded her, and she knew without any practical basis that the words were true.

She let Fial take her to Geraint, where he lifted her arm and turned the palm to face the leader. Geraint placed the blade against her flesh, giving a sad smile before the metal did its damage. A fiery sting followed the blade, bringing tears to her eyes. She bit her bottom lip to keep from crying out. When Geraint pulled back she squeezed her fingers against the wound, pushing past the bright snap of pain to focus on the blood that fell to the ground.

"*Bendith y Mamau.*"

The instant the third drop touched the ground world around them began to change.

A strange, disconcerting trembling in the base of the enormous trees started, the roots throbbing, and eventually lifting from their protection coverage in the earth to flop about like a handful of frightened snakes. With much awkward maneuvering the displaced trees walked themselves out of the way to reveal a narrow, but perfectly cleared pathway that led deep into the heart of the hidden forest. Just visible to the naked eye, yet still some miles in the distance, was the slope of the backing mountain range and supposed home of *Eirianwen*.

All members of the group turned their expressions of wonder and astonishment in her direction, and Sophie felt a flush in her cheeks. She had no explanation for the occurrence.

"Who are you?" Owain asked, drawing a sharp look from Geraint.

"So-phie," Fial said, as though her name constituted some type of answer.

"I don't know," she said. To discourage any further questioning she stepped onto the now apparent trail. She felt someone take the hand she had extended behind her, knowing it was Fial without having to turn around. The strange creature had grown on her, and she took an odd, and perhaps misplaced comfort from his presence.

Owain had led Jili, along with his own horse, passing the reins over to Sophie without comment. Like the others, his attention was captured by the harsh, wild beauty of the place they had discovered. Once the last member of their party had passed over the invisible border to the forest within a forest, the displaced trees quickly closed in behind them, replanting themselves back into the rocky soil. Looking back the view of the pristine lake had been obscured by a wall of foliage, so dense the only light that touched them came from high above the tops of the enormous trees. Sophie fidgeted with the charm about her neck, its touch like ice against her warm flesh.

After she'd mounted Jili, Fial was pulled up to reclaim his place behind her. Almost immediately he began to babble, and even though she could not understand she did recognize several words that the creature repeated. Owain listened with a tight puzzled look on his face until at last the talkative creature came to a rest.

"He says that long ago this area was a free land, and many of the different life forms in Annwn came to hunt and gather, and to swim in the lake. They were all aware of the tales that *Eirianwen* lived somewhere nearby, though none had ever seen her. One day a small group of *Ellyllon* came to collect berries and they found a beautiful, young woman bathing in the lake. They turned away to allow her to come ashore and dress.

When clothed they offered to share the fruit they had collected. Though she refused the woman promised to remember their kindness. She touched the leader, discovering a truth from far in both their futures. The vision showed her that their kind would one day be of great assistance in leading an important person to her location. She showed them the spot and told them how the trail could be accessed and then disappeared."

Sophie listened, taking in the meaning. "So they had come upon *Eirianwen* herself, bathing in the lake?"

"So it would seem."

She felt Fial snuggle against her back and couldn't help but smile. Owain let out a soft chuckle and them pushed ahead to join Geraint at the head of the procession. Where the previous area of forest they'd traversed had been dank and foreboding, this section offered beauty at every turn. Flowering vines climbed over rock and tree limbs, blossoms thrusting toward the yellow-orange warmth above. The serene blue sky stretched far and wide, with a soft wind dancing through the tree tops. Sophie felt the tension drain from her body.

Her mind wandered from the immediate circumstance, far past the borders of her adoptive world. She drifted back to the time before coming to Knob's End, of her mother, not so long passed and never far from her thoughts. She contemplated the damage the woman's death had wrought on the lives of father and herself. It had been a long, terrible year watching helplessly as her mother had succumbed to the cancer that would eventually kill her. She had drawn her emotions inward, so afraid to upset the women, who already had such a burden to carry. Likewise her father had been quiet, never complaining and giving till the last possible second.

The year after had been even worse. She and her dad had barely talked. He'd become a ghost of his former self, simply going through the motions of life without actually living. None of her friends had been through anything like what she had, and though they'd been supportive, they simply couldn't understand her pain. She'd felt so alone.

Her grandmother, her father's mother, had been great. She'd been welcomed into her home with open arms, and it had been so wonderful to have a feeling of connection again, something that had been missing from her life. In a quiet, unobtrusive way her grandmother's love had started healing the wound she'd been keeping raw by not letting her anger and sadness work its course. Instead she'd kept the feelings deep inside herself, letting them fester and sour every aspect of her life.

And now she'd found an even bigger family, one that accepted her, respected her and would even die for her. She had to let her strength shine through, not just for Annwn, but for herself.

"Halt," Geraint called out.

Sophie gave the reins a sharp tug, stopping Jili short. Owain had been riding alongside her, and after a small shrug he joined his leader. They conversed quietly, and Geraint pointed something out that Sophie didn't understand. A lazy, haphazard group of tiny butterflies flew past, leaving the scent of citrus in their wake. Sophie smiled, following their meandering voyage over the group until they passed by the head of Geraint's horse. About ten yards on they abruptly disappeared. She scanned about, sure that she'd missed something but they were simply gone.

Several of the horses whinnied, and Jili's startled movement almost unseated Sophie. "What's wrong, girl?" she whispered, patting the animal on side of her head.

"Nothing, my child," said the woman who materialized at Sophie's side aside. Sophie looked down on her, vaguely aware of the movement and cries about her.

Fial had dropped from the horse, and was kneeling before the woman, soon joined by the other Ellyllon who all bowed in reverence of the stranger. The woman smiled, offering her hand to Sophie. As recognition grabbed hold she found herself smiling back, and with the woman's assistance dismounted Jili. They two regarded each other, Sophie all but drowning in the other woman's beauty and radiating goodness. The sun caressed her form, shining off the waves of her long, dark hair.

"Eirianwen," she said.

"Yes, child. I have waited a long time for you." Then she reached one delicate hand forward and cupped the charm.

Her touch was warm silk, sending a pleasant shiver through Sophie's body. "I knew this would guide your way."

Geraint rushed forward, a rude and defiant move that Eirianwen acknowledged with a small smile. "You have the dagger?" he demanded.

"I do," she answered. Then without further explanation she walked away from the group, ebony hair swaying. Once she'd reached Geraint's horse she looked back, beckoning with one finger. A few more steps and she vanished from view.

Sophie ran after her, ignoring the cries of protest. As she passed Geraint's horse she snatched the map from the carrying case, unsure why she felt compelled to do so. Seconds before she reached the magic shield she felt it calling out to her. Her skin tightened, the air warm and thick. The small hairs on her arm rose to attention, as the world about her began to swirl and dim. A brief, panicky moment passed where it wasn't possible to breath, but she kept moving, knowing the truth was finally within her grasp.

She pushed through what felt like an invisible Jell-O wall to step into the small, meadow where a narrow path led to a small building some ways in the distance. Along the path stood several men and horses, which Sophie quickly passed by. When she caught sight of a Coraniaid, caught with his sword thrust out before him she stopped. Her touch found the body still warm, yet eerily still.

"They're not dead. Simply frozen. When the time comes I will return them from whence they came," Eirianwen said before ducking inside the cramped dwelling of Sophie's visions.

She gave the Coraniaid a last look, then followed Eirianwen inside. A fire burned in the same stone hearth, and the table was still laden with herbs and other strange items.

Eirianwen had taken a seat, and was now holding a small knife on her lap. She gestured to the other chair, which Sophie sat down on. She clutched the map as though her life depended on her keeping hold of it. The strange flapping sound coming from the parchment made her realize how badly she was shaking, but with determined effort she unclenched her hand and managed to spread the map out across the table.

Eirianwen leaned forward, drawing her finger along the map to rest at the area they were at. "We are here. A long way from the lovely territory of Rhiannon." Again the finger traced along the age-worn parchment to stop at the crest representing Nerys's homeland.

The faces of those she'd met in Rhiannon flashed before her eyes. Brynmor, so excited to have Nerys home, the loving embrace shared between Mairwen and her daughter. She thought of the handsome Gethen and the way he'd watched Nerys, unable to completely conceal his amorous feelings for the beautiful girl. Even the faces of the many workers at the castle haunted her, knowing that is she were to fail her quest it would be their lives the consequences would fall upon.

Next the finger tapped the small island of *Anffrwythlon*, where the tragic Tegwen resided, waiting for release from her terrible fate. "You have many people helping you. Many who wish you to succeed." Eirianwen looked up, for a moment her face replaced with Tegwen's, tears streaming down her porcelain cheeks.

"The power to end this is within you. For it is not just the dagger, but the power of truth needed to wield the weapon. Truth can be both dark and light. That is why I have interfered as I have. The dagger cannot come to be in the wrong hands. Such a thing will cause pain for many."

"But why me? I am just a girl."

"Yes, you are. But you are also a daughter of Annwn." Her hand lifted to place the dagger upon the map. "I have never experienced a prophecy as powerful as yours. The night your ancestor was brought to me I knew she had to be saved. Her life was but the first step in bringing you to this moment."

"I don't know what to do!"

"Close your eyes and let the magic come to you. Your visions have given you the secrets of the past. Let them do the same for the future. There is so much more you are capable of."

Sophie's lids slipped closed, and the gentle, melodic timber of Eirianwen's voice lulled her into a state of calmness. Her breathing eased, with her heart and pulse dropping to a normal pace. From this dark cocoon of tranquility emerged a small point of light, a distant, almost unnoticeable intrusion. Once it touched her she felt the compulsion to move toward it, feeling the sensation of the earth beneath her feet and the soft increase in temperature as surely as if her physical form had been transported to the place in her mind.

The tiny point of light open like a doorway, casting her out into the blazing afternoon sun. She found herself in a muddied field, where cries of anguish and determination filled the air. Far off in the distance she spied the same rock crest, the stream, and the oddly-shaped building from the vision inspired by Tegwen's touch. She now understood the significance. Albanach and his followers had been keeping watch from the structure, and adjacent to it lay the land where the great battle with Llyr was fully underway.

When her gaze found Cadoc her breath caught in her throat. He was on foot, engaged in sword battle with one of the enemy. He'd been hurt, blood soaked one sleeve of his shirt, and she could tell the wound was hindering his performance. The one he fought with kept coming at him from his injured side, gaining the advantage.

A massive shadow suddenly swallowed the battlefield, followed by a cry so shrill and far-reaching it blocked out all other sounds for several seconds. Instinctively Sophie dropped to her knee, and searched the sky for the source of the intrusion. High above the continuing violence a giant bird flew, and as it swooped lower, turning to approach the distant castle Sophie spotted a figure on its back. The distinctive red-gold hair streaming behind the figure brought her breath back with a painful gulp.

"Sophie," a voice called out to her.

She looked back, finding nothing but darkness. A creeping, insistent pressure played at her back, drawing her away from the vision. Her last wild glance about the battle showed Cadoc on the receiving end of a vicious blow. He crumpled to the ground as Sophie began to scream, fighting to stay in the time yet to come, but unable to hang on. She was yanked back to the present, coming to with a concerned Eirianwen looking down on her. It took a few seconds to understand she was sprawled on the dirt floor of the small cottage, the intensity of the vision having knocked her from her chair.

"I have to get to Cigfa. Now!"

"I know. It is much too far for your party to make it on foot."

"Eirianwen, you are the most powerful Gwiddonod Annwn has ever known! You must have some kind of magic that can get me there! Please, I must save…" Her tears burst forth with fury, ending her ability to speak clearly.

"The power to save Cadoc is within you, Sophie. Trust in this."

"Help me!"

Eirianwen grabbed Sophie by both wrists, forcing her to meet her gaze. The blue fire of her eyes captured her, draining away her anguish. The charm at her throat warmed against her skin, and the dagger tucked into Eirianwen's belt glowed white-hot.

"Do your best, Eirianwen. She'd going need all the help she can get!"

Both women startled at the unexpected addition. The woman from the clearing stood beside the table, hand resting on the map. "Ceridwen," Eirianwen said, like the word left a bitter taste in her mouth.

"Always underestimating me. This time it will cost you everything." She smiled and made her move, managing to snatch the map away and disappear in a whirling flash of crimson light.

"Noooo!" Eirianwen screamed at the nothing left in the map's place.

"But we have the dagger," Sophie said, not understanding what the loss of the map meant.

"Sophie, the map has been enchanted. It once belonged to Llud LLaw Eraint and holds the power to keep the pact in place. The only thing that can break it is the dagger. You must get it back." Without explaining further the witch hurried about the small space grabbing an odd assembly of items that she began to measure and mix in a crude wooden bowl. Her lips moved reciting words that Sophie did not understand, but made her cringe.

Several drops of blood from a cut she made across her own inner arm set the concoction frothing. A terrible stench assaulted Sophie's nostrils, the frothy mist coming from the mixture burning her eyes like someone had pressed a freshly-cut onion directly against them. Eirianwen lifted the bowl with one steady hand, and grabbed Sophie's arm with the other.

"This is a most dangerous spell, one that does not always have the best results. Invoking this kind of magic, like Ceridwen must have done to get into my private dwelling, is dangerous. Yet it is the only thing that can help you now."

Sophie didn't like the sound of that but she let the witch lead her back to the area where Geraint and his men waited for her. As the emerged from the protective spell about Eirianwen's dwelling Owain rushed toward them.

"Now this is only enough to transport four of you. Even then there may be repercussions, but we don't have time for that now. Choose wisely."

Geraint and Owain would of course be needed, but the last spot caused her pause. Two of the Giants remained, as well as several of Geraint's soldier, all with the power and experience needed in a battle of the type they were to face. She looked over the tense faces staring back at her, weighing her option when she felt a warmth brush her lower leg. Fial had come to her, and when their gazes met the answer was found.

"I choose Geraint, Owain, and Fial," she said with confidence.

"I believe you have made a wise a choice."

Owain leaned in, giving her a smirk. "Fial?"

Sophie smiled, but didn't explain. Eirianwen guided then into a small circle and instructed them to clasp hands. She walked about them, reciting a spell that nipped at Sophie's skin. At last she tossed the contents of the bowl into the air, where it floated in the most unnatural for several seconds before becoming an angry, liquid tornado swirling about their group, pressing them against one another in a decidedly unpleasant way.

"Come back to me, Sophie. We have other things to discuss," Eirianwen's voice called after her.

A fiery wind blew up through the centre of the group, a

terrible counter-pressure to the magic ring keeping them captive. The ground beneath their feet fell away, where invisible tentacles pulled them down into a shocking cold darkness. An abrasive whirring rang in her ears, a sound so powerful it seemed to be suffocating her.

Sophie emerged from the darkness coughing and clawing at her throat in a desperate attempt to allow air to flow into her body. She hit the damp ground with a heavy thud, the impact hard enough to make her teeth rattle. She'd barely enough time to recover her senses when powerful vibrations in the earth warned her of the approach of something large and fast-moving. Looking up she found herself in the path of several horses whose riders were pushing them for everything they were worth. She scrambled out of the way amidst a shower of mud, narrowly missing a collision.

Once she found her footing she took off running, her path guided by the destination burned into her mind. Geraint had pulled one of the riders from his horse, taking the animal for his own use. He rode by Sophie, eyes on the battle raging several hundred yards from where they'd landed. Owain took off on foot mere seconds behind her, but moving in a different direction. Peripherally she was aware of him slashing his way through the onslaught of enemy soldiers. Fial had followed her, his boisterous chatter lost in the sounds of action all about them.

Then she spotted him. Cadoc was engaged in sword fight near the edge of the battle closest to the castle. As in her vision she could see that he was wounded and his continued efforts were taking their toll. Without thinking Sophie grabbed the charm with one hand, and threw the other out before her. From her fingertips emerged a blast of light, a phenomena that hit Cadoc's opponent like a cannon ball. The man's back bowed, and with a grunt of surprise he toppled to the ground.

Cadoc whirled about in shock, meeting the gaze of an equally surprised Sophie. Once facing her direction she could see that in addition to the gash across his arm, the back end of an arrow protruded from his chest. Upon recognizing her he broke out in a mad grin, causing Sophie to run even faster. As she closed the distance he fell to his knees.

"Cadoc, no!" She skidded across the remaining ten feet, pulling his sagging form across her body.

"Sophie," he said, blinking rapidly.

"Yes. And now that I'm here you are not going to wuss out on me."

Fial chirped at her, then seeming to realize that his attempts at communication would have no affect straddled himself over Cadoc's body and snapped the shaft of the arrow close to chest. From the small satchel worn over his bony shoulder he pulled out a handful of a sticky, greenish substance that he smeared about the injury. Then he flitted to the other side to neatly remove the head of the arrow lodged between his ribs. Cadoc cried out, and struggled to pull away from Sophie. She held tight until Fial had finished tending to him. Returning to her side, the Ellyllon handed Cadoc a small bit of another substance pulled from his satchel, then pointed to his mouth.

Understanding, Sophie took the slimy, peanut-sized item and pushed it between Cadoc's lips. Before he could protest she pressed her mouth over his, feeling him swallow what she hoped was a pain killer of some kind. He shuddered and pulled back from her.

"How do you feel?"

"Like I just got shot with an arrow," he barked. Fial flitted about, speaking his usual gibberish.

"The bleeding stopped," she said, placing her hand over the wound on his chest.

His hand closed over top of hers, the warmth sending tingles up her arm. He leaned in to kiss her again, causing Fial to squeal in delight. They both laughed, and rose to their feet, where Cadoc scrutinized her more closely.

"What in the world happened to you, girl? You look terrible."

She bit back the sharp retort that sprung to mind. After being dragged through the forest and the tumble down the rocky embankment she must have looked quite a sight. The sudden plunge into darkness erased her attempt at an explanation.

The scurrying, chilling sensation of déjà vu danced along the nape of her neck, and as she looked up into the sky she found exactly what she'd expected. Cadoc and Fial followed her gaze, taking in the unexpected appearance of an Adar Llwch Gwin being ridden by a young woman with a blaze of golden hair trailing out behind her.

"Is that Nerys?" Cadoc asked.

"No, but I have a good idea who it is."

CHAPTER 17

Cadoc knew better than to ask any more questions. When Sophie started running in the same direction as the Adar Llwch Gwin he fell in step beside her. Fial came along with them, racing ahead only to come back to them time and time again. They charged through the cascades of flying arrows and clanging swords with blind determination, moving as though they'd grown wings on their feet. In the distance the giant bird touched down, delivering its passenger to an area devoid of immediate danger.

Once on her feet the girl dared a look about, and upon seeing Sophie and company heading in her direction she turned to the creature at her side. As they closed the distance the girl leaned in to whisper at the side of the bird's head, an action prompting a rippling, fluid shudder to ride the length of the creature's form. The feathers shook violently, their colour somehow bleeding into the air about its body. Then as though it had liquefied the creature dissolved into an ebony puddle on the rocky ground.

From this pool emerged a human form, at first devoid of definitive features, which then began to take shape before Sophie's eyes. Left in the place of the Adar Llwch Gwin was an almost identical version of the woman who'd been the creature's rider. The second woman stood a few inches taller, yet the similarity was startling.

Sophie came to an abrupt stop. Cadoc and Fial remained with her, the looks on their faces belying their astonishment at what they'd witnessed.

The first woman stepped forward. "Sophie, I presume?"

"Yes, and you must be Eira?"

She nodded. "Yes, and this is my sister Aderyn."

The two sisters put their hands out before them, stacked one upon the other, reaching in Sophie's direction. Before making any conscious decision to do so, she found her hand meeting theirs, igniting a shock of supernatural power so profound it forced a painful jolt up her arm. Her bones grated against one another at the elbow, yet despite the intense pressure fighting against her Sophie maintained her connection with the sisters, embracing the phenomenon that had captured them.

The progression of Nerys, Eira, and Aderyn from childhood to present day, including the emergence of their individual magical gifts, played out before Sophie's eyes as clearly as if it had been captured on film. In ways that words could not have given her, the imagery provided a poignant understanding of the scope and limitations of their gift, and the depth of their commitment to one another. Sophie saw the sisters through the other's eyes, absorbing a love and loyalty so deep it proved difficult to experience first-hand.

The wondrous occurrence soon deflated, falling away like the layers of an onion to leave the three back in their real time and place. It was a moment of urgency and with no place for mistakes.

"What are you doing here? Isn't it dangerous?" Sophie asked.

"Yes, but whether the pact is enforced or not, Albanach still has our sister. With one, the enemy takes all three. We must save her," Eira answered.

"We must get into the castle," Aderyn said.

Sophie looked to where she pointed, taking in the numerous and challenging obstacles that could prevent such an accomplishment. Before them lay several hundred yards of field filled with armed men and galloping horses, and beyond that was a steep embankment to a level area where the castle sat. In addition to the guard visible patrolling along the top the stone wall encircling their destination, a wide moat prevented easy access. Unless an underground passage existed, the only way to enter was through the front gate.

"Nerys is inside and we have to save her."

"I'm certain this is where they've taken the map, too. We have to get it back," Sophie said.

"I thought the quest was for the dagger," Aderyn asked, pointing to the dagger tucked into Sophie's belt.

"Long story. We need both and Ceridwen has stolen the map. I had a vision of this place, so I assume it's been brought here."

"Ceridwen?" Aderyn asked, shocked.

"It would make sense. This is where the pact was made after all." Eira made the last comment as though it were common knowledge, but Sophie had never heard such a thing before.

Yet it made sense. As Nerys had told her magic leaves a residue, sometimes so subtle as to be unnoticeable, yet has the potential to make a permanent change in the places or people it has touched. As such the words instigated a sudden glimpse of the past. A blink of her eye and she saw the land as it was in the time of Llud LLaw Eraint, the castle yet to exist. Instead there stretched an endless expanse of desolate land, the sharp, scraggly brush protruding from the hard-packed dirt. Even this poor excuse for plant life faded out, leaving a rocky barren stretch for many miles until reaching the border with Coranis. It was there that the fate of those now battling for their future had been sealed.

"What I don't understand is why Ceridwen is playing for Gaidheal's side?" Sophie said as she trotted along behind the sisters.

"She and Eirianwen were close once, like sisters, but Ceridwen was always jealous of her power. When the prophecy was spoken of Ceridwen disappeared. She must have thought it was her chance to get the upper hand."

The densely-packed field and the urgent, unpredictable nature of the activity slowed their progress. Cadoc and Fial kept close to her side, with the sisters leading the charge.

They moved in unison, with a hypnotizing stealth and precision that Sophie could not have copied in her wildest dreams. She did alright to remain on her feet and out of the way of oncoming arrows.

Coming over a small crest the group came upon a large

group of the enemy faction lying in wait, with smaller groups advancing from either side to offer additional resistance. They were in effect trapped, a truth that Sophie realized as she narrowly avoided colliding with Eira. A bright surge of fear shot through her body, leaving her feeling as though her skin had shrunk two sizes too small.

"Follow us," Aderyn called out seconds before dropping into the shape of a large cat. She charged ahead, moving much lower than the level at which the fighting took place and with a speed that left Sophie in awe.

Following her sister's cue Eira flung both hands out before, letting forth two towering strips of fire. She gestured that they should follow her as she bolted down what essentially was a private passageway through the centre of the most intensive fighting. Just as she slipped between the protective walls of fire she caught sight of Ysbaddaden slashing his way through a hoard of armor-clad men. He didn't see her, but the fact that he was still alive and fighting gave Sophie a rush of thankfulness and hope.

The heat licked along Sophie's side, but she reserved her worry for what might lay at the end of their safe passage. They ran for several minutes before the magic waned, dropping in level until it was completely extinguished. Within seconds a mass of angry soldiers descended upon them, wherein Sophie narrowly missed being impaled on a long stake being maneuvered by a Coraniaid man with a quick duck and roll.

When she stopped rolling she sat up to an eerie silence. Cadoc offered his hand and pulled her back onto her feet. Once standing she realized that a sheet of ice had been cast over the rivals in close proximity, capturing everyone in a series of hostile poses. Aderyn, still in cat form, appeared between a set of men who'd been frozen mid-thrust with their long swords. She growled in their direction before disappearing from sight once again.

"Let's get a move on. It won't last," Eira said.

True to her word, Sophie noted the condensation sweating along the frozen forms, a warning of their impending release. The group scampered around the figures, toward a ragged rock embankment leading to the plateau where the castle sat. Beyond that the moat was less than a hundred feet away. Aderyn scampered up the hill with ease, transforming back to her human form at the level top. With decidedly more difficulty the other four came to join her.

With a hand shading her eyes Aderyn surveyed the structure's defenses. Sophie followed her line of sight to a handful of men pacing the length of the section of wall facing them. One had sighted them also, and in pointing their presence out to his comrades a warning horn sounded.

"They're not going to make this easy, are they?" Sophie asked as a shower of arrows rained down on them, making them scramble back over the edge of the embankment.

From the new vantage point it could be seen that most of those who'd been frozen had freed themselves, and joined the ranks of a much larger group marching toward the castle. Sophie's heart thumped, and for a moment she lost her grip, slipping about half way down the hill. She caught one hand around a rock protrusion bringing her slide to an abrupt halt. Her breath came in ragged gasps.

"Sophie, look out!" one of the sisters called from above.

The warning came just in time for Sophie to scuttle free of the pathway of a blood- crusted sword. With one hand she pulled herself up the rocky ground, as the other wrapped around the cold comfort of the charm. A hand grasped her ankle, giving a vicious yank.

"*Bendith y Mamau!*" she cried.

The familiar ruffle in the atmosphere touched her, the coldness seeping into her flesh. The ragged hem of the dress of the *cyhyraeth* dragged an icy trail along the front of her body, the connection sending a ripple of disgust through her body. She felt bile burning in the back of her throat. The man at her feet screamed, and in his desperation to get away from the horrible creature pitched himself backward. He hit the ground at an awkward angle, rolling the rest of the way to the ground. There the *cyhyraeth* descended on him, draining him of his life force. When nothing but an empty husk remained the creature moved on in search of another victim.

A glance over her shoulder as she made her way back to where the others waited let her know that several more of the creatures had joined the first, and were spreading out into the advancing army like a pack of hungry locusts. No doubt there were some among Albanach's legions who had magical abilities, and who might be able to fend them off or offer something as terrible in return, but the creatures should help hold the group off the time being.

"I hate those things," Cadoc said as she climbed alongside him.

"Me, too," Sophie agreed. "I'm glad they're on our side."

Aderyn was surveying the castle with a careful, guarded focus, unwilling to allow anything to be missed. After a few seconds of tense silence she spoke her plan. "Eira, I am going to leave you to get Sophie and Fial to the landing by the castle's main gate. From there you should be able to access the interior through the small door beside it and let yourselves in. Once inside lower the bridge so that our army can gain entrance."

"What about Cadoc," Sophie asked.

"He's coming with me. I'm going to let him down in an advantageous spot on the wall, where he can take out some of the guards. We need as little resistance as possible. We can regroup inside."

Everyone took a moment to swallow their fear, and let the details of their intended actions settle in. Sophie let her gaze travel along the massive stone wall, looking for the door Aderyn had referred to. In the first pass she missed it. As the sun emerged from behind the protective cover of passing clouds the light reflected off the small bit of metal in the door's handle, giving away the door's all-but hidden location. It sat to the right of the enormous wooden gate, with a small ledge underneath that protruded from the wall. It must have served some kind of safety or service function, Sophie surmised.

"Ready?" Eira asked her.

She didn't feel ready, but she nodded anyway.

Eira turned to Fial and addressed him in what Sophie took to be the same peculiar language the creature had been muttering in since she'd met him. He must have understood as he responded to the words, and then proceeded to climb onto Sophie's back. Eira took Sophie's hand, immediately instigating a change in the atmosphere about them, dropping the temperature dramatically. An urgent pressure appeared, wrapping itself around Sophie's body and presenting a lop-sided, uneven view of the space about them. Her feet lifted from the ground and she felt herself rising up, spinning more and more quickly, until there was nothing to be seen but a blur of colour. Fial was still with her, as she could feel his arms clamped about her neck, but she could not be certain what had happened to the others.

The cyclonic motion came to an abrupt end, dropping she and Fial onto a hard surface. It took a moment to get her bearings, so the hand that touched her arm startled her and she scurried away. Her vision cleared about the same time as her hand slipped over the edge of landing, sending her reeling backward into nothingness. Eira grabbed her a second time, getting a tighter grip than her first attempt and pulled her back to safety. They had landed on the ledge as planned, where Sophie had a clear view of Cadoc riding on the back of Aderyn in her Adar Llwch Gwin guise.

They sailed up the height of the wall, making a hard dive to the right and out of Sophie's line of sight. Cadoc's sword had been drawn, and she silently wished him well in his part of the plan. A sharp chirp from Fial drew her attention back, and she turned to find him fiddling about with the lock, much to Eira's annoyance.

"Can you control him, please?" Eira snapped.

Before Sophie could reply and small spark emerged from one of Fial's hands, hitting the lock and thrusting the door open. The turn of events was as silent as they were surprising, eliciting an ear-to-ear grin from the Ellyllon. They slipped inside like phantoms, evading the notice of any of the castle's inhabitants. Inside they found themselves in a small storage space, dank and pungent with odors Sophie didn't want to know the origin of. Eira took her hand, leading her across the small space toward the thin line of light coming from under the door opposite the one they'd just entered.

A loud thud, followed by the raucous clatter of a hostile altercation filtered in, drawing their advancement to a halt. Several heartbeats passed before the sound become less distinct, fading as those involved moved away from their hiding spot. With hesitation Eira opened the door, peeking her head out to take a quick perusal of the space and any possible obstacles. A quick flick of her hand let Sophie know that she and Fial should follow as she stepped from the relative safety of their present location.

Once past the door, Sophie found herself in an enormous courtyard, the drawbridge to her left, and the main castle structure several hundred yards in front. The outside space was littered with weapons, carts, and a row of saddled horses. Eira moved to the release for the drawbridge, pressing the lever to start the descent. Surprisingly the action did not draw any unwanted attention. If the *cyhyraeths* did their job, at least some of Llyr's men would be able to gain access to the castle.

"We should do our best to pass by unnoticed and without the use of magic. Anything out of the ordinary will draw attention," Eira instructed before setting off in the direction of the castle.

A terrible squawking and a chorus of angry voices sound ahead and above them, making Sophie's heart sink like a stone. Surely the sound had been Aderyn and Cadoc coming into contact with members of Albanach's assembly. As she faltered Fial gave an impatient chirp and tugged at her hand. Swallowing hard and refusing to give in to the tears welling in her eyes, Sophie pressed on. Moving as one, they travelled along the perimeter of the great wall, managing not to draw attention and making quick time to the castle. Once at the closest entrance, Eira used a small burst of fire to open the door and ran inside.

Like the sisters' home in Rhiannon the inside of the castle was a confusing labyrinth of hallways and rooms, but Eira charged ahead as though certain of her destination. Sophie had to run to keep up with the girl, the endless space about her blurring past without comprehension. A stairway appeared and Eira shifted direction, taking the steps two at a time. Once at the top she made an abrupt turn to the left, for a moment vanishing from sight. Sophie gulped, choking on her breath. Taking the same turn, Eira came back into view, her long hair streaming out behind her like red-gold fire.

A set of guards came into sight, startling Sophie, but seeming to have no effect on Eira at all. Both of the men drew their swords and charged at them. Eira, still running, gave a wave of her arm and a rush of water came at the guards, taking their feet out from under them. They both crashed to the floor, swords slipping away on the flow of water. As they struggled to right themselves, Eira grabbed one of the swords and pressed it to the throat of the man closest to her. Her arm trembled, and for the first time she looked wan and unsteady.

The other sword had delivered itself to Sophie, and snatching it up she mimicked Eira's action with the other man. The water turned to mist, evaporating as though it had never existed at all.

"Get to your feet. And watch yourselves, we know how to use these." Eira's words were not to be argued with.

Sophie wasn't so sure she could come through with that threat, her arm was already aching just from holding the heavy weapon. Having to swing it about might prove more than she could handle, but the men didn't know that. She kept her expression hard, faking it. The guards took the threat seriously and relented to being taken prisoner.

Eira instructed them to walk ahead, with she and Sophie following right behind.

They passed several doors, were weary eyes peered out at them, and a few called for help. At the very end of the hallway the men stopped before the last door.

Eira gave the one in front of her a sharp poke with the sword. "Open it."

"We don't have the key," the man answered, defiance burning in his eyes.

"I don't believe you."

"It's true," came a familiar voice from inside the locked room.

Eira cried out and rushed to peer in the small opening near the top of the door. "Nerys, are you alright?"

"Yes, I'm fine. The guards speak the truth. Only the one

who comes at night with my meal has a key."

"I understand," Eira said. "Do you know where it's kept?"

"A floor below this is the main guard room, where only the most senior men are allowed to enter. It is kept there, but access is all but impossible."

"What do we do, Eira?" Sophie asked.

The girl's face had lost all its colour. Her gaze wandered over the guards, the locked door and the long hallway behind them. At she settled on Fial, and the barest of smiles crossed her lips. She knelt down, coming face to face with the creature. "We need you, Fial. Annwn needs you. You must go and retrieve the key. Do you understand?"

His eyes, already large and shiny, grew to the size of saucers. He nodded, slowly, tiny feet tapping. Sophie ran her hand over the sparse hair atop his pointy head, garnering a smile. Then he turned on his heel, and disappeared in a blur of movement.

"Do you think he can do this?" Sophie asked.

"He has to," Eira answered, her tone not entirely convincing.

Ten long, painful minutes passed, enough time for Sophie to begin fearing the worst. Then moving so quickly as to seem to have appeared out of thin arm, Fial was back with key in hand. Eira took it from him, opening the door and allowing her sister to jump out into her arms. The sisters embraced, crying.

Knowing they were not out of the woods yet, Eira pulled away and ordered the guards into the room, locking it behind them. For good measure she tossed the keys out of the nearby window, and after grabbing her sister's hand headed back the way they'd come.

"Are you well, Eira? You looked drained." Nerys regarded her sister with concern. "Too much magic in too little time," Eira answered.

Sophie must have looked confused For Nerys addressed her. "Performing magic drains the individual, sometimes to the point of exhaustion. If one is too strained they may not be able to use their gifts at all."

"Ok."

"It happened to me as well. My first few days here I tried to influence all those I had contact with, even managing to make one believe he wanted to let me go. I only made it to the courtyard before I was recaptured. After that they changed the guards at my cell often, so I could not affect any one person to any degree."

They'd reached the lower level, running head on into a group of armed soldiers.

Sophie skidded to a stop, almost toppling over. Fial raced ahead, flitting about the men and managing to cause one to tumble to the ground. Eira pointed at the fallen man, sending a coating of ice about his body, but not quite covering him as she had the ones in the field. Nerys grabbed his sword and the three women entered into dangerous hand to hand combat. A she suspected, swinging the sword about was almost more than she could handle, each thrust about taking her to the floor and making her should feel as though it had been ripped from her body.

Fial had managed to climb onto a large chandelier above them, where he jumped about and chirped incessantly. He seemed to be trying to convey some important information to Sophie, but while trying to keep herself from being impaled the message alluded her. When her heel caught on a protrusion in the floor, dropping her onto her back side, she finally got it.

A rope was tired to the shaft of wood lodge in the stone floor, leading to the chandelier and holding it in place. Seeing that she understood, Fial jumped out of harm's way. With a swift chop from the sword the rope severed, bringing the large fixture down upon the men, disabling two. Sophie snatched the now dangle length of rope and from behind looped it over the neck of the man fighting with Nerys. She yanked back, taking him to the floor. The two women dropped on him, immobilizing his hands and feet with the rope. That left two.

After reclaiming her sword, she and Eira charged the one closest to them. He whirled about at the last second, his weapon clanging against Sophie's with such force she lost her grip. As he was about to take a fatal thrust at her, she clasped the charm. In the moment she vanished from view, Eira stepped up and brought her sword down on the man's broad back. He cried put, pitching forward and coming to rest in a pool of his own blood. Sophie let go of the charm, having not moved an inch and watched as the liquid spread out in her direction.

Eira looked crushed, letting her sword fall from her grip. It hit the stone, and Eira went down. Nerys had managed to disarm the last man, and with Sophie's help, tied him to other wrapped in the length of rope.

"Eira," Nerys said, shaking her sister's still form.

Eira jerked, her eyes snapping open. "I'm ok."

"No, you're not, but we have to get out of here."

Sophie and Nerys helped her to her feet. Pounding hooves and battle cries had begun to filter in from the courtyard, bringing Fial's excitement to an almost manic state. The three women made their way to the outside, moving past those rushing through the castle's front foyer without raising any flags. Steeping out into the courtyard was another matter entirely.

The group stumbled out into the midst of a roaring battle. A quick scan brought Ysbaddaden, Owain, and several others of Geraint's men to Sophie's attention. She didn't see Geraint himself, or Cadoc, a worrying truth. In amongst the clashing swords, racing horses and barrage of arrows, several of the *cyhyraeths* wandered, falling on the wounded. In her peripheral vision she caught a large object racing in her direction. She whirled about, sword drawn and determined to protect herself.

Instead of one of the enemy she found herself looking at Cadoc, who even covered in dirt and blood, his sweat-soaked hair plastered to his head, was one of the best sights she could imagine. He didn't stop moving until he had his arms wrapped around her, and his lips were pressed to hers. As he pulled back the smile on his face vanished.

"Get down," he barked.

She did, feeling the air displace as his sword swung over top of her crouched form. When she heard the meaty connection it made with something behind, she knew he'd just saved her life. The still body on the ground confirmed it.

Sophie had barely risen to standing again when a large shadow swept over them, and looking up she found herself underneath Aderyn, flying overhead. She dodged the arrows flying at her, swooping down to knock men from their horses. Eira remained drained, sagging against Nerys for support and she needed to be their foremost concern.

"Papa!" Nerys cried out suddenly, pointing a shaky hand at a nearby group of men.

Sophie followed her finger, finding the man in question on foot, engaged in a vicious fight. He had been holding his own until a second man tackled him from behind, taking them both to the well-trodden ground. His sword slipped away, leaving him with only his hands to protect himself. A mean left hook caught his opponent under the jaw, sending him spiraling face-first into the mud. With a quick roll the sword was reclaimed, and springing to his feet he took down the second man with one strike.

Without missing a beat Llyr raced over to the wayward grouping, hugging both daughters. He then nodded to Cadoc, before letting his gaze settle on Sophie. Fial scuttled behind her, peeking out at the rugged, domineering male presence. Extending his free hand in her direction, he came to where she stood.

"You must be Sophie," he said in a gravelly voice.

"Yes," she answered.

The action spilled over into their area, one man bumping into Sophie's back before diving back into the battle. When a second knock took her she spun about in annoyance, only to find a much-worse-for-wear Ysbaddaden behind her.

"Badda!" she cried, giving the man a squeeze.

The giant flushed all the way to his hairline at her show of affection. "Now, now girlie. I'm alright."

"Ysbaddaden, I am entrusting you with the safety of my daughter Eira. She is too weakened to be of further help here. You must take her to safety," Llyr said.

He made an awkward bowing motion in response to the address. "Yes, Tywysog Llyr. I will protect her at all costs." Without another word he slung the girl over his shoulder and made his way back through the sea of bodies.

"Now what?" Sophie asked.

"We continue fighting. We must find Albanach," Llyr said.

"And the map!" Sophie added.

"We lost the map?" Cadoc asked.

"I thought the dagger was key the ending this," Llyr said at about the same time.

"It's complicated," she said as she ducked out of the way large spear that had been tossed in her direction.

"If Albanach is here, he'll be in that tower," Llyr said, pointing to a part of the castle set to the back of the structure, and blocked by a multitude of obstacles, the first of which was the numerous members of Albanach's army in the near vicinity.

"Hopefully Ceridwen is with him and we can figure out a way to take the map back," Sophie said.

"Cadoc, help me clear the way," Llyr commanded and took the lead in escorting them across the bustling courtyard.

Sophie's heart hammered as she followed the two men. Her blood ran like fire through her veins, though her flesh was cold and clammy. *This is it*, she thought.

CHAPTER 18

Llyr and Cadoc fought through the masses attempting to
block their advancement, at times aided by the members of
their army who'd made it to the courtyard, and Aderyn who
continued her swooping assaults against the enemy faction.
Several times she passed so closely overhead that her enormous
wing feathers brushed the top of Sophie's head. Her strikes
were unpredictable and very precise, taking many a man from
his horse.

Geraint suddenly joined the group on horseback, a sight
Sophie couldn't have been happier to see. Owain came in on
his heels, the grimace on his face, and the tight way he held his
sword arm showing the strains of a difficult fight.

"How can we assist, Tywysog?" Geraint asked, his words
heavy.

"We need to get to the south tower," Llyr said, straining to
be heard over the roar of the battle. "I believe Albanach hides
there, and this will not end until he hands over the map."

"Or dies," Cadoc added.

"Yes, that may well be the case."

"If we retrieve that map no one has to die." The shrillness
of her voice was alarming, even to Sophie. She let her fingers
brush over the cold steel of the dagger kept safe inside her
leather satchel.

"Let's go then," Geraint said. He made a gesture to Owain,
receiving a sharp nod in return and the men were off.

In a series of well-practiced moves the men pushed aside
a large number of the enemy, also allowing more of their own
to file through and keep up the resistance. Soon they stood

before the south tower, erupting from the ground in show of impenetrability. The smooth stone exterior could not be scaled by hand, and the staircase rising along one side was heavily lined with archers. A nearby section contained a second battalion of archers, who immediately began firing.

Llyr led them behind the relative safety on a straw-topped horse shelter, placed close to the main entrance to the tower. At the door stood a group of burly men, armed with swords and other menacing looking weapons. Cadoc dared a quick peek around the side of the shelter, his action calling forth another shower of arrows. The ground rumbled and loud swoosh filled the air. Before anyone could formulate a thought about what might be the source behind such a sound a giant boulder came crashing to the ground, killing several people in its path. It had missed the group by less than twenty feet.

"They've a catapult. We are sorely out-armed here," Llyr said.

Cadoc chanced another look. "I think we can get in from the top."

"And how do you propose to get there? The stairs are blocked."

"I suggest we fly."

As if in response to Cadoc's words, Nerys's eyes slipped closed and her hand clenched into fists. Her concentration touched Sophie, gouging into her brain in a surprising and most unpleasant way. She tried to protest, but the pressure was so intense she could not speak, her tongue lolling about like a dead fish. Then the feeling vanished, allowing her sight to clear so that she could see Aderyn perched before her. Cadoc grabbed her hand and motioned to Nerys, leading them both to the giant bird. There he helped them onto the bony but sturdy back, joining them at the base of the creature's tail.

"We'll meet you inside," Llyr called as the giant wings began to flap, raising the trio high into the air.

Sophie's stomach lurched with the near vertical ascent, not at all soothed by Cadoc's arm about her waist. All she could think about was plummeting to her death, and the fallout of her death on the inhabitants of Annwn. Cadoc spoke against her ear, but the rushing wind ate his words, leaving nothing but the warmth of his breath against her skin. A mere twenty seconds later, they made an abrupt change in direction and came to rest atop of the multistory tower. Far below the rest of their people continued to fight; she could see that Llyr and his men had made it to the base of the staircase, despite being outnumbered.

Aderyn made a quick change back to her human form, staggering just a bit as her talons became delicate feet. Her skin had taken on a pasty, unwell hue. Like Eira she seemed to have been pushing herself too hard, draining the well of her magical talents. Upon seeing Nerys alive and well Aderyn scooped up her sister and spun her around, their combined laughter like pearls in the wind. Sophie couldn't help but smile.

Fial rushed over and hugged both the women's legs, making the sister chuckled even harder. Aderyn patted the rambunctious creature on the head, and made a quick swipe at the single tear that fell down her pale cheek.

"Alright, we need to get back to task here. The map must be located, and Sophie needs to…do whatever it is she needs to do," Aderyn said, giving her an intense look.

Four pairs of eyes were staring at her, making her wish the top of the tower would crumble beneath her feet, swallowing her away from their expectations. She had no idea what she was supposed to do, but like the events that had happened thus far she supposed she'd wing it.

"Let's go," she said, putting a confidence into the words she didn't feel.

No one needed further prompting. Single file, with Cadoc taking the lead, they open the roof's hatch and lowered themselves into the unknown. A small, dank room lay beneath, uninhabited and unfurnished. Below it a small staircase brought them into a hallway that dissected a grouping of four rooms. In silence they travelled to the first set, waiting for any signs of occupancy. Both rooms were empty, the heavy coating of dust showing them to have been in such a state for some time.

One of the next rooms had the doors slightly ajar and a pair of voices filtered out into the hallway. As Cadoc attempted to step ahead with sword drawn, Nerys laid a hand on his arm and gave him a pointed look that all understood to mean 'wait.' Her eyes slipped closed as she grabbed her sister's hand, and a dreamy half-smile came across her rosecoloured lips. A soft, yet insistent sensation brushed over Sophie, and like a fog drifted past their grouping. She couldn't help it, despite the anxiety of the situation, she suddenly felt lighter and experienced a misplaced happiness. The change in tone of the two unseen persons indicated they'd been affected as well.

The two people, both young men dressed as though prepared to enter the battle below, sauntered out into the hallway. Tough they were both armed, neither attempted to reach their weapons. Instead they looked to Nerys, smiling and undisturbed by their presence. Nerys came to them with hands outstretched. "Your swords, please."

Without a word both men handed over their swords, which Nerys handed back to Cadoc and Aderyn. Then she led them back into the room, where both sat down as instructed and allowed themselves to be tied together with a section of rope. Nerys placed a finger to her lips as she backed out of the room, both men nodding their agreement to be quiet.

Closing the door behind her, Nerys said, "The effect won't last long, maybe twenty minutes. After that they'll start hollering."

"Understood," Cadoc said, once again taking the lead.

They only made it about halfway down the stair case, putting them on the second floor by Sophie's estimation, when a group of voices came to their attention. Cadoc took a few tentative steps forward, daring a quick peek about the archway, leading into the main area. He came back with brows furrowed.

"There are at least twenty people, as far as I could see," he whispered. "It sounds like a few more beyond where I could see."

"A good bet that Albanach is here," Aderyn said.

"We need a better understanding of the layout before we charge in," Cadoc warned. "Agreed," Nerys said. She gave the group a look over, finally settling on Fial. With acrook of her finger she had them retracing their steps to the floor above,stopping by the window at the landing. She pulled off the leather strip about her waist and with a quiet execution of words turned the item into a length of chord. "I think we can lower Fial to the window below, where he could slip inside and take a look about. He's small and fast, hopefully he can go unnoticed."

"I can go," Aderyn said.

"No, you need to save your strength. We will need you if this comes down to a face-to-face battle."

She agreed and helped secured the bit of chord about Fial's waist. Together the sister's carefully lowered him to the window below, with Cadoc and Sophie watching for movement from above and below. Several fretful minutes passed until a tug on the chord let the women know he'd returned. After untying him, Nerys set about getting the information. She listened to his nonsensical chatter intently, another skill Sophie hadn't been aware her friend possessed.

"He says there are about twenty people in the main space. On this floor, there is only one additional room, guarded. Another ten are inside, and from his description it is Albanach and Ceridwen included."

"This is dangerous, sister," Aderyn said, pulling at her bottom lip.

"Yes, but letting Albanach win is not a possibility."

"Agreed, sister," Aderyn said. "We should split up and come from as many directions as possible."

"Cadoc, Sophie, and I will go down the stairs. You and Fial take the window."

With a determined nod Aderyn slipped up onto the window edge. Nerys tied the chord to a nearby fixture on the wall and gave her sister a wave goodbye as Aderyn wrapped the loose end about her waist. Fial scrambled onto her back, and together they rappelled down the side of the tower. Cadoc led them down the steps once again, where a few from the landing, Sophie gave him a light tap on the arm

"Let me go first," she whispered, pointing to the charm.

He gave a smile of understanding and stepped aside. She wrapped her sweaty hand about the charm, whispering the magic words and immediately feeling the effects. Looking down she saw nothing of her lower half, and knew she had managed the trick of invisibility. With trembling legs she wandered into the enemy group, doing her best to keep her breathing light and noise-free. One man took an abrupt step backward, nearly colliding with her. She took a quick sidestep, almost loosing grip on the heavy sword in her right hand.

She followed the outer edge of the room, all the way to the guarded double doors, which luckily stood open. As carefully as she could she slipped past the two men in armor. She felt the tip of her sword connect with one man's lower leg, causing him to look down, but finding nothing amiss he again raised his gaze. Sophie was holding her breath so tightly she thought she would choke.

Inside the smaller room, Albanach, Ceridwen, Domnall, and several others she didn't recognize sat about an oval-shaped table, studying the map. Ceridwen traced her hands along various lines, and invoked a number of incantations, all to her frustration. Nothing magical was triggered from her efforts. The King and his son were both displeased at her lack of success.

"You said you would be able to reap the secrets of this map for my benefit, Ceridwen. I took you at your word."

"You must be patient. This is old magic, very powerful. I need time to study it."

"I will not worry of this matter—yet. Now is the time to keep the document safe."

"Once twelve hours has passed the pact will be true, and Annwn will be ours." The King smiled at his proclamation, confident he would win.

In the next few seconds a number of things happened; Sophie tripped over a discarded cup on the floor, drawing attention to her presence, one of the guard's ran into the room to warn them of intruders, and a loud crashing, like wood splintering filled the air. Ceridwen looked directly at where she stood, as though she could see through the magic cloaking her, unleashing a powerful beam of energy that shot from her fingertips like fire.

Sophie was struck in the chest, immediately crumpling to the ground and losing her invisibility. On the heels of this action, Llyr and several of his men burst into the room.

"Get them!" Albanach cried.

Domnall and then other seated at the table rose and jumped into the fight. Ceridwen leapt over the table, coming straight at Sophie who'd had the wind knocked out of her.

Within steps of being in the witch's clutches a large black shape flew over Sophie's head, the mass connecting with Ceridwen and sending them both flying. It was enough time to get to her feet. Without waiting to see what have saved her she raced to the table where Albanach stood holding the map in one hand. With the other he drew the sword from his side, making Sophie realize she'd left her own on the floor where it had fallen from her grasp. At the last possible second she dropped, passing under Albanach's blade as she slid along the table top on her side.

Owain burst into the room, further distracting Albanach, so that Sophie managed to pluck the map from his grasp and jump from the table. She shoved the map in her satchel and attempted to make her way through the mass of people. The black shape that had taken Ceridwen down was Aderyn in cat form, she could now see. One particularly brutal blow from the witch sent the girl sailing across the room, and as she hit the wall she slipped back into her true form. The end of Aderyn's strength had almost been reached.

Owain and others kept the enemies busy, allowing Sophie to escape into the main room, where she found Llyr and his men had broken through the guards and were engaged in a bloody show of force. Cadoc and Nerys had both joined the fight, and Fial flitted about the perimeter of the space, oddly silent in his obvious terror. Sophie didn't know what else to do, she retraced her steps to the upper level. The urgent chirping from behind let her know that Fial had followed.

She'd forgotten about the two men behind until they came bursting out of the room they'd been left in. She screamed, in the same instant throwing out her hand before her. A ball of light flew at the two men, as she had on the battlefield with Cadoc, taking them both down. Whether they lived or not she could be sure, and she didn't have time to check. She raced into one of the empty rooms and lay the map on the dusty floor. Her eyes blinked in rapid succession, her chest burning.

What I am supposed to do?

Footsteps pounded up the steps and angry voices called out. There was no time to falter. She ripped the dagger from her belt, feeling the power swell about her. The map transformed before her eyes, taking on a three-dimensional quality, and sending forth bursts of images from times long past that played out on the air like supernatural videos. She saw Lonnog and the line of Coraniaid solders, Eirianwen, Llud LLaw Eraint, and many others she did not recognize, time flying past until one face ran into another, and the swirling, urgent pressure of the magic in the map threatened to topple her. She raised the dagger above her head, suddenly certain what action she must take.

"Nooooooo!" screamed Ceridwen from the doorway.

Ignoring her, Sophie brought the dagger down with all her might, stabbing it through the parchment and into the wood floor beneath. Like the flick of a light Sophie was transported past the boundaries of space and time, to a place that existed only for her.

There she found herself with two others—Lonnog and Llud LLaw Eraint.

She came to them in a void of darkness, a place of limbo between the past and present. Both had grim expressions on their face, regarding her.

"You have broken the pact," Llud LLaw Eraint said, his voice so deep it crawled along her skin.

"Yes," Sophie answered, unable to believe it to be true.

"This is the end for now," Lonnog said, as his figure began to slip away. "But not for good." Then he vanished in a wisp of smoke.

"He speaks the truth. Annwn is safe for now, you have stopped the Coraniaids from gaining access to our lands, but it will not stop the hatred that drove the pact to come to be. Gaidheal is still our enemy. Do you understand?"

"Yes."

"Keep the map safe. There are secrets in it still. What part of myself I have managed to leave behind may help you still."

Then Llud smiled and with a sweeping bow pressed a kiss to the back of Sophie's hand. As his lips pulled away from her skin the man evaporated in a sound like the air rushing from a balloon and Sophie was sent hurtling back to where she'd come from. At the last possible second before emerging back into the present she felt someone take her hand.

She came to sprawled across the map, her hand firmly in the grasp of another person. She looked up shocked to find Eirianwen standing beside her.

"You," snapped Ceridwen from the doorway. "I will not let you get away with this!"

"This is our fight now, Ceridwen. Let the other be."

The witches came at each other, meeting in a shower of crimson light. A terrible screech filled the air, gouging into Sophie's brain. When she thought she could not stand the sensation any longer it was ripped away from her, taking the women with it. Without missing a beat she sprung to her feet, tucking the dagger in her belt and the map inside her satchel. It was only then she realized Fial was still in the room with her, his small form lying motionless near the doorway.

"No," she cried. She scooped him up in her arms, alarmed by the way his head lolled and his complete lack of response to her touch.

With him clutched in arms, she raced back down stairs where to her utter surprise the battle was still underway, though they appeared to have gained the upper hand. Several of Albanach's men lay on the floor. She spotted Cadoc and raced to his side.

"Help me. Fial's been hurt."

"Is he breathing?" Cadoc asked.

"I...think so."

"C'mon then. Aderyn and Nerys followed Llyr down to the lower level a few minutes ago. If anyone can help it's them. Where did you go?"

"To do what I thought I had to, but the fight is still on. I don't understand."

Neither did Cadoc from the look on his face, but he didn't push the matter. He steered them through the remaining men, and down the stairs. On the lower level, more men were down, including a few that Sophie recognized as those who'd been fighting on Annwn's side. Their deaths pained her, but she couldn't let it distract her with danger still looming. A quick scan of the room did not locate either sister, or Llyr, and she assumed they'd fled out the massive front doors standing ajar.

The battlefield had cleared considerably since they'd entered the tower, either through death and injury, or those who'd fled. Untethered horses stampeded about the courtyard, in their fright trampling anything in their path. Across the open space Sophie spotted Llyr and his daughters, closing in on a cornered Albanach.

"There," she cried and started running.

She dodged the litter strewn space, clutching Fial's still body. Aderyn caught sight of her, eyes wide. She cried out, but the distance was too vast for Sophie to hear her clearly.

When she started waving her arms in her direction she realized it was a warning of some kind, though the clarity came a bit too late. The blow took her from the left side, knocking her to the ground and spilling Fial from her grasp.

She looked up at the sharp end of a blood-soaked sword, pointed directly at her face.

Domnall grinned. "Now I have you just where I want you."

Cadoc skidded to a stop, sword drawn. "Leave her alone, Domnall. Take me instead."

Domnall snorted. "You're nothing, boy. She's the one who must pay."

The blade came racing at her, only to stop short of actually piercing her chest. A strange look passed over Domnall's face, and then the front of his shirt became a bright, crimson stain. He turned, showing Sophie the sword protruding from his back. In agony he shuffled away, his own weapon dropping from his grip. To no avail he attempted to dislodge the metal from the wound, but could not manage it from the angle at which he'd been hit. He screamed.

"You are not the only one who has magic," he spat out through his tightly clenched teeth. From his pocket he pulled a small sack and sprinkling the contents about his form he vanished before Sophie's eyes.

"Sophie," Cadoc cried, falling to his knees.

"Fial," she answered, crawling along on her hands and knees.

From her vantage point she could now see who had thrown the weapon that had saved her life. Ysbaddaden, with a much recovered Eira, stood about twenty feet away. She also saw Llyr strike a fatal blow against Albanach. His death did little to assuage the guilt squeezing at her heart.

At last she made it to Fial and pulled him against her tired, aching body. Cadoc, Eira, and Ysbaddaden joined her, soon flowed by Aderyn, Nerys, and Llyr. They all looked down on the little creature, pain in all their eyes.

"He fought the good fight, lassie," Ysbaddaden said. Sophie nodded, not sure of her voice.

Aderyn dropped to her knees and pressed her ear to Fial's chest. "I don't think he's dead," she said.

"Can you save him?" Sophie asked.

"I don't know. What happened to him?"

"Ceridwen."

Aderyn sighed. "Sisters, I need your help."

Aderyn took Fial's body from Sophie grasp, a feeling like having her heart ripped from her chest. She then gently place him on the ground, and the three woman clasped hands in a small circle. Once closed the power lashed out, lifting Fial's body and prickling along those watching the occurrence as it unfolded. They sister began to walk in a clock-wise motion, eyes closed and grips on one another firm. Eira let forth burst of fire, ice, and wind as Aderyn fluctuated between various animal-human forms. Nerys emitted a sweet fog, that ruffled Sophie's hair and made her smile despite her pain.

The individual energies fused together, forming a super-magical ability that proved as draining as it was difficult to control. The three sisters struggled to focus the energy on the fading Fial, with limbs trembling and tears pouring down their faces. Eira, already weakened, slipped to her knees and a thin trickle of blood began to leak from one ear. She cried out as the sisters continued moving and were forced to drag her along the ground, but refused to break her contact.

A blinding flash erupted, shooting straight into the sky. The force knocked everyone back several feet, and as Sophie hit the ground she heard something in her shoulder crunch. For a few seconds she floundered overcome by the scorching pain, gritting her teeth until her vision cleared and her breathing no longer sounded as though she were about to hyperventilate.

She couldn't see Fial. Aderyn had Eira across her lap, with Nerys kneeling at her side. Sophie struggled to get herself into a seated position, helped by Cadoc who'd recovered with no ill effects. She leaned on him as they made their way to the sisters, her stomach like a sponge that had been squeezed dry.

Eira gave a sudden jerk, eyes flying open. The other two sisters reacted with tears and grateful laughter. Another sound came behind the women's voices, one that Sophie never imagined she'd be happy to hear. Fial came racing around Nerys's side, and jumped straight in her arms. He wrapped his thin arms about her neck and hugged her with surprising strength, before scampering off to hug everyone else in close proximity.

Sophie started to laugh, jolting the pain in her shoulder back to life. She winced, catching Cadoc's attention.

"We need to get you back to Rhiannon, where you can be taken care of," he said. "What are you talking about? You've been shot and hurt in goodness knows how many other ways." Truth was the pain was so intense she didn't know if she could stay conscious.

"I'll be alright, Sophie. I have a reason to be strong."

When he looked into her eyes the pain vanished. Somehow she'd done it. Annwn was safe. Nerys had been rescued and all her new friends were alive.

Better still, she had Cadoc at her side.

BACK IN KNOB'S END...
THREE WEEKS LATER

"Sophie!" Nerys called out, catching her attention just before she ducked into the change room to get ready for field hockey practice.

"Hi, what's up?" she asked.

"I wondered if you want to come over for dinner on Friday night?" By the twinkle in her friend's eye, she already knew what Sophie's answer would be.

"Of course."

"Ok, see you later."

Sophie smiled, shaking her head as Nerys walked away. Of course she wanted to come over; after all it was an opportunity for some alone time with Cadoc. This happy thought led her back to the end of the crazy adventure she'd had in Annwn, and the how what happened there had changed her life forever.

After rounding up the remaining Gaidheal supporters and marching them back to their own lands, Sophie and company had returned to Rhiannon, all exhausted and battered to various degrees. She had indeed separated her shoulder, a situation that Mairwen had quickly fixed along with her other more serious injuries, but three weeks later she was still sore and bruised. Her grandmother had admonished her for being so careless after she'd "explained" her taking a tumble in Nerys's back yard.

Ysbaddaden had parted ways with them, intent on returning to his own land and his daughter. He promised to keep in touch, and assured Sophie she was always welcome in Matholwch.

Mairwen had raced from the castle to meet them, weeping

and hugging her husband and daughters multiple times before letting them continue on. Eira was the most affected, and even with the knowledgeable care of her mother and others had remained bedridden for almost a week after Albanach's fall. Gethen, who'd they'd found hurt, but still alive on the blood-soaked battlefield had thrown all caution to the wind and professed his not-so-secret love for Nerys. She reciprocated, and the two were enjoying the early stages of their courtship. Mairwen had been delighted and hoped the pairing might lead to a wedding in the future. She'd been so happy, in fact, it had taken little to convince her to keep Fial in the castle with the rest of her family. Though she'd been sad to leave him behind, she was pleased that he was safe and with those who would care for him.

Surprisingly, Nerys had decided to come back to Knob's End with Sophie to finish out the school year. For whatever reason, she enjoyed human life and wanted to continue on with her fictitious existence. Of course, she could slip back to Annwn at any time, and enjoy the company of her new boyfriend and family whenever she wanted. More often than not Sophie joined her, always delighted at the new and wondrous things she experienced with each visit.

Magic was in her blood and she had much to learn, like the fact that having such gifts did not mean that one was infallible or that things would always work out as planned. The supernatural world was unpredictable and sometimes uncontrollable, and even with the best of intentions things can go terribly wrong. The inability to be completely healed of the injuries they suffered during battle was one such fallout for Sophie, Geraint, and Owain from the use of the transportation spell exercised by Eirianwen.

Cadoc had joined Nerys about two weeks later, or a few days on Annwn time, coming to live with her as her "cousin" and new student at the nearby Harold J. Elusious Academy for Boys. Though the battle was over, Llyr and others suspected the war was not. Domnall and Ceridwen were still at large, and both the Gaidhealians and the Coraniaids would surely be firm enemies of Annwn. Cadoc would act as protection for Nerys and Sophie, as he had been inducted into Rhiannon's Noble Guard. His past wanderings would come to good use and the honour had fulfilled his need for a place to call home.

Coming back to Knob's End had been both terribly heart-wrenching and welcome. It had been hard to leave her new friends behind, but she had missed her normal life. Truth be told, the uneven balance in the passing of time between worlds was draining, and Sophie had to be careful with how much time she spent in Annwn. She was human after all, at least for the most part.

The map had come with her, and was kept safe by Gruddyeu. The man was delighted to have opportunity to study the magical piece, and Sophie and he worked diligently at uncovering its multiple secrets. Many adventures of the past were locked in the worn bit of parchment, some that were sure to spill into the future.

The very last thing Sophie had done before coming home was to meet with Eirianwen. She'd travelled with Cadoc to the witch's homeland.

"So good to see you well, Mistress Sophie," Eirianwen had said upon seeing her.

"You, too."

Cadoc had protested, but Sophie had insisted she'd be fine when Eirianwen had asked her to come inside her private area.

"She will be kept safe," Eirianwen had assured him.

Once alone the two walked to the small cottage, choosing to sit in the velvet green grass to speak. There had been one thing Sophie had not been able to let go of and she knew that only one person could help her.

"I thank you for your bravery and willingness to help a land not your own," the witch had said.

"I'm glad I could help and I wonder if I might have one request?"

"Ask."

"Could you release Tegwen from her curse?"

"You ask for help for another, and not reward for yourself?" Eirianwen smiled, a dazzling display.

"Yes, I do."

"Then it will be done." Eirianwen leaned forward and touched one fingertip to Sophie's forehead. A spark of energy escaped from the connection, drifting to the sky and burst into a flock of hummingbirds. "Be safe, Sophie. Annwn has need for you yet."

She'd blinked and Eirianwen was gone. Instead of the land about the witch's humble shelter she found herself at the shore of the lake, before a curious Cadoc. When he didn't ask what had transpired she felt her feelings for him grow.

The vary last thing Sophie had seen as she stood at the edge of the pond and the portal back to her own land was the ghostly image of Tegwen. She had been holding hands with a man Sophie assumed to be her true love, the one she'd been taken from so many years ago. They had both waved their hands good-bye and vanished.

Now, as she emerged from the school in her cut-off sweat pants and tank top, she spied Cadoc sitting in the bleachers next to the field where her team practiced, waiting with infinite patience. His smile rivaled the sun as he caught sight of her. The sudden realization of how much she cared for him stopped her in her tracks. Her chest ached, and it took everything in her not to race over and throw her arms about him.

I think I've fallen in love, she thought.

Cadoc gave her a quizzical look, making her realize how absurd she looked as she stood staring at him. She waved and joined the other girls on the field.

"Alright, ladies. Three laps," the coach called out.

Sophie was glad for the distraction. One adventure was firmly behind her. Many waited for her to find them.

ABOUT THE AUTHOR

Liz Strange is the published author of ten novels and several short stories. She has also written multiple scripts for both film and television.

Curious about other Crossroad Press books?
Stop by our site:
http://store.crossroadpress.com
We offer quality writing
in digital, audio, and print formats.

www.ingramcontent.com/pod-product-compliance
Lightning Source LLC
Chambersburg PA
CBHW030303200626
46816CB00002BA/739